BOOKS BY CHARLES G. IRION

Project: RESCUE Adventure Series
FREE FIRE

Stand Alone
FOUR

Murdered by Gods Series
Machu Picchu
One World
Timbuktu

Summit Murder Mystery Series
Murder on Everest
Abandoned on Everest (prequel to Murder on Everest)
Murder on Elbrus
Murder on Mt. McKinley
Murder on Puncak Jaya
Murder on Aconcagua
Murder on Vinson Massif
Murder on Kilimanjaro

Hell Series
Remodeling Hell
Autograph Hell
Car Dealer Hell
Divorce Hell

Roadkill Cooking for Campers
"The Best Dang Wild Game Cookbook in the World"

Amazon Author Page: amazon.com/author/charlesirion
Facebook: www.facebook.com/MBGOneWorld
www.facebook.com/charlesgirion
Twitter: @AuthorIrion
Instagram: @charlesirion
YouTube: Charles G. Irion
Website: www.charlesirion.com
IMDb: Charles G. Irion

This book is a nonstop ride! Will and his team face non-stop action and surprises. Great if you're into thrillers that keep you on your toes. — Marie M.

"At the heart of Project: RESCUE Adventure series lies a bold new approach: 'Their expertise would lay, not in the art of war, but in the art of survival and negotiation.' With this mindset, Irion unleashes a gripping world of heart-pounding international drama, where every encounter balances on the edge of triumph or catastrophe. I couldn't put FREE FIRE down!" — Joseph Cox

FREE FIRE offers high-stakes action and tough ethical dilemmas in Ethiopia's Tigray region. Will Irons leads a gripping rescue mission that spirals into a deadly conspiracy. Fast-paced yet reflective, it's a must-read for those who love action-packed thrillers with depth. — Tyler J.

This story takes off right from the start and doesn't slow down. Will and Deke face danger at every turn. Great if you like thrillers that are fast and full of action. — Noah C.

This intense tale of survival and friendship brings the Tigray region to life. Will and Deke face danger from all sides in an action-filled, character-driven story that blends military thrills with rich settings. A perfect pick for fast-paced thriller fans. — Leah M.

This story has everything: action, suspense, and strong friendships. Will and Deke make a great team, and their bond brings real heart to the story. A solid pick for thriller lovers! — Longtime fan of Charles Irion and Scott Devlon

FREE FIRE is a real page-turner! The action is intense, and the story pulls you right in. Will and Deke make an awesome team. Definitely worth picking up! — Nora D.

This thrilling adventure follows Will Irons and Deke James as they try to save a Doctors Without Borders team. Tension mounts when they uncover a conspiracy, blending intense action with strong emotional bonds. A captivating page-turner for fans of military thrillers. — Emma R.

This book's an adrenaline rush! Will and Deke are on a dangerous rescue mission that spirals into a wild conspiracy. The story's got intense action but also real friendship, which makes it even better. If you like military thrillers, this one's a winner. — Trevor E.

FREE FIRE starts off as a rescue mission but quickly turns into a mystery. Will and his team find themselves in a messy situation, uncovering a plot with big consequences. It's suspenseful and keeps you guessing. Perfect for anyone who loves action with a bit of mystery. — James A.

FREE FIRE has everything you'd want in an adventure: suspense, action, and characters you can root for. A highly entertaining read that's hard to put down! — Layna J.

I have a new favorite character...Deek!
— Wayne M.

Will and his team are thrown into a high-stakes mission with unexpected twists. The action is intense, but the story has real emotion too. A solid pick for thriller fans who like a good story. — Gage T.

Wow! What a fantastic literary ride of suspense, intrigue and cosmic venture. I think it's Irion's best work to date – and that's hard to top. I look forward to the next novel. — Jackie Fontaine, Actor

"Once again, the intrigue and imagination of Charles Irion is beyond belief. This is probably the best story he's written to date, and that's a very high bar to surpass. I only have three words to sum this book up...I WANT MORE!" — Elaine York, Owner of Allusion Publishing

In the spirit of Clive Cussler's high-octane thrillers, *FREE FIRE* delivers action, intrigue, and danger at every turn. When a diplomatic team's mission for peace turns into a fight for survival in Ethiopia's unforgiving highlands, the FAST Team is called to action. Led by Will Irons, a man with unbreakable resolve and unmatched skills, the team faces relentless enemies and lethal traps, racing against time to save the diplomats from a catastrophic fate. But as they dig deeper, they uncover a dark conspiracy that could change the fate of an entire region.

From the mountain shadows of Tigray to a thrilling rescue under fire, *FREE FIRE* is a pulse-pounding adventure that won't let you go. —Sean Ellis author of **INTO THE BLACK**—A Nick Kismet Adventure

FREE FIRE

A Project: RESCUE Adventure

CHARLES G. IRION

IRION BOOKS LLC — ARIZONA

REVIEWS FOR BOOKS
BY CHARLES G. IRION

STAND ALONE

FOUR: *"It must be good when you're
still pondering the plot and trying to figure out
how to fix the world so this doesn't happen in real life."*

MURDERED BY GODS SERIES

MACHU PICCHU: *"That ending!
This book will stay with me for a while!"*
ONE WORLD: *"Terrific read. Scary that it's totally plausible...!"*
TIMBUKTU: *"Very exciting! The outcome is
not what I thought it would be!"*

SUMMIT MURDER MYSTERY SERIES

EVEREST: *"An intriguing beginning to what
promises to be a stellar series!"*
ABANDONED: *"A clever story told from
a character's point of view."*
ELBRUS: *"Another highly entertaining mystery from Irion!"*
Mt. McKINLEY: *"A vivid tangle of murder,
intrigue and danger."*
PUNCAK JAYA: *"Thoroughly enjoyable!"*
"Couldn't put it down!"
ACONCAGUA: *"One of the best protagonists I've ever read."*
VINSON MASSIF: *"Sometimes the book was so realistic I was as
freezing as the characters! Grab a blanket and tuck in!"*
KILIMANJARO: *"WOW! What a way to end it with a bang!"*

HELL SERIES

AUTOGRAPH HELL: *"I've been a collector for years
and thought I knew it all—I was wrong. A great read!"*

CAR DEALER HELL: *"Buying a car? Get this book!"*
DIVORCE HELL: *"This book is as real as it gets about a tough subject!"*
REMODELING HELL: *"A must read for those brave enough to conquer their own home repair and remodeling!"*

COOKBOOK

ROADKILL COOKING FOR CAMPERS—'THE BEST DANG WILD GAME COOKBOOK IN THE WORLD':
"More than just a fun novelty item—great recipes too!"

CHARLES G. IRION
"One World One People"™
www.charlesirion.com

Published by Irion Books, LLC Copyright © December 2024
Charles G. Irion C.I. Trust First Edition 2024
10 9 8 7 6 5 4 3 2 1

Library of Congress Control Number: 2024921207
ISBN paperback: 9781734718584

Cover Design — Thomas Rodriguez, TJR Designs
Book Design — Elaine York, www.allusionpublishing.com
Project Manager and Assistant to Charles G. Irion — Julie Bailey
Audio Book Director — Greg Lutz, Murder Ink Productions

Irion Books, LLC
4462 E Horseshoe Road
Phoenix, AZ 85028
Email: charles@charlesirion.com

FROM THE AUTHOR
CHARLES G. IRION

When I wrote *FOUR*, I thought Scott Devlon's storyline had reached its conclusion, his son, Marc, stepping in as my new protagonist. Then life threw a twist my way. A planned trip to Ethiopia's Tigray region for a Project C.U.R.E. hospital assessment was canceled due to a U.S. Department of State Level 4 Travel Advisory:

"The Tigray Region and the border with Eritrea are restricted for travel by U.S. government personnel, with limited exceptions to support humanitarian capacity and priority diplomatic engagement efforts. Border roads with Eritrea are closed and conditions at the border may change with no warning."

Despite the warning, I was ready to go. Even with the risk, I was determined and ready to face the challenges. But in the end, the "powers that be" came back with a firm and unequivocal, "NO!"

Frustrated but undeterred, I decided to channel my energy into creating something new. Drawing inspiration from Scott Devlon's company developed in my *Murdered By Gods* series, I'm excited to introduce the *Project: RESCUE Adventures*. If I couldn't embark on the journey myself, I'd travel through the power of storytelling. The result is *FREE FIRE*, the first book in a thrilling series that delves into the world's most dangerous places, where missions can take a disastrous, if not deadly, turn. This isn't a one-man job—it's a team effort. Enter the FAST Team: a group of highly skilled individuals who rely on each other to overcome extraordinary challenges and rescue those whose survival hangs by a thread.

I'm excited for you to meet the team and hear your thoughts on their first adventure!

Just like the FAST Team depends on each member's strengths, I couldn't have brought this book to life without the incredible support of my family and friends. To everyone who offered feedback and reviews, big or small, thank you—your input made all the difference.

PROLOGUE
ESPERIA
October, 1935 — Abyssinia

THE STARS SHINING in the expanse were so bright, the soldiers didn't need lanterns to light their way as they marched stealthily out of the ancient city and into the foothills of the Adwa Mountains, a fact which greatly pleased Captain Renzo Moretti. Even though the military forces of the Kingdom of Italy, under the command of Marshal Emilio De Bono, now controlled the city of Axum, enforcing a curfew on the local population, the secrecy of Moretti's mission—a task given him by *Il Duce* himself—was paramount. If even a whisper of what they had done this night got out, there would be hell to pay.

Moretti led his men with the confidence of one who had traversed much harsher paths. Despite being more than two-thousand miles from Italy, he felt oddly at home in the highlands of Abyssinia. The landscape, with its crisp air, soaring peaks, and ancient rock-hewn churches, reminded him of the Alpine vistas of his youth. Born and raised in Cortina d'Ampezzo, amidst the rugged peaks of the Dolomites, his childhood was spent traversing steep trails and learning the secrets of the highlands, which had instilled in him an unshakeable fortitude and a deep reverence for nature's grandeur.

He had begun his military career as an enlisted soldier in the *Alpini* Corps, the elite mountain warfare unit of the Italian Army, where his alpine roots gave him an edge fighting Senussi rebels in the Jebel Akhdar region of Cyrenaica. His indomitable spirit and reputation for bravery quickly caught the attention of the *Servizio Informazioni Militare*—the Italian Military Information Service—and soon a freshly commissioned Moretti was conducting covert operations in North Africa, gathering intelligence that would prove crucial in the Italian campaigns across the continent. Though he never lost his love for the mountains, his adventures in Africa, walking in the footsteps of such greats as Julius Caesar, Septimus Severus, and even Napoleon Bonaparte—whom Moretti admired even if he was a Corsican—awakened in him a fascination with history. In the stone churches of Egypt and Libya, he pored over nearly forgotten texts and maps, uncovering a history of Christianity older even than Rome, and rumors of forgotten kingdoms, like that of the legendary Prester John, waiting to be rediscovered.

His martial prowess and scholarly curiosity made him the ideal choice to lead this mission. As DeBono's army swept down from Eritrea, easily defeating the poorly equipped Ethiopian forces, Moretti and his select team of commandos had been dispatched on a daring expedition that would, he felt certain, become the stuff of legend.

Navigating by the stars, an art older than war itself, Moretti guided his men south through the undulating terrain. The highlands surrounding Axum were a labyrinth of shadows and whispers, the rustle of the wind through the acacia trees the only sound in the stillness. They avoided the well-trodden paths, lest some rural goat herd espy them, choosing instead the cover of the low-lying shrubs and the occasional rocky outcrop. Every man felt the weight of the silence; the secrecy of their mission was a shroud that cloaked their every move.

Eight miles southwest of the outermost edge of the city, Moretti called a halt. The plateau where they now stood was more exposed than he would have liked, but it was the only terrain suitable for the rendezvous. As they approached, Moretti signaled a halt, his hand raised in the air—a silent command heeded instantly. The men fanned out, securing the perimeter with practiced ease, and settled in to wait.

The vigorous cross-country march had kept the night's chill at bay, but now that they were idle, the cold air gripped them in an icy fist. Moretti hugged his arms about his chest and began searching the sky impatiently.

He gradually became aware of a low rumble, barely audible at first, but growing louder with each passing second until it was unmistakably the drone of aircraft engines. The commandos, sensing the change, shifted their gaze upward, their breaths visible in the cold night air.

And then, there it was, coming in from the lowlands to the south—a dark silhouette against the glittering backdrop of the cosmos—the airship *Esperia* emerging as if birthed from the night itself.

The *Esperia*'s tale began as the LZ-120 *Bodensee*, a passenger airship constructed by Luftschiffbau Zeppelin GmbH shortly following the end of the Great War.  Designed by Paul Jaray and powered by four Maybach Mb.Iva engines, the LZ-120 first took to the skies on August 20, 1919. With its innovative hull shape and luxurious accommodations for up to twenty-seven passengers, it represented a new mode of long-distance travel—through the air. It was a symbol of hope and progress, ferrying passengers between Berlin and Friedrichshafen, and even completing a remarkable seventeen-hour voyage from Berlin to Stockholm.

However, the *Bodensee*'s period of service as a German passenger liner was short-lived. In 1921, as part of war reparations, the airship was handed over to the Italian Navy, where it was renamed *Esperia*, and for a time served as a proud testament to Italy's expanding aerial capabilities, completing a fifteen-hundred mile journey from Rome to Barcelona and then on to Toulon, in twenty-five hours. The *Esperia* continued to soar until 1928, when it was officially decommissioned and, as far as anyone knew, broken up for scrap.

Yet, *Esperia*'s story was far from over. In a secret, outside the reach of treaties and hidden from international scrutiny, the Italian Intelligence Service, recognizing the airship's potential as a platform to conduct clandestine operations in places where airplanes could not land, had the *Esperia* secretly mothballed at an airbase in Pontadera, near Pisa, held in reserve for a mission exactly like this.

When Moretti had received his orders to accompany DeBono's army to Axum, *Esperia* had stirred from its secret hangar like a leviathan of the air, cruising across the Mediterranean and down the coast of the Red Sea before turning west toward Abyssinia, rising into the highlands to meet Moretti and his commandos, and bear them, and their secret cargo, triumphantly back to Rome.

As *Esperia* descended onto the plateau, its massive frame backlit by the stars, Moretti's men sprang into action, seizing the airship's mooring lines, which dangled like the tendrils of some great celestial jellyfish. When the lines came within reach, the soldiers seized the thick ropes with gloved hands, and then their comrades rushed to add their weight to the effort. Their bodies braced against the pull of the *Esperia*'s lighter-than-air lifting gasses, they began reeling the airship as if it were a prize fish.

Captain Moretti watched in fascination as his men worked like a well-oiled machine of flesh and determination to bring the airship to heel. The low rumble of the engines mixed with grunts of exertion, a symphony of man and machine working in harmony. With a final heave, the soldiers drew *Esperia* down until its integrated cabin banged loudly on the rocky ground.

After a brief pause to ensure that all the mooring lines were secure, Moretti approached the airship with a measured stride. Although the vessel remained shrouded in darkness, he could feel its awe-inspiring immensity looming above him. At nearly four-hundred-feet long and sixty feet in diameter, it was like walking under a battleship in drydock.

As he neared the forward end of the cabin, the hum of the idling engines still resonating in his ears, a figure stepped down from the control car, his silhouette framed by the soft glow of the cabin lights.

Moretti extended a hand. "Captain Ricci. Punctual as ever."

Ricci, a distinguished flyer from the Naval Air Service, ignored Moretti's hand. As a naval officer, his rank of captain held considerably more authority than Moretti's army commission, but Moretti was in command of the overall mission, an arrangement that clearly did not please the airship captain. "Let's move this along," Ricci growled irritably. "We've got a long, hard night ahead of us."

Moretti turned and gestured for his men to come forward, then returned his attention to the airship's captain. "Your journey went well, I take it?"

"For the most part. The ship flies best at two- or three-thousand feet. Up here in the mountains, where the air is thinner, maintaining buoyancy is a challenge. We've had to release ballast to compensate for the loss of lift. Now that we're adding all of you and your..."

He glanced over Moretti's shoulder as the four soldiers bearing a large crate suspended atop a pair of litter poles, advanced toward the rear of the cabin.

"Cargo," Ricci continued, "will require us to shed even more if we're to get aloft again."

"You will be able to take off though?"

"Mmhmm," replied Ricci equivocally. "The problem is that as the night cools, the hydrogen gas contracts, giving us even less lift.

At sea level, we would simply ride low through the night, but up here, that's not an option. Come tomorrow, when the sun's heat expands the gas again, we'll wish we still had that ballast."

"But you can do it?" Moretti pressed. "I want to be at least five-hundred miles away when the sun rises."

"If it can be done, we'll do it."

Moretti did not like the sound of that but knew the cautious Ricci would not make promises he couldn't keep.

"At least the weather is on our side," the airship captain went on.

Moretti reflexively glanced skyward, the cloudless sky confirming Ricci's assessment. At that moment, one of the soldier's bearing the cargo litter tripped on the raised lip of the doorway and nearly dropped his burden.

"Careful with that!" hissed Moretti, his eyes narrowing as the crate tilted precariously.

The other commandos struggled to steady the precious cargo until their comrade regained his footing and equalized the load. Moretti breathed a sigh of relief as the crate stabilized, and then began moving again, disappearing inside the cabin.

Ricci uttered another grunt. "Well, let's hope that's the most excitement we see tonight."

RICCI'S COMMENT LINGERED like a dire premonition in Moretti's thoughts as the crew of the *Esperia* set to work preparing to take to the skies once more. Engineers checked gauges and dials, ensuring that the four Maybach engines were operating at optimal capacity. Ballast bags were hoisted and crewmen stood by, awaiting the command to empty their contents, lightening the ship's load. At a signal from Ricci, the soldiers at the mooring lines let go, unleashing the behemoth from its earthly tether, and then sprinted for the open cabin door. The lines fell away, slapping the ground, but the airship was slow to rise, even when Ricci gave the command to release ballast and engage the engines.

The dual-bladed propellers churned the still mountain air, the engines now roaring at full intensity, moving the airship forward in order to create lift under the immense envelope and break the grip of inertia.

In the control cabin, standing beside Ricci, Moretti gazed out into the darkness, his heart pounding in his chest as the airship began moving forward blindly. There were mountains out there much taller than the plateau beneath them, and if they did not rise above them, his secret mission would end in disaster.

Then, one of the crewmen called out. "We're rising steady, captain. Passing 7,200 feet."

Moretti held his breath, as if by so doing, he might somehow further increase the ship's buoyancy. A minute later, the crewman announced another hundred feet of rise.

"Steady as she goes," said Ricci, his gaze fixed on the instrument panel, hands steady on the wheel. "Increase pitch," he commanded crisply, his voice cutting through the din of the engines.

"Aye, sir," replied another crewman, manipulating the elevator controls to angle the nose of the *Esperia* upward, aiding their ascent.

"Altimeter reading 7,500 feet and rising," called out the first crewman.

Ricci nodded, his focus unwavering. "Prepare to adjust trim as we clear the mountains," he said, anticipating the need for balance once the airship was free from the mountain's updrafts.

For nearly half an hour, captain and crew remained in a state of heightened awareness as they navigated through the darkness, battling invisible air currents while the landscape fell away beneath them. Then, without any warning, the altimeter needle wavered and then began to fall, causing a murmur of concern to ripple through the crew. Ricci's eyes narrowed as he observed the instrument's unusual behavior.

"Are we losing altitude?" Ricci's voice was a low growl, barely audible over the roar of the engines.

Moretti, who had not felt the airship's very gradual ascent, now strained his senses for any sign that they were falling.

The crewman manning the altimeter shook his head, uncertainty etched on his face. "It's hard to say, captain. The barometer's showing a sudden drop in pressure. We're either losing altitude or we've entered a low-pressure area."

Ricci's jaw clenched. "Keep a close eye on it. Have the engineer check the gas cells for leaks."

As crewmen scrambled to comply, a new voice came over the ship's communication tube. "Cloud cover ahead, Captain! It wasn't there a moment ago."

Ricci and Moretti exchanged a glance. "I thought the skies were clear," said Moretti.

"They were," growled Ricci. "But that's the thing about the weather. It changes."

"Can the ship handle it?"

"We'll find out, won't we."

No sooner had he said it than the airship began to shudder violently. Moretti clutched a rail like a lifeline as the deck began rising and falling, flinging him around like a rubber ball at the end of a string. While all around him the crew fought to maintain control, their faces set in grim determination as Esperia sailed blindly into the teeth of the unexpected tempest.

Suddenly, the world lit up as lightning forked across the heavens, the flash revealing a swirling gyre of clouds outside. A fraction of a second later, a deafening thunderclap shuddered through the deck beneath them.

"Mother of God!" gasped Ricci in the sudden darkness that followed.

The oath... Or was it a prayer?... Struck a primal chord in Moretti's thoughts. He was not a devout man, viewing scripture and dogma in a historic context, but he had never forgotten the stories and sermons learned in childhood—accounts from the Old Testament and the New of storms sent by God to punish the wicked and test the faith of the devout.

Is this our punishment? He thought. *Divine retribution for our act of desecration?*

Then another flash of lightning tore the darkness asunder, revealing the stark outline of a mountain peak—immense and unforgiving—looming directly in their path.

"Brace for collision!" Ricci shouted. In the fading glow, Moretti saw the captain's hands spinning the wheel in desperation. Then the thunderclap hit, and the world turned upside down.

ONE

Present Day — Tigray National State, Ethiopia

THE RUGGED LANDSCAPE of the Simien Mountains seemed to reach out and embrace Taneisha Hayes as she stepped out from the Range Rover that had borne her and the other members of her diplomatic team up the old mule trail—there were no roads here—to the village home of Alem Tekle.

That was how Taneisha had begun to think of the settlement—Alem Tekle's village.

Located about thirty miles southwest of Axum and a good ten or fifteen miles from the nearest paved highway, surrounded by irregular fields sown with teff, sorghum, and maize—subsistence crops that barely provided enough for the residents—the settlement had no official name and did not appear on any maps. The inhabitants, in keeping with local custom, simply referred to it as '*Bet*', a Tigrinya word that roughly translated as 'home'.

The cool mountain air was a stark contrast to—and a welcome relief from—the sweltering heat of the Ethiopian lowlands where she'd spent ten long days making the final arrangements for the expedition north into the Tigray region.

Nestled in the northern reaches of Ethiopia, Tigray was a land of striking contrasts. From the rugged peaks of the Simien and Gheralta Mountains to the sprawling plains of the Adwa Highlands, the terrain was as diverse as the people who call the land home. Its borders touching Eritrea to the north, the Amhara Region to the south, the Afar Region to the east, and Sudan to the west, Tigray stood at a strategic juncture, a meeting point of diverse cultures and historical narratives.

It was also a warzone.

That wasn't really anything new. The two-year-long conflict, now generally referred to as the Tigray War, which had tentatively ended with a ceasefire in November of 2022, was just the latest in a long series of conflicts both localized to the Tigray region, and more broadly in the nations comprising the Horn of Africa, that had almost completely stifled economic and social development in the region.

And yet, like many previous conflicts in the Horn of Africa, the Tigray War had largely gone unnoticed by the outside world. This ignorance of African affairs was only partly due to the coincidental arrival of the COVID-19 pandemic. Mostly, it had to do with the chronic apathy of Westerners toward people who, in the infamous words of one American president, lived in "shithole countries."

That perception, to say nothing of the stagnant economic conditions and abysmal quality of life for the inhabitants of the region, was something Taneisha Hayes was dedicated to changing. She believed, as did the other members of her all-volunteer team from the Africa in the 21st Century Initiative (A21I)—an international non-governmental organization dedicated to the goal of "bringing Africa into the 21st century"—that the so-called "dark continent," once the cradle of humanity, would play a much greater role in human history moving forward.

But first, the killing had to stop.

The declaration of the ceasefire had mostly curtailed the violence, but it had done little to address the underlying issues. That, Taneisha knew, would take a lot more than a simple agreement to lay down arms. It would take actual dialogue—bringing all the stakeholders to the table, and making them understand that they, and only they, had the power to decide their future. Some of the revolutionary fighters, notably a former Tigrayan National Front commander named General Tadesse, were already beating the war drums, and gathering considerable support.

She turned away from the mountains and instead took in the small collection of mud-brick huts that Alem Tekle and about two hundred or so of his kinfolk called home.

From what Taneisha had learned, in talking to many of his former comrades-in-arms, Alem had been fighting for the independence of the Tigrayan people for nearly all of his adult life. Born in these rugged hills he still called home, he had witnessed the struggle for independence against the Ethiopian monarchy and later the Soviet-sponsored Derg regime. His father, a simple farmer, had instilled in him a deep love for the land and a fierce pride in their Tigrayan heritage. Inspired by stories of warriors who fought against the oppressive Italian Fascist forces during World War II, Alem joined the Tigray People's Liberation Front, or TPLF, during their struggle against the Derg in the 1980s. His charisma and strategic mind quickly earned him respect among his fellows.

His leadership abilities had not gone unnoticed. When the TPLF—which had for years been a major party dominating Ethiopian politics—lost its position of power in the democratically elected government, and in the face of growing anti-Tigrayan sentiment, transformed into the Tigrayan National Front, TNF, Alem emerged as a key figure leading the army of the nascent rebellion—the Tigrayan Defense Force. Navigating the complexities of guerrilla warfare, he coordinated supply routes, rallied villagers, and strategized ambushes against Ethiopian forces.

Yet, despite his successes on the battlefield, Alem had paid a heavy price for his decision to fight, losing friends, family, and comrades. His eldest son was killed early on in the conflict. Later, a trusted lieutenant sold him out, revealing his location to Ethiopian troops, who in a midnight raid, captured Alem, dragging him away from his village.

He spent the remaining months confined to a dark cell, tortured and interrogated. Released during negotiations following the ceasefire, the sixty-seven-year-old Alem had returned to his village in the mountains, where he assumed the role of revered elder. He was, Taneisha felt certain, someone that others would listen to, and if she could convince *him* to reject Tadesse's hawkish message and support the existing peace, he would convince his fellow Tigrayans.

Thankfully, Taneisha was not alone in making her case.

Her diplomatic team consisted of Miguel Sanchez, a seasoned negotiator with expertise in conflict resolution; Pierre Dubois, an economist with a keen understanding of regional economies; and Fatima Khan, a human rights advocate with a passion for justice. Taneisha, the nominal leader of the group, was the expert on Ethiopia, with a Master's Degree in African Studies, six years at the US Department of State's Bureau of African Affairs, and conversational fluency in Amharic, the national language of Ethiopia. Each member of the team brought a unique perspective to the table and was prepared to lay out a roadmap for a better future for Tigray, but which ideas, if any, would resonate with Alem Tekle and other leading figures in Tigrayan society remained to be seen.

The remaining member of the team was no diplomat. Rajesh Raj, a former Ghurka, now working as a security expert—read "bodyguard"—was under contract with A21I to protect the team from harm. Rajesh, with his steely gaze and a no-nonsense demeanor, commanded a force of five men—all former Ugandan soldiers, now working in the private security industry—armed with Kalashnikov automatic rifles. Rajesh and his men, divided between two more Range Rovers—one ahead of Taneisha's and one behind—had already exited their vehicles and spread out to form a secure perimeter around the diplomats. Their presence was a stark reminder of the ever-present dangers in Tigray—a region under a Level Four Red "Do Not Visit" travel advisory from the State Department.

But going into dangerous places was the only way to—hopefully—make them a little less dangerous. Everyone on Taneisha's team knew the risk and accepted it. There had been a few tense moments, but by and large, the Tigrayans they had encountered had been hospitable and welcoming.

Taneisha's gaze was drawn to a light-skinned young man striding out from the collection of huts to greet them. His features were sharp, with pronounced cheekbones and a narrow nose, his face framed by a wispy beard. He wore a loose white Zuria, the traditional male attire in the region, draped about his upper body, with a matching turban wound about his head. When his eyes met hers, he smiled broadly and opened his arms in an inviting gesture.

"Greetings," the young man said, his voice warm and welcoming. He came forward and reached out, offering his hand to Taneisha. "I am Ezana Sengal. Welcome to the home of my grandfather, Alem Tekle. Please, come inside and enjoy the *merhaba*."

Ezana spoke in Tigrinya rather than Amharic, but there were enough similarities between the languages for Taneisha to get the gist of the introduction. The people of Ethiopia, including the Tigray, used a patronymic naming convention, in which a person received an individual name and then took their father's name as a surname, thus Ezana was the son of Sengal, who in turn was the son of Alem, the son of Tekle. Taneisha wondered if Sengal was the son Alem had lost during the recent war.

Merhaba, she knew, was the Tigrinya word for 'welcome' but as used by Ezana, it referred to the *Buna Tetu,* the celebrated ritual coffee service. Though many Americans thought of coffee as being primarily a South American export, Ethiopia was truly the birthplace of the beverage. According to a time-honored legend, an Ethiopian goatherd named Kaldi had observed his goats becoming highly energetic after eating the berries of a certain tree, and soon people in the region began brewing the hot beverage that would eventually become a daily mainstay for billions. It was just one example of how much the world owed to Africa.

Taneisha accepted Ezana's vigorous handshake and replied with a few words she had practiced, "*Selam! Bezihe beti b'tam astemari new,*" which roughly translated to, *Hello. May your home be blessed.*

Ezana's smile broadened and then he proceeded to go down the line, shaking hands with the other members of the A21I team. Miguel Sanchez replied with a few words of Amharic he'd been practicing. The others just nodded and smiled.

When the introductions were complete, Ezana beckoned the group to follow him into the settlement. As they all started after him, Raj broke away from the perimeter and called out to Taneisha. "Can I have a word with you?"

Taneisha hid her impatience behind a smile. "Yes, Rajesh?"

He waited until he was close enough that he could speak in a low voice, almost a whisper. "I don't like this. We're too exposed out here. If something happens, we won't be able to cover all the approaches."

She wanted to say, *Nothing's going to happen,* but knew better. Despite the seeming placidity of this remote setting, Tigray remained a dangerous place. Moreover, it was Raj's job to worry about such things. She'd worked in enough dangerous places to know the importance of trusting the people who had sworn to protect you.

But this meeting *had* to happen. "I know it's not ideal," she said patiently. "But we're going to have to make do."

Raj gave a resigned sigh, as if he had expected no other answer. He then regarded Ezana for a long moment, as if trying to decide whether he was trustworthy. "My men can only do so much," he said finally. "All of you need to be on the lookout for trouble. Complacency will get us all killed. If things go sideways, you need to be ready to get out of there."

"Understood," replied Taneisha, and then, leaving Raj to worry, turned to Ezana and gestured for him to continue.

The Tigrayan brought them into a small courtyard, overhung with a broad shade canopy. In the center of the courtyard, sitting on the ground before a low table was an older man who bore more than a passing resemblance to Ezana, and a young woman, who held a wooden bowl full of small green coffee beans in her lap. An older woman emerged from a hut with an assortment of breads and pastries which she placed on the table.

Ezana indicated the old man with a gesture. "This is my grandfather, Alem Tekle."

Taneisha approached the old man, greeting him in Tigrinya and offering her hand. Alem did not rise, though Taneisha felt sure this had more to do with his advanced years than an intentional choice to insult her. Although reportedly only in his late sixties, Alem's hard life had aged him prematurely, adding twenty years to his physical age. His weathered face bore the scars of battles fought, both on the front lines and in clandestine meetings.

Taneisha knew that any serious conversation would not begin until the guests were served their first of three cups of coffee, so she directed her colleagues to sit around the table. The preparation of the coffee was as much a part of the ritual as its consumption, beginning with the rinsing and roasting of the raw coffee beans, a task which would be performed by the young woman—possibly Alem's granddaughter or Ezana's wife. Although this ritual, like most things relating to Ethiopian culture, fascinated Taneisha, today she found herself wishing they could just skip ahead to the real reason for their visit. But trying to rush things would only get the discussion off on the wrong foot, so stifling her impatience, she did her best to be attentive to the process.

When they were all seated, the woman gestured for them to partake of the repast laid out on the table—an assortment of breads, dried fruit, roasted grains, and, of all things, popcorn. As they all snacked, the woman began rinsing the coffee beans in the bowl, rubbing them with her fingers to remove the husks. After patting them dry, she took them over to a corner of the courtyard where she poured them into a cast iron skillet sitting atop a woodburning stove and immediately began stirring so that the contents would heat evenly. In a matter of minutes, the beans began crackling and popping. The young woman began fanning her hand over the skillet, wafting the distinctive aroma of roasting coffee in the direction of her guests. The smell always took Taneisha back to her childhood in Seattle, and weekend visits to Pike Place Market where the original Starbucks location still roasted small batches of coffee on site.

The young woman poured them into another small bowl, and using a blunt stick like a pestle, began grinding the hot beans to the desired coarseness. After that, the grounds were poured into a long-necked, bulbous clay vessel—  called a *jebena*—after which water was added and the *jebena* was placed on the stovetop. When the coffee came to a boil, she poured it into a cooling vessel, then returned it to the *jebena* for a second boil. As this process was repeated a third time, Taneisha felt her impatience rising along with the temperature of the beverage. Finally, when the coffee reached its final boil, the young woman brought the *jebena* over to the table, and after fitting a horsehair filter over the end of the spout, held the vessel about a foot above the line of small ceramic cups arrayed before them, and began to pour. The stream of dark liquid moved from cup to cup, with only a few drops splashing out, and then the young woman beckoned them to enjoy.

Taneisha thanked the woman, took a sip, and then faced Alem Tekle. "Mr. Alem, thank you for inviting us into your home. And thank you for your willingness to talk with us. I have heard that you share our commitment to keeping the peace in Tigray."

Alem's tired eyes regarded her for a long moment. "When I was a young man," he began, speaking in Amharic. "I dreamed of a free Tigray. Nothing was more important to me. Now that I am old, I still dream of a free Tigray, but more than that, I dream of peace. Peace for my grandchildren and their grandchildren. I wonder. Can both ever exist in the same world?"

The words seemed formal, rehearsed, but when he spoke them, his world-weariness was palpable.

Taneisha was careful with her reply. "Mr. Alem, I can't promise you that Tigray will ever become a sovereign nation. That's something over which we have no influence. But peace *is* possible, if we work for it."

Something of the young man he once had been stirred in old Alem. "Peace with a boot on our necks is no peace at all. To accept such a peace would dishonor all those who fought before us."

Taneisha raised her hands. "It doesn't have to be one or the other. There is a middle way, but someone must be courageous enough to break the cycle of violence and oppression."

Alem gazed back at her. "How would you do this?"

"This isn't something that we," Taneisha gestured to indicate her colleagues, "can do for you. It is the people of Tigray who must make it happen. I have spoken with your leaders in Mekelle, and they have told me that the peace cannot hold without the support of the people. Men like you."

Alem waved a dismissive hand. "I am old."

Taneisha shook her head. "The young men will listen to you. In the villages, and in Axum town."

Alem narrowed his gaze. "What would you have me tell them? Simply to lay down their arms?"

Taneisha couldn't entirely suppress a satisfied smile. With his question, Alem had opened a door, and Taneisha was going to stick her foot in before it slammed shut. "That's why we're here, Mr. Alem. My friends and I want to hear about what concerns you. Together, we can begin laying the foundation for lasting peace *and* prosperity in Tigray."

Alem appeared to consider this for a moment. Then he turned to the young woman who had served the coffee and spoke in rapid Tigrinya. She nodded, and then indicated with gestures that everyone present should return their cups to the table in order to begin the second of three servings.

This time, Taneisha made no effort to hide her smile. Things were finally moving in the right direction. She started to offer her thanks to Alem, but before she could speak the words, a distant but very distinctive, rapid popping noise cut her off.

It was, she knew, the sound of gunfire.

Alem's eyes flashed angrily in recognition of the sound. He met Taneisha's gaze and hissed, "Is this the peace you would promise?"

TWO

ALEM DIDN'T WAIT for a reply, but leapt up with unexpected vigor and began shouting to his family members. A moment later, they were gone, retreating into the huts, leaving Taneisha and her colleagues to fend for themselves.

DuBois was the first to react. Jumping to his feet, he started back down the path they had followed into the settlement.

Taneisha rose as well. "Pierre, wait. We don't know what's happening."

There were more reports—long bursts of automatic weapons fire, some overlapping, indicating multiple shooters. The air snapped and crackled with the sound of bullets passing overhead.

The economist glanced back. "We're being attacked. What more do you need to know?"

Sanchez, who in the course of his diplomatic career had visited any number of hostile environments, was ready with an answer. "Pierre, think about it. We don't know where the shooting is coming from."

"We have the safety protocols for a reason," Taneisha added. "Rajesh is in charge of our security. We take our cues from him."

"I think Rajesh may be a bit busy just now," countered DuBois.

"All the more reason to wait here," retorted Sanchez. "Rajesh and his men don't need us getting in the way."

Almost as if summoned by the repeated mention of his name, Raj appeared on the path, running toward them, clutching his assault rifle in both hands. His face was streaked with sweat and grime, and the smell of sulfur hung about him.

"Raj!" shouted DuBois. "What's happening?"

Raj waited until he was standing in their midst to reply but he did not answer the question directly. Instead, he made a come-along gesture. "We have to leave. Right now. Follow me and keep your heads down."

Taneisha and the others had rehearsed hasty evacuations, but those drills had not prepared them for the emotional experience of moving under fire. Like DuBois, Taneisha felt a mixture of both fear and curiosity. Who was attacking the settlement? What was their intention? Was this a bandit raid aimed at Alem Tekle and his kin? Or were Taneisha and her team the actual target?

She knew that, ultimately, it didn't matter. The only appropriate response was to follow the protocols Raj had established, but the reality of the situation, with adrenaline exciting the nervous system, short-circuiting rational thought, made compliance with Raj's protocols a monumental effort. Nevertheless, the four of them lined up behind Raj and followed him through the settlement, staying hunched over to provide less of a target to any hostile gunmen.

As they moved closer to the perimeter, the noise of gunfire grew louder. A haze of smoke, stinking of gunpowder residue smudged the air directly ahead. Raj raised a hand as they reached the last hut. "Stay here," he advised. "And keep your heads down."

"Rajesh!" said DuBois, pleading. "Tell us. What is happening?"

Raj gave an impatient frown. "Two lorries full of armed men came up the trail. When we challenged them, they opened fire. One of my men was wounded."

"Who are they?" asked Taneisha, prompted by more than just curiosity. The identity of the attackers would bear heavily on their mission. If the aggressors were Eritrean or Ethiopian military, it would be a hard sell to convince men like Alem Tekle to continue to observe the ceasefire. But there was also a very real possibility that the attacking force might represent an extremist faction in the TNF, targeting Alem for supporting the ceasefire. Either way, things weren't looking hopeful for the peace effort.

"I'm not sure. They aren't using military vehicles, but that doesn't mean a whole lot. I called defense command to report the contact. They aren't aware of any hostile activity in the area, and the nearest help is two hours away. I'm afraid we're on our own." Raj eased out from behind the cover afforded by the hut for a quick look at the battlefield, then just as quickly drew back and faced the group. "Be ready to move when I give the signal."

"Move?" asked DuBois.

"To the Rovers. We're getting out of here." Then, as if sensing that his charges were getting lost in the fog of war, he went on. "We're going to be taking fire, so stay down. Get in on the right side. Keep the vehicles between you and the enemy. Once you're inside, keep your heads down. Don't give them a target."

DuBois swallowed nervously but managed a nod.

"Just follow my lead, and we'll get through this," Raj added, and then hefting his rifle, ventured out into the open, making a mad dash to rejoin his men.

Curiosity overcoming fear, Taneisha edged forward to have a look for herself. She immediately spotted the three Range Rovers, parked right where they had left them, about twenty yards away. She then picked out the figures of Raj's hired guns, attired in military surplus green and brown camouflage fatigues, kneeling down at the corners of the SUVs, firing their assault rifles at an enemy force Taneisha could not yet see. A moment later, she found Raj, crouching beside one of the Ugandan mercenaries, engaged in an animated discussion.

"What are you doing?" asked DuBois, horrified. "Raj said to stay here."

"He said to watch for his signal," argued Taneisha without looking back. "We can't very well do that if we can't see him."

DuBois started to protest, but Sanchez cut him off. "He also said to be ready to move, Pierre. Are you ready?"

DuBois stammered out an affirmative.

Sanchez then addressed the quietest member of their group. "Fatima, are you ready?"

"Yes," came the soft but confident reply. It was not the first time Fatima, who had escaped political violence and oppression in Afghanistan at an early age, had faced mortal danger.

Taneisha returned her attention to Raj just in time to see the former Gurkha waving his hand, urging them to make the crossing. She took a deep breath, muttered, "You got this," and then took a tentative step toward the waiting vehicles.

A loud boom—like close thunder—shook the world. Taneisha saw Raj's eyes go wide in horror, his head turning in the direction of the sound, and then he was flung through the air like a rag doll, propelled ahead of and then engulfed in the expanding cloud of smoke and dust occupying the space where the Range Rover had been an instant before.

Then a wave of pressure caught up to her like a slap from the hand of God, and everything went black.

THREE

DR. ELENA RAMIREZ'S hands moved deftly as she packed her black medical bag. More a backpack than the traditional Gladstone bag depicted in old movies and TV shows where doctors actually made house calls, with its contents, she could perform interventions for most injuries and medical emergencies, and treat any number of maladies common to the region. While it was a poor substitute for the resources available to her back at her parent hospital in San Francisco, California, with her backpack, she was the closest thing for hundreds of miles to a top-tier medical center.

Her colleagues from the Doctors Without Borders mission were similarly engaged, preparing for their expedition to bring vaccines to nearby settlements.

They were a cosmopolitan bunch. There was Dr. François Laurent, a pediatrician from Marseille and Dr. Amina Hassan, an infectious disease specialist from Nairobi; and three registered nurses—Carlos Ortega, a cheerful and resilient RN from Mexico City; Jessica Miller, a nurse from Chicago; and Haruto Tanaka, another RN from Tokyo.

There had been some friction at the beginning—there always was—as they got to know each other and their respective approach to practicing medicine, but all of them were veterans of numerous missions abroad, and the hardships of primitive living in the remote Tigrayan town of Adi Gebru posed little difficulty.

The clinic was little more than a repurposed house, partitioned into examination rooms. The beds and other medical equipment looked as though they might have been taken from a museum exhibit of doctors' offices from the 1950s but had, in fact, been provided by another international non-governmental organization that built hospitals in developing nations using donated medical equipment. There were two rooms in back with hospital beds that could be used for longer-term care, but as it was their practice to bring care to the patients in their homes—most were unable to make the long journey down from their settlements in the mountains—the beds had served a different purpose. The medical team had taken turns bunking at the clinic. While the rationale for this arrangement could be justified as protecting the clinic from thieves and vandals, in fact what they most liked about overnighting in the clinic was the opportunity to sleep in a real bed, instead of in a sleeping bag on a foam pad in the nearby Orthodox Tewahedo Church—their host for the six-week assignment.

Elena had just zipped up her bag when she heard the distinct rumble of vehicles coming up the road. She looked up, instantly alert. The arrival of a vehicle rarely brought good news. Very few locals had cars and would never use them to drive to the clinic unless it were an emergency. The Ethiopian military had trucks, as did some of the rebel fighters who still lurked in the hills, training and planning for the next round of the Tigray War. A visit from either group was nothing to celebrate. At best, they would bring a comrade in need of treatment either from a extreme illness or a combat injury. At worst, it might mean a shakedown. They had money set aside for that purpose, and usually a small bribe was enough to send the unwanted visitors on their way. That was just the cost of operating in a place like Tigray.

Hefting her pack onto one shoulder, she moved to the door and, steeling herself to face whatever might lay on the other side, opened it.

The vehicles pulling up in front of the clinic were neither military trucks nor the beaters typically used by locals. Instead, she saw a pair of forest green Toyota Land Cruisers, streaked with dust but otherwise in good repair, at least to judge by appearances. Land Cruisers were well suited to the rugged environs of Tigray. The logistics contractor working for Doctors Without Borders had supplied the medical team with two of the four-wheel-drive sport utility vehicles, though they were older models with years of heavy use and showed it.

This is different, she thought.

As the SUVs came to a stop, four people emerged—two from each. Elena's attention was immediately drawn to the driver of the nearest.

If Elena had a "type," he would have been it. He was tall, at least six feet, and well proportioned, with sun-bleached, shaggy blond hair, a deep tan, and exuded a rugged charm. Attired in a white photojournalist-style shirt and khaki cargo pants, he definitely had the look of someone whom she wouldn't at all be opposed to buying her a drink, though in her experience, such men were seldom to be found hanging about upscale watering holes, trolling for dates; they were outside, doing *real* things.

Not that Elena frequented those places either. There just wasn't enough time in her busy schedule for such distractions.

The second man to emerge was a good half-a-head taller than his companion, a black man built like a linebacker. His gold and black daishiki looked more like something a tourist might purchase than a traditional African costume, and when taken with his short dreadlocks, Elena would have bet good money that he was an American.

The two who got out of the second vehicle were less distinctive. The driver was a petite woman of indeterminate age, with short blonde hair and elfin features. She was the sort of woman who could, if she wanted, become almost invisible. Her passenger was a dark-skinned man who, judging by his thick black beard and blue turban, practiced the Sikh religion and....

"Dr. Singh," Elena said, a smile of recognition forming. Some of her apprehension over the unexpected visit abated. Sanjeet Singh was a physician who, like her, took on assignments from Doctors Without Borders. "What brings you here?"

The bearded man smiled. "Dr. Ramirez. You remember me."

"Yemen, wasn't it?"

"Yes, two years ago. It's good to see you again." He gestured to the others. "These are my colleagues: Maisy Cole. Will Irons, Deacon Jones. We're from Project: RESCUE."

"Call me Deke," added the big African-American.

"Project: RESCUE?" asked Elena. "What's that?"

The good-looking man—Will Irons, she remembered—fielded the question. "Project: RESCUE works with NGOs like Doctors Without Borders, or Médecins Sans Frontières (MSF), to provide logistical support in hard-to-reach places. Guides, drivers, translators. And a security assessment. We're the ones who arranged logistical support for your team and performed the initial security assessment."

Elena's brow furrowed in confusion. "Well, thank you... I guess? That doesn't explain why you're here."

"Project: RESCUE also provides, as the name suggests, rescue. Emergency evacuations for those hard-to-reach places."

Elena shook her head. "There's nobody here who needs to be evacuated."

"I'm afraid that's not correct, Dr. Ramirez. The US State Department has issued a Level Four Red notice for Tigray, warning all Americans to leave. Your organization asked us to bring you out. We're here to take you home. "

Elena felt her cheeks go hot with anger. "That's absurd! We know Tigray can be dangerous, but we're doing fine."

"You may not have been affected yet," said Sanjeet patiently, "But there has been an uptick in armed robberies and kidnappings, as well as reports of increased activity among the rebel groups which may endanger the ceasefire."

"All the more reason we're needed here. Do you have any idea how hard the war hit these people?"

Will met her gaze steadily. "Dr. Ramirez, I admire your dedication, but this isn't up for debate. Doctors Without Borders made the decision. It's not up to me or you. We're here to take you and the rest of your team back to Axum and put you on a plane for home."

Elena clenched her fists in frustration. Part of the appeal of Doctors Without Borders was being able to work without the constant oversight of management. "This is unacceptable. I'm calling headquarters."

"You'll have to do that from Axum," said Will. "Right now, we need to get moving. Please tell the rest of your team to get packed."

"Wait, we're leaving right now?"

"That's right." He gestured to his companions. "Tell us what we can do to help."

ELENA FELT LIKE a piece of driftwood being swept along by a fast current, completely at the mercy of forces beyond her control.

She hated feeling that way.

A call by satellite phone to headquarters had verified what Will had told her. The decision had been made with haste, and efforts to contact Elena directly had failed because it was her practice to keep the sat-phone turned off except for emergencies and a weekly check-in, to conserve the battery. Electricity in Adi Gebru was inconsistent at best.

Grudgingly, she had passed the news along to her colleagues and had been somewhat dismayed by their almost eager acceptance. For their sake, she went along with the decision, and working together with help from the Project: RESCUE personnel, they began loading up their equipment and belongings, and were ready to roll out inside of half an hour.

As they were preparing to leave, Elena asked Sanjeet why Project: RESCUE had sent four people in two vehicles to deliver the news and escort them out.

"Redundancy," Sanjeet replied. "This way, if one of our Land Cruisers breaks down, we have a backup."

"Will's Rules number one and two," intoned Deke, overhearing their conversation. "Always have a plan. Always have a Plan B."

"I notice you guys aren't carrying any guns. What if we run into trouble?"

"In my experience," explained Will, "Running around a foreign country with a gun is more likely to invite trouble than keep it at bay. Project: RESCUE can and does hire local security providers for clients working in extremely dangerous areas, but our group prefers to leave a lighter footprint."

Despite her irritation with Will, Elena was impressed by this enlightened attitude, which she shared. In her experience, guns caused more problems than they solved. One had only to look at the present situation in Tigray to see it.

With the four-by-fours loaded up, they set out heading north on the highway. Will and Deke took the lead. Elena, along with Dr. Hassan and Jessica rode in the second vehicle, followed by Dr. Laurent, Carlos, and Haruto in the third. Maisy and Sanjeet brought up the rear.

The mood in Elena's vehicle was tense as they drove, though she suspected the others were more concerned with the threat level than the fact that they were leaving behind important, unfinished work. Her mind raced to come up with some way to reverse this decision so they could go back to the clinic and, at the very least, finish the vaccine program.

They had only gone about ten miles when Will slowed and then stopped his vehicle, and Maisy drove up from the rear to pull up beside him. They conversed for a few minutes, and then Will did a U-turn and headed back the way they'd come, while Maisy took his place at the head of the convoy.

Elena didn't like being left out of the loop, so instead of following meekly, she honked her horn several times and began flashing her lights to get Maisy's attention. When Maisy stopped, she pulled up alongside the green Land Cruiser and rolled her window down.

"Where did they go?" she asked, making no attempt to hide her irritation.

Maisy, calm and composed, explained, "We picked up a radioed distress call from a settlement up in the mountains. A group of visiting diplomats is under attack and pinned down."

"And your friend decided to just go charging to the rescue?" Elena asked, incredulous.

Maisy gave her a wry smile. "We're Project: RESCUE. That's what we do."

FOUR

WHEN TANEISHA CAME to, she was on her back, staring up at the blue sky, surrounded by her three colleagues. For a blissful few seconds, she couldn't figure out why. Then, she remembered the explosion. Remembered the Rover disappearing in a flash. Remembered Raj....

Raj?

Sanchez's face drifted close to hers, his mouth moving. He was talking, maybe asking if she was all right, but all Taneisha could hear was a persistent ringing sound. Her head felt thick, as if someone had stuffed it with sawdust, but aside from that, she wasn't aware of any injuries.

"I'm okay," she muttered, or maybe just thought she did, and then tried to sit up. Her limbs felt like bags of cement, but with a little assistance from Sanchez and Fatima, she managed to raise her upper torso.

The shift in position brought the flaming wreckage of the Range Rover into view. Taneisha's heart sank. Whatever had caused the explosion had not merely destroyed the SUV in the middle, but also dealt severe damage to the other two. Worse, there was no sign of the security detail.

Sanchez was tugging at her arm, urging her to get to her feet. His shouted exhortation sounded like someone screaming into a pillow, but she was able to get the gist. "We have to go!"

But go where? she wondered. There was no way to leave, and no one left to save them.

Nevertheless, she allowed Sanchez to help her stand and then followed him and the others back into the settlement. The air was thick with the acrid scent of gunpowder and fear. They passed several men in local attire—presumably Alem Tekle's kinsmen and neighbors—armed with Kalashnikov rifles and running into the fray. She could see the determination in the eyes of Alem's neighbors as they took up arms to defend their homes, but she also saw the grim acceptance of the inevitable. Even if Alem's kinsmen somehow repelled the enemy, incalculable damage had already been done. The ceasefire was finished, and with it, any hope of a peaceful future for Tigray.

Just then, a stray bullet struck the wall of the hut they were passing, spraying Taneisha with dust and debris, reminding her that the failure of their mission was the least of her immediate concerns.

Sanchez led the way, his experience in hostile territory supplying the lifeline to which the rest of them clung. DuBois stayed close behind him, leaving Fatima and Taneisha to bring up the rear. They moved quickly, ducking between huts and weaving through narrow alleys, the sounds of battle echoing all around them, and soon found themselves back in the courtyard where they had held audience with Alem. Flies swarmed about the plates of food prepared for the coffee ceremony. Taneisha's gaze lingered on the forgotten *jebena*, a symbol of hospitality now forever tainted by the violence that engulfed them.

Another deep boom shook the ground underfoot, and a plume of smoke rose into the air, marking the site of the explosion near where they had been only a moment before. A few seconds later, debris began raining down on them, prompting everyone to duck and cover.

"We need to get inside," wailed DuBois. "Find some place to hide and wait this out."

"They are using RPGs," remarked Fatima.

RPGs, Taneisha knew, were Russian-made, shoulder-fired anti-tank rockets, used extensively by insurgent forces in battlegrounds around the world against everything from helicopters to houses. She had never previously seen them used, but knew Fatima probably had.

"What does that mean?" countered DuBois.

"It means," Sanchez supplied, "that if we stay here, we're dead."

"Where's Raj?" Taneisha asked, although she knew the answer.

"Raj is dead," said Sanchez, grimly. "They're all dead."

"Where are we supposed to go?" wailed DuBois.

This time, Sanchez had no answer. His face was stoic, but his eyes betrayed a flicker of despair. Taneisha felt her heart begin to pound as the reality of the situation descended on her.

"We run," said Fatima. Her hand found Taneisha's, a small but welcome comfort amid the encroaching dread. "Leave the village. Flee into the hills."

"What's to stop them from following us?"

"They may not care about us," said Sanchez. "This attack might have nothing to do with us."

Taneisha heard the doubt in his tone. Even he didn't believe the timing was a coincidence. Nevertheless, he went on. "But we'll stand a better chance out there than we will in here."

"Very well." DuBois's voice was shaky, but he nodded in agreement. "Into the hills then."

Sanchez gestured to the far end of the courtyard, and the path leading through the part of the settlement farthest from the fighting. "Let's move fast and keep low. Stick together, no matter what."

As much as she knew it was the right choice, Taneisha felt a sudden foreboding. While they cowered in the courtyard, it was almost possible to cling to the illusion of sanctuary, that they were safe within these confines, while leaving would mean admitting the danger was real. But the danger *was* real. Staying where they were was like hiding under the bed while the house burned down around them. She nodded and then, still gripping Fatima's hand, started after Sanchez.

Beyond the courtyard, the settlement seemed to have been completely abandoned, but as they neared the edge of the inhabited area, they caught sight of some of the residents—women, old men, and young children—crossing the open fields of waist-high teff grass, making their way toward the craggy foothills a good two-hundred yards distant.

The sight buoyed Taneisha's spirits. These people were survivors. She and her colleagues could do a lot worse than to simply follow their lead.

That glimmer of optimism guttered quickly as the sound of gunfire intensified. Bullets sizzled through the air around them, some of them decapitating long grass stems. A glance back showed half-a-dozen armed African men wearing dark green camouflage fatigues, moving along the perimeter of the village, a good hundred yards to their rear, firing their assault rifles on the move as they gave chase.

Terror gripped Taneisha's heart. *They're here to kill* us.

Any doubts regarding the attackers' motives had been swept away.

"Run!" shouted DuBois, already heeding his own advice.

It seemed like a futile endeavor. The nearest crags were still a couple hundred yards away, and while they might conceivably outpace the pursuing gunmen, they could not hope to outrun their bullets.

Still, they had to try.

"Run," Sanchez shouted, though unlike DuBois, he remained with the two women, urging them on as much with his presence as his words. "We can make it!"

Taneisha broke into a run, but was soon winded. She thought she had been acclimating to the rarefied high-altitude atmosphere, but this was the first time since arriving that she had engaged in any sort of physical activity beyond a short walk. Nevertheless, she struggled on and did not let go of Fatima's hand. Fatima, too, held on fiercely, drawing strength from the connection. If death was to be their lot, then at least they would face it together as they attempted to flee.

A bullet struck the ground practically at Taneisha's heel, showering the backs of her legs with debris, eliciting a cry more of alarm than pain. In some remote corner of her mind she wondered what it would feel like to be shot. Would there be searing pain? Or would the shock overwhelm her nervous system, leaving her numb to the injury? She'd heard stories of shooting victims, in the grip of an adrenaline surge, completely unaware that they had been wounded.

It occurred to her then that, barring a miracle, she would soon have an answer to the question whether she wanted it or not.

She wanted to scream. Rage at the world and it's cruelty. This wasn't what was supposed to happen. She had come to Tigray to help preserve the peace, not die with a bullet in her back.

I don't want to die!

Panic and despair gripped her. Her thoughts swirled with conflicting imperatives.

Keep running... Drop to the ground and hide in the tall grass... Play dead... Give up and beg for mercy....

She had no idea which, if any of these, held the key to salvation. Had she been forced to choose, she might have done the latter, but her colleagues were still running and so she put aside her misgivings and let herself be carried along.

Suddenly, a massive shape appeared in the corner of her eye, rising mountain-like from the midst of the teff stalks. Taneisha reflexively glanced in that direction and felt a new wave of hopelessness crash over her as she beheld a battered and dust-streaked green Toyota Land Cruiser charging across the field on what appeared to be an intercept course with her and her colleagues. They might be able to outpace the gunmen and their reports, but they could not hope to outrun a four-by-four.

But no sooner had she determined this than the SUV swung to the left, crossing the path they were blazing, and coming to a full stop just a few yards behind them. It took Taneisha a moment to realize that the vehicle was now between them and the pursuing gunmen, a moment in which she heard an urgent shout over the din of the persistent gunfire.

"Get in!"

She glanced back and saw a huge African man—easily six-foot-five, broad chest and muscular arms straining the fabric of his multicolored daishiki—standing beside the open passenger side doors of the Land Cruiser, waving his hand in an urgent come-along gesture, and repeating his exhortation.

It took Taneisha another moment to grasp the significance of this development. The man from the SUV was trying to help them.

Sanchez figured it out a fraction of a second before Taneisha and immediately pivoted toward the Land Cruiser. "Taneisha! Fatima! Get in," he urged, and then turned back to shout after a still-running DuBois, who had either failed to notice the SUV's arrival, or misunderstood its intent. "Pierre! Come back. Help is here."

Taneisha and Fatima were already heeding the advice, coming about to make a mad dash back to the waiting vehicle.

"Let's go, let's go" urged the big African man, but then, as they reached the SUV, he broke into a broad smile. "You folks looked like you could use a ride."

The comment caught Taneisha off guard, eliciting a nervous laugh. "What gave us away?" she replied, though she was so out of breath the intended quip came out as a hoarse whisper.

"Get in and keep your heads down. The doors are armored, and the windows are supposed to be bullet resistant, but between you and me, I wouldn't bet my life on it."

As if to underscore this point, the interior of the SUV reverberated with the sound of bullets striking the opposite side. Each impact sounded like a hammer blow.

"I will try to remember that," said Fatima, climbing into the Toyota's rear passenger compartment, ignoring the plush bucket seats to instead crouch down on the floor.

Taneisha was right behind her, but as she scrambled into the vehicle, it finally sank in that to the man had spoken unaccented English.

American English.

Before she could comment on this, Sanchez and DuBois arrived and clambered into the vehicle's rear compartment with them. Their savior slammed the door shut behind them and then climbed into the front passenger seat. "Good to go!" he called out, shouting to be heard over the din of bullet strikes.

As if on cue, the driver of the SUV craned his head around to look at the four refugees huddled in the back. He was, Taneisha saw, a white man with a mop of unruly sun-bleached hair and blue-gray eyes. His face had the bronzed, weathered look of someone who spent more time outdoors than in. He regarded them for a moment and then cracked a smile. "On behalf of the crew, I'd like to thank you for choosing us for your emergency transportation needs. Please keep your arms and legs inside the vehicle at all times, and remain in your seats until the ride comes to a full and complete stop."

"What he's trying to say," said the big man in the passenger's seat, "Is hang on to your butts."

FIVE

THE LAND CRUISER jolted forward, all four tires throwing up rooster tails of grass and dirt as it shot across the field. The driver cranked the steering wheel hard to the right, carving a tight U-turn to bring the vehicle back around and onto the trail it had blazed when making its entry. Bullets continued to hammer into the door panels and pock-mark the laminated coating on the thick bullet-resistant windows. After a few seconds, however, the intensity of the incoming fire seemed to slacken, and then fell off altogether, prompting Taneisha to raise her head just enough for a glance back at the settlement.

The first thing she noticed was the armed men, now moving in what looked like a full-blown retreat back from where they'd first appeared. Taneisha, recalling Raj's earlier report of two lorries bearing the armed attackers, did not allow herself the luxury of hoping that the hostiles would give up. The column of black smoke rising skyward from the far side of the village, marking the place where the three Range Rovers continued to burn, served as a powerful reminder that the enemy's arsenal was not limited to assault rifles.

The big man in the passenger seat glanced back at them. "Anyone get hit?"

Taneisha took a moment to check herself for injuries before answering. "I'm okay." She was relieved to hear her colleagues answering in similar fashion.

Then DuBois, sounding slightly irritated, asked, "Who are you? Where did you come from?"

"I'm Deke," answered the passenger. He jerked a thumb toward the driver. "That's Will. We picked up a radio transmission about a village being attacked, and since we just happened to be in the neighborhood, we thought we'd check it out. See if anyone needed a hand."

"Lucky for us that you were close by," said Sanchez.

"'Just happened'?" echoed DuBois, skeptically. "Nobody *just happens* to be in Tigray. Not foreigners, at any rate. You are Americans, aren't you?"

"If it's all the same," intoned Will, the driver, "I'd prefer to answer your questions over a cold beer at the hotel lounge in Axum. Right now, I need to focus on driving this beast, so if you could, please keep the chatter down."

The passenger—Deke—shrugged. "You heard the man."

DuBois huffed in irritation, but Taneisha was more than happy to postpone any discussion if it increased their chances of survival. She raised her head just enough to look through the windshield and saw the path ahead, a mule trail similar to the one they had negotiated to reach Alem Tekle's village.

Will slowed the SUV almost to a full stop and shifted the four-wheel-drive into low range. The engine growled like a caged beast eager to break free as Will maneuvered the vehicle with the precision of a seasoned mariner navigating treacherous shoals. The old mule path, cutting through rocky, uneven terrain, even overgrown in places, was a relic of a bygone era, now a serpentine adversary that tested the limits of man and machine.

After the initial haste of their rescue, the unexpected slowdown was excruciating. The SUV seemed to crawl like a snail over the rocks. As it traversed the terrain, the vehicle tilted up and down and from side to side at impossible angles, forcing the passengers to cling to the bases of the vehicle's bucket seats to avoid being tossed about the interior.

"You got this," Deke said, his voice a calm counterpoint to the tension that filled the cabin.

Will just nodded, his hands firm on the wheel.

In the back, Sanchez, Fatima, and DuBois were a study in contrasts. Sanchez's eyes were alert, scanning for any sign of their pursuers. Fatima's expression was stoic, a silent prayer perhaps on her lips. DuBois, however, was a bundle of nerves, his every twitch betraying the fear that clawed at his insides.

As the Cruiser dipped into a particularly vicious rut, DuBois couldn't contain a whimper. "At this rate, they'll be on us in no time," he blurted. "We're sitting ducks. Unarmed and—"

"Pierre!" Sanchez's voice rang like a bell, sharp and commanding. "Quiet."

But the economist just moaned. "I think I'm going to be sick."

"Focus on the horizon," suggested Deke. "It'll help with the nausea."

The vehicle lurched, wheels spitting out stones and dust as Will navigated a narrow ledge, the drop-off threatening to swallow them whole. The silence that followed DuBois's outburst was filled only by the sound of crunching gravel.

Then, they heard the all-too familiar sound of rifle fire.

"And there they are," DuBois muttered, more to himself than anyone else.

"There's a ravine ahead," replied Will, his tone betraying no hint of doubt. "If we can make it there, we'll be home free."

Taneisha wasn't sure how reaching the ravine would solve all their problems, but it didn't seem like the right time to ask.

The Land Cruiser crested a rise, and for a moment, the world seemed to pause, the beauty of Tigray sprawling before them, a stark contrast to the imminent danger nipping at their heels. Then gravity reclaimed its grip, and the vehicle tilted down. Before them lay a maze of challenges which Will met with a perfectly synchronized dance of steering and throttle. His jaw set in determination, he guided the Land Cruiser with an expert touch, the vehicle responding as if it understood the gravity of their situation.

DuBois, pale as a ghost, ducked his head between his knees. "I should never have come here," he whimpered, his voice barely audible over the din of their escape.

Ignoring the despair of his passengers, Will focused on the path ahead. The ravine was in sight now, a narrow gash in the earth that promised a sliver of safety—or a disastrous end.

"Will!" Deke shouted. "Behind us."

"I see them."

Curious despite herself, Taneisha looked back. Through the cloud of dust rising behind them, she could see a pair of four-by-four pickups making their way across the terrain the Land Cruiser had just traversed. Harder to see were the armed men standing in the beds of the trucks, firing their weapons over the tops of the cabs.

Another loud boom split the air, simultaneous with an eruption of white smoke behind the lead pickup, and from the midst of the dust cloud, a projectile, trailing a bright orange flame and a long smoke tendril, sliced through the air racing toward the Land Cruiser. Taneisha ducked reflexively as the rocket whooshed past, just barely missing them. A moment later, the projectile detonated against a rocky outcropping fifty yards ahead of them, sending a plume of dirt and debris skyward.

"Jesus," Deke exhaled, his eyes wide with the realization of how close they'd come to oblivion.

Sanchez peered back at the rising dust cloud. "That was too close. We need to move!"

With the ravine just ahead, Will pushed the Cruiser to its limits. The vehicle's tires clawed at the rocky ground, propelling them forward with a desperate urgency. Then, with almost no warning, they reached the edge. From Taneisha's perspective in the rear compartment, it looked as if they had come to the end of the world, and that advancing forward even a single inch would send them plummeting into oblivion.

Will, however, did not hesitate.

"Hold on," he said, his voice steady despite the immediacy of their peril, and then eased the SUV forward.

The Land Cruiser went almost completely vertical, tipping over the precipice and plunging down the slope. Taneisha felt certain that, at any moment, they would tip forward and began somersaulting end over end, but somehow, Will managed to outrun disaster. His descent into the ravine was a masterclass in controlled chaos. His hands seemed to float above the steering wheel, making rapid corrections, guiding the vehicle as it surfed down a cascade of loose rock. The Cruiser's tires bit into the shifting gravel, its frame groaning against the strain, yet it held firm under Will's deft control.

"Keep it steady," Deke murmured, his voice barely audible above the crunch of stone and earth. "You've got this, brother."

Behind them, one of the pursuing trucks breached the precipice with a roar, daring the treacherous descent, but almost immediately, it began to slew wildly, its tires losing grip amid the rubble.

"They're losing it!" Deke shouted, his eyes locked on the rearview mirror.

Will glanced back, his eyes narrowing. "Not good," he muttered.

Taneisha looked back, too, just as the driver of the truck lost control. The vehicle peeled away from the decline and tilted over, then began to tumble end over end down the slope, engulfed in the roaring tide of rock and dust that coursed down the ravine.

Taneisha's eyes went wide in horror as she watched the landslide race toward them.

Will, sensing the impending collision, cranked the steering wheel hard to the left. The Cruiser fishtailed, and for a heart-stopping instant, Taneisha believed that they would also roll over, but Will's instincts were true. The SUV straightened out and shot up the sloping wall of the ravine like a snowboarder carving up the side of a half-pipe. The tumbling truck, riding the wave of rock and debris, missed them by mere inches, its metal body screeching a cacophony as it continued its doomed plunge down the ravine. Will quickly turned the Land Cruiser downslope again, riding the edge of the ravine just above the slide.

For a long moment, the noise of the rock fall reverberated through the Land Cruiser, rising to a crescendo, but then, as quickly as it had begun, the tumult died away. In the silence that followed, the only sound to be heard was the labored breathing of the Cruiser's occupants and the steady rumble of its engine.

Taneisha gazed up the slope to where the second pickup sat idle, its driver evidently unwilling to risk the fate of his comrades. Then she let out the breath that she hadn't even realized she'd been holding and looked forward, her eyes meeting Will's in the mirror.

"Nice driving," she said with a grateful smile.

Will just nodded, then turned his focus to what lay ahead.

DuBois lifted his head, his eyes meeting hers with a silent question. "Is that it?" he asked, his voice a hoarse whisper. "Are we safe?"

Taneisha stared at him for a moment, then gazed out at the rugged beauty surrounding them. They were still a long way from anything remotely approaching safety, but thanks to the timely intervention of two strangers—Will and Deke—she was liking their odds of making it out of Tigray alive. "For now," she said, patting him on the arm. "For now."

But as Will brought the Cruiser back to the mule trail that would eventually cross the main highway leading back to Axum, and the adrenaline of the close call drained away, Taneisha's initial sense of relief gave way to a dark mood. They might have walked away with their lives, but their mission of peace had ended in disaster. She could only pray that the attack on Alem Tekle's village would not be the first battle and precursor of a second Tigray War.

SIX
Belém do Pará, Brazil

BORIS IVANOVICH PETROV sat in the cavernous lecture hall located in Hangar Two of the Hangar Convention and Fair Center of the Amazon, and thanked whatever gods might be listening for the miracle of air conditioning. The tropical humidity was a living thing, a suffocating blanket that had left him nearly soaked through in the brief time it had taken him to move from his hired limousine to the convention center entrance where he dutifully took his place in the Hangar Two auditorium, along with the other attendees of the 30th Conference of the Parties to the United Nations Framework Convention on Climate Change—more commonly known as COP 30.

Converted from actual aircraft hangars, the venue consisted of two interconnected pavilions enclosing a floor area of 24,000 square meters, under capacious free span skylights and ceilings which maximized natural light while maintaining the comfortable controlled climate inside. The interior was cool and artificially crisp, a welcome relief from the sweltering Brazilian humidity that lay just beyond the paneled glass walls.

The organizers of COP 30 had transformed this space into a nexus of debate and decision, where every utterance and idea might tip the scales of the planet's future. For the next twelve days, the Hangar Center would serve as a modern colosseum of knowledge where the world's leading environmental experts gathered to wage war on an invisible enemy: climate change.

Also present were representatives of the leading industrial nations, men and a few women, who had been given the unenviable task of finding a way to balance the urgency of the climate crisis with the economic needs of their respective governments. And then there were men like Petrov—working behind the scenes to ensure that any measures taken by the member nations would not upset the decades-long flow of natural resource wealth into the coffers of their benefactors.

As Senior Vice President of Global Operations for VEK—*Volga Energeticheskaya Korporatsiya*, Russia's largest publicly traded petroleum producer—Petrov was no stranger to this shadow dance. While the company proudly proclaimed a commitment to reducing its carbon footprint—with a stated goal of achieving net carbon emission neutrality by 2050—it continued to push for increased oil production.

Petrov had not gotten where he was by trying to please everyone. He had climbed the ranks of Russia's energy sector with a combination of shrewd political maneuvering and a deep understanding of the global oil market. As Deputy Minister of Energy, he had been instrumental in shaping Russia's oil policies and had played a pivotal role in expanding the country's energy influence abroad. His tenure at VEK had seen aggressive expansion and a relentless pursuit of Russia's energy interests, often at the expense of international relations. And now, here at a conference dedicated to putting his company out of business, he would execute his boldest maneuver yet.

A hush fell over the assembly as a climate scientist from the host nation stepped up to the podium, his presence commanding the room's attention. His voice, clear and resonant, cut through the silence, welcoming the gathered dignitaries and imploring them to embrace the urgency of their collective mission.

Petrov listened, his expression unreadable, as the scientist painted a vivid picture of a world on the brink. His ice-blue eyes held a glacial detachment as he listened to the impassioned pleas of the Brazilian climate scientist. The man's voice rose and fell with the cadence of a preacher, urging the assembly toward a covenant of carbon neutrality, of bold sacrifices for the greater good. But where others heard a call to arms, Petrov heard opportunity knocking with a rhythm only he seemed to recognize.

"As we stand here today," the scientist proclaimed, "the Amazon breathes for the world, but it is suffocating. We must act now or face a future where the lungs of our planet wither into a barren wasteland."

The crowd erupted in applause, a thunderous wave of approval that reverberated through the conference hall. Petrov clapped along, a slow, deliberate beat that belied the machinations whirring behind his stoic façade. He was not here as a mere steward of Russia's vast petrochemical wealth; he was the harbinger of a plan so radical it would send a tidal wave through the echelons of power across the globe.

As the applause died down, Petrov rose from his seat and made his way through the auditorium. From past experience, he knew that the opening days of the conference would be more of the same—an endless procession of climate Cassandras, naively imagining that this time it would be different, this time people would take note of the warnings and stop kicking the can down the road. He straightened his tie, a sartorial noose that felt tighter with each passing moment, and decided that, despite the early hour, he needed a drink.

"Boris Ivanovich," came a familiar drawl from behind him. "Fancy seeing you here, among all these tree-huggers and Chicken Littles."

Petrov turned and regarded the other man—an American lobbyist named Johnathan "Jack" McAllister. With his silver hair immaculately combed back, bespoke suit tailored to a fault to accentuate his broad shoulders, and the air of confidence he wore like a second skin, McAllister knew how to blend the charm of a southern gentleman with the cutthroat acumen of a Wall Street trader.

Petrov's response was a nod, measured and unreadable. "Jack," he acknowledged, the single word an entire conversation in itself. Then he added, "Chicken Littles? I am not familiar with the reference."

McAllister chuckled. "A children's story about a little chick who gets hit on the head by an acorn, and then runs around telling all his friends that the sky is falling."

Petrov nodded. "Ah. Yes, I know the story."

"You know, it's almost comical," McAllister went on, gesturing around them. "Here we are, talking about cutting emissions, and yet our very presence here is a testament to the power of oil. How many of these folks do you think flew in on private jets?"

Petrov's smile was thin, noncommittal. "A necessary evil," he replied.

"Sounds a lot better than 'naked hypocrisy'," said McAllister, laughing, He leaned in. "I've been meaning to ask you about your recent shopping spree."

Petrov feigned incomprehension. "I don't follow you."

"Locking up oil shale leases in Africa and Asia. Here I thought you were more interested in *exporting* your oil to those places. Why on earth would you be snapping up reserves in the places that are supposed to be emerging markets?"

Petrov shrugged. "I would think it obvious to a smart man like yourself, Jack. If we control those reserves, then nobody else can develop them. Basic economics, no? Limit the supply to increase demand for our product."

McAllister regarded him skeptically. "Any other day of the week, and I'd say that's a sound strategy. But if these climate nuts get their way, you're gonna be sitting on a pile of stranded assets."

There was a beat of silence as Petrov regarded the American. The leases McAllister was referring to weren't exactly a closely guarded secret, but Petrov was dismayed to hear that his activities had attracted the attention of industry insiders. He had hoped that the acquisitions would seem merely routine.

He waved a hand in the direction of the auditorium. "Do you really believe anything will come of this? They will beat their chests and make more empty promises to change, but the world keeps turning, and we both know runs on petroleum."

McAllister cocked his head to the side. "This time might be different. It's getting harder and harder to shift the blame. Right now, my clients are a lot more worried about ensuring that they aren't going to be held liable for future climate-related damages than in preserving the status quo. Yet here you are doubling down on oil futures. You know something the rest of us don't?"

Petrov felt his heart rate quicken. In a few days, the entire world would know what he knew, but the success of his plan depended on keeping his true motives secret a little while longer. He managed an indifferent shrug. "Maybe you are right," he said. "But then again, maybe not. Everything is a gamble, no?"

McAllister's smile widened, but it didn't reach his eyes. "Just making conversation, Boris. After all, we're all friends here, aren't we?" He patted Petrov's shoulder, a comradely touch that felt more like a warning, and then took his leave.

Petrov watched him walk away, the American's words a buzzing fly in the ointment of his plans.

Stranded assets, indeed.

He has no idea.

THE BAR WAS a dimly lit oasis of polished wood and gleaming glass, a departure from the stark formality of the conference hall. Petrov navigated through the clusters of delegates to a secluded corner booth. The low murmur of conversations, punctuated by the clink of ice in crystal tumblers, was a welcome change from the hive-like buzz in the auditorium.

As he settled into the banquette, the vibration of his encrypted satellite phone disrupted his tranquility. He glanced at the caller, tapped the button to accept the call, and pressed the phone to his ear. "Tell me something good."

"I'm afraid the news is not good."

The voice belonged to Mikhail Andreyevich Sokolov. A former operator in the Spetsnaz—Russian special forces— Sokolov had found a new purpose—not to mention substantial wealth—working in the private security industry, doing very much the same thing he had in the service of the GRU, Russian Military Intelligence, but now for a much more generous master. Sokolov was the linchpin of Petrov's master plan, tasked with carrying out a series of moves that would, like preliminary moves on a chessboard, guarantee the success of that plan. That he was calling to report bad news set Petrov's pulse soaring. "What do you mean?"

"Things did not go entirely as planned." Sokolov's voice was tinged with frustration, a rare crack in his otherwise stoic demeanor.

Petrov's hand tightened around the phone, his knuckles whitening. "Just say what you mean, Mikhail."

There was a long pause, and Petrov imagined Sokolov taking a breath and trying to find the words to explain away his failure. "The attack on the village went as planned. We disrupted the meeting. Unfortunately, the foreigners... Got away."

"Got away? How did they manage that?"

"They had help. I don't know from whom."

"I don't care about your excuses. Just take care of it."

Sokolov affirmed with a curt, "Understood," before the line went dead.

Petrov remained motionless, the weight of the moment settling upon him. The failed attack was a setback, but not a defeat. He was playing a long game, and there were still many pieces to maneuver into place before he made the decisive masterstroke. Victory would bring him wealth beyond measure, and who in their right mind didn't want more wealth?

But if he failed, his life wouldn't be worth a counterfeit kopeck.

SEVEN

Axum, Tigray National State, Ethiopia

 **THE AFTERNOON SUN** bathed the ancient city of Axum in a warm, golden light as Will Irons and his best friend Deke James stepped into the cool refuge of the Atse Kaleb Hotel bar. The walls were adorned with photographs of the iconic stelae which had been discovered nearby, and the ancient ruins of the palace and baths that had once belonged to the Queen of Sheba—a silent homage to the city's storied past. A low murmur of conversation filled the air, a blend of languages and accents that spoke of the diverse clientele the hotel attracted.

The Atse Kaleb was a modest yet comfortable establishment, known for its welcoming atmosphere and strategic location at the edge of the old city where many of Axum's historic and revered churches and landmarks were located. Once a destination for adventure tourists with a love of history, Axum was beginning to see a revival of interest, and the Atse Kaleb Hotel was already benefiting from it, though how much longer that state of affairs would last now seemed in doubt.

Will surveyed the bar, letting his gaze drift over the occupied tables until he spied his colleagues, communications specialist Maisy Cole and Dr. Sanjeet Singh, sitting at a table in the back of the establishment. Upon seeing them, he breathed a sigh of relief.

Deke, ever the more extroverted of the two, continued to the bar where he ordered a couple of cold St. George beers—a local favorite—and then brought them over to the table where their friends were sitting.

The four of them worked for Project: RESCUE, the international non-governmental organization founded by humanitarian-adventurer Scott Devlon. Project: RESCUE provided logistical support, security, and if necessary, emergency evacuation for international travelers, and especially for people providing humanitarian relief in the world's most dangerous places.

Project: RESCUE primarily utilized local resources to ensure client safety and success during the course of day-to-day activities, whether those clients were adventure tourists or relief workers trying to build hospitals in remote parts of developing nations. Recognizing that certain crises could easily overwhelm the resources of the local agencies working with Project: RESCUE, Devlon had tapped Will Irons to create a rapidly deployable field team—nicknamed "the FAST Team"—to quickly go wherever they were needed and do what the locals could, or would, not.

Devlon wasn't looking to create a paramilitary hostage rescue unit to go in with guns blazing. While some situations might require that sort of response, Devlon, a former Army Ranger with combat experience in Afghanistan, had come to believe that violence often created more problems than it solved. A reputation for strongarm tactics and rogue operations might very well result in travel restrictions in countries where Project: RESCUE's services were most needed. Much like the International Red Cross and Red Crescent, it was imperative that Project: RESCUE be perceived as a neutral, non-violent entity.

Devlon envisioned a small group that could navigate the treacherous terrain of crisis zones with the agility of mountain goats and the calm of seasoned diplomats. Instead of battle-hardened warriors loaded for bear and ready to engage in close-quarters combat, his team would be made up of explorers, mountaineers, and adventure athletes, men and women who had scaled the highest peaks and traversed the most unforgiving landscapes. Their expertise would lay, not in the art of war, but in the art of survival and negotiation. They would know how to read the land, converse with local leaders, and find safe passage where none seemed to exist. They would be linguists, capable of communicating in local dialects; medics, able to patch wounds and mend broken spirits. They would be the swift arm of Project: RESCUE, reaching out to foreign aid workers, journalists, and any others whose lives hung in the balance. And Devlon could think of no one better suited to lead his FAST Team than Will Irons.

The two men had first met when Devlon attended Will's High Altitude Mountaineering Course at the American Alpine Institute, AAI, in Washington state in preparation for his first ascent of Mount Everest. Devlon had been impressed with Will's leadership abilities, as well as his infectious optimism and willingness to push boundaries for the greater good. Will was resourceful, resilient, ready for anything, and even though he had never worn a military uniform, Devlon had recognized him as a kindred spirit.

Will had always been magnetically drawn to the world's wild places. His childhood was a tapestry of camping trips under open skies and days spent exploring the forests and streams near his home in the Cascade Mountain Range of Central Oregon. It was this love for the natural world that led him to pursue a Master's Degree in Ecology, a field that allowed him to understand the planet he so cherished.

Following graduate school, Will had applied for and was selected to be a NASA astronaut candidate, but when, after completing the program—two years of relentless physical and academic training—governmental budget cuts led to the cancellation of the mission he had been assigned, Will faced a choice. He could take an administrative position at the space agency while waiting for another flight slot to open, or he could chart a new course. He chose the latter, leaving NASA behind with no regrets, and sought a different kind of adventure—one that did not require a journey to space, but rather a deep dive into the human experience on Earth. He began this new phase of his life by honing his skills in wilderness survival and environmental ethics at the National Outdoor Leadership School. Afterward, he lived the life of an itinerant adventurer, guiding climbs, fighting wildland fires, and eventually taking a job with the AAI, where he crossed paths with Scott Devlon.

Always ready for a new challenge, Will had jumped at the opportunity to create and lead Project: RESCUE's FAST Team, and had immediately enlisted his best friend—and former AAI student—Deacon James.

Deacon "Deke" James was a man of contrasts. His imposing physical presence, honed during his days as a linebacker for the Detroit Lions, belied the warmth and approachability that radiated from him.

After a promising, but tragically short-lived, athletic career—sidelined by an injury that cut his NFL journey short—Deke had found a new purpose. Armed with a degree in psychology, he decided to channel his minor celebrity status into something meaningful, lending his time and influence to a social work program aimed at uplifting the lives of at-risk urban youth.

Much as with Devlon, Deke's friendship with Will had taken root when the former had taken Will's AAI Mountaineering course. Deke's dream was to climb the world's tallest mountains, not just for the thrill, but to defy stereotypes. There were very few African-American mountaineers—of the nearly 7,000 climbers who had summited Mount Everest, less than twenty were black. Deke aimed to change that narrative.

Will admired Deke's determination and unwavering spirit, and the two became fast friends. Everest loomed on the horizon, a challenge they both yearned to conquer. Deke hadn't stood on its summit yet, but he and Will had a pact: someday they would stand together on the roof of the world and write a new history.

When Will Irons approached his friend with the idea of helping him create the FAST Team, Deke didn't hesitate. The opportunity to save lives, to be part of a team that transcended borders and politics, resonated with him. He believed that negotiation, not brute force, was the key to unlocking doors in the most dangerous corners of the world.

As Will's second-in-command, Deke brought a unique skill set to the table. His deep voice could command attention, yet he preferred to disarm tense situations with humor rather than threats. When faced with armed militants or desperate warlords, Deke would crack a joke, catch them off guard, and find common ground.

Together, Will and Deke had carried out a number of spectacular rescues.

In the Peruvian Andes, they'd responded to a distress call from a team of climate scientists monitoring glacial retreat that had been stranded by a landslide and menaced by Blinding Path insurgents. Will and Deke had parachuted into the treacherous terrain and navigated ancient Incan trails teeming with hostile wildlife to reach the archaeologists, whereupon Deke had negotiated safe passage through a local village under the control of a notorious narco-trafficker.

On the mighty Congo River, an expedition of biologists studying endemic species—and under Project: RESCUE's protection, was attacked by pirates. Will and Deke, after executing a daring night-time approach, had managed to board the vessel, scatter the pirates using non-lethal distractions and Deke's imposing presence, and effect the rescue of the scientists.

Helping out Taneisha Hayes and her team of diplomats was just another day at the office.

As Will pulled out a chair at the table where Maisy and Sanjeet were sitting, the former grinned up at him. "So, you two Boy Scouts did your good deed for the day?"

Maisy's joke was in reference to Will and Deke going off-script—leaving the convoy escorting the Doctors Without Border team to answer the distress call from the besieged diplomats.

Before Will could respond to Maisy's quip, Deke arrived at the table, setting the two ice-cold bottles down before taking the remaining empty seat. "Two good deeds, actually," he said. "We helped an old lady cross the street. But then it turned out she didn't want to go, so we had to help her back again."

Will, however, was less sanguine. "We got the diplomats out safely. I'm afraid we can't say the same for their security escort. Or the villagers."

The comment brought the mood at the table down a few notches. In a somewhat more subdued manner, Maisy asked, "Any idea who was behind the attack?"

Will shook his head. "Actually, I was wondering if you'd heard anything."

The suggestion did not surprise the diminutive Maisy. Although her role on the FAST Team was communications officer, her background was in intelligence gathering.

Maisy Cole was the only member of the team with a military background. Prior to working with Project: RESCUE, she had served in the US Air Force as an intelligence officer. Her ability to decipher and speak multiple languages wasn't just a talent; it was an art form she practiced with the dedication of a virtuoso. After achieving the rank of major at a relatively young 32 years of age, Maisy had made a lateral transfer to the Defense Intelligence Agency, her expertise in language theory dovetailing perfectly with her ability to achieve easy rapport with strangers to make her an exceptional case officer.

When Scott Devlon went looking for a communications specialist for the FAST Team, Maisy was his unequivocal first choice.

Her military and intelligence training had equipped her with skills in clandestine action and asset recruitment. In the field, Maisy was more than a translator; she was a bridge between cultures, a key that unlocked the nuances of communication that went beyond words. Her ability to "read" people made her an indispensable member of the team, her insights often providing the clarity needed in the most chaotic situations.

Petite and elfin, with short, strawberry blonde hair and a spray of freckles across her nose, her looks were deceiving. Between assignments, Maisy's love for strategy and risk found an outlet at the poker table. As a semi-professional tournament player, she wielded her ability to read her opponents with the same finesse she applied to her work. At the poker table, as in the field, Maisy was a force to be reckoned with—a woman whose cards were played close to her chest, and whose moves were always one step ahead.

Maisy, however, just shook her head. "I haven't heard anything, but I'll keep an ear out." She shifted in her seat, and then went on. "You should probably know that Elena's pretty pissed off at us."

Will's hand instinctively found the cold bottle of St. George, the condensation a brief respite from the heat of the conversation. "I'm not surprised," he said. "But it wasn't up to us. Her organization made the call."

"Good luck telling her that," retorted Maisy. "Because she didn't listen to me when I said it. I believe her actual words were, 'We all knew what we were getting into. Now go the hell away and let us do what we came here to do.'"

Sanjeet, who had been quietly following the exchange, added, "She's a tough one, that Dr. Ramirez."

Coming from the usually reserved Sanjeet, that was the highest compliment. As the team's medical officer, his calm, stoic demeanor was a stark contrast to Deke's more playful approach to life. Sanjeet also had the added insight of having previously worked with Dr. Elena Ramirez during an earlier international mission for Doctors Without Borders.

Born to a Punjabi family that had emigrated to the United States from Pakistan, Sanjeet's path was marked by a blend of steadfast tradition and bold independence. Despite his family's hopes that their only son would adopt a more conventional lifestyle, Sanjeet had chosen a path that kept him on the move, always heading out to the next emergency, the next group in need. His adherence to the fundamentals of Sikhism—a faith that emphasized service and justice—was unwavering, even if it meant defying expectations. The cobalt blue turban which he always wore when in the presence of others, signified that he was a 'warrior', but in a spiritual rather than literal sense—defending his faith and upholding righteousness. He was a healer. If he fought anything, it was an ongoing battle against death and despair.

An accomplished cardiac surgeon, he had worked for more than a decade at New York's Bellevue Hospital, often accepting challenging assignments with Doctors Without Borders and other international NGOs. A brief encounter with Scott Devlon in the high altitudes of the Ladakh Plateau on the Indian border had been a turning point. There, amid the rugged beauty of the Himalaya and Kunlun Mountain ranges, Sanjeet's work at the Ladakh Heart Foundation had caught Devlon's attention. It wasn't just his medical acumen that impressed Devlon, but also his ability to connect with people, to offer solace to those suffering.

"Elena's dedication is what makes her exceptional," he added, his voice a soft baritone. "It is the same fire that drives all of us here."

Deke, having just drained his beer, set the bottle down with a clink that punctuated the moment. "Well, she might blame us now, but if things go to crap here the way it looks like they might, she'll thank us."

Maisy raised an eyebrow as she looked past him toward the entrance. "Speak of the devil."

All eyes turned in the direction of her stare and beheld the topic of their conversation, Dr. Elena Ramirez, striding across the bar, heading straight for them like a heat-seeking missile, her gaze laser focused on Will.

She was, as Deke had observed when they'd met her for the first time earlier that day, an attractive woman, but it was a beauty that defied convention—a beauty born of resilience and purpose. In a more familiar setting, say a fundraising cocktail mixer on Fifth Avenue, made up and dressed to the nines, she would probably have been considered runway-model glamorous. But here, in the heart of remote Tigray, with her long black hair pulled back in a no-nonsense ponytail, her olive complexion unenhanced by cosmetics, and wearing khaki trousers and a long-sleeve work shirt, her beauty was something more than just skin deep.

She strode up to their table, and with hands planted firmly on her hips, squared off against Will as if she intended to fight him. "I just thought you should know, I'm going back to the clinic tomorrow."

Will took a slow sip from his beer and then rolled the bottle between his palms. When he didn't reply, she went on, "Don't even think about trying to stop me."

He set the bottle down and looked up at her. "Elena, as I told you this morning, Doctors Without Borders contracted Project: RESCUE to put you and your medical team on the first flight out of Axum, and that's what I intend to do. So, if you have a problem with that, take it up with the head office. They're the ones who made the decision to pull you out. They're worried about your safety, and frankly, they're absolutely right to be."

Elena flashed a triumphant smile. "I guess you haven't heard. The airport is shut down. Due to the increased instability in the region, all flights to and from Axum are cancelled."

"All the more reason for you to sit tight here," Will countered. Sensing that his admonition would go unheeded, he continued, "Look, if you can convince your director back home that it's safe for you to return to the clinic, I'll be happy to drive you back. But I'll need to hear it from them."

Elena's stance softened ever so slightly, the fire in her eyes flickering with a challenge. "I don't need their permission. Or yours."

"Then why are you here?" he retorted coolly.

She worked her jaw in irritation. "I'm here," she said slowly, "to let you know to stay out of my way."

Will took a patient breath. "Elena, if you go back there, you'll be putting yourself *and* your patients at risk. Whoever was behind today's attack was targeting foreigners, but a lot of innocent people got hurt in the crossfire."

"I can take care of myself," she asserted, but the slight quaver in her voice suggested that maybe she hadn't considered the implications of her decision.

Will leaned back, the chair creaking slightly. "I know you can," he admitted. "You don't have to prove anything."

For a moment, their eyes locked, a silent acknowledgment of the respect and the unyielding spirit they both shared. Elena broke the gaze first, turning away as if to dismiss the gravity of the moment. "Then there's nothing more to discuss," she declared, but the slight pause before she turned to leave suggested exactly the opposite of her parting statement. Whatever it was she had hoped to accomplish by confronting Will evidently remained unfinished.

Will watched her go. He knew that behind her tough exterior lay a woman driven by a fierce compassion, a woman who might just need someone to watch her back, even if she'd never admit it.

"I think what she really wants is for you to try to stop her," remarked Deke.

Will shook his head. "What she really wants is for me to go with her."

Deke shrugged. "Either way, she's totally into you."

Will rolled his eyes.

"Are you going to?" asked Maisy.

Still following Elena's exit, Will shook his head. "I'll talk to Scott. See what he wants us to do."

EIGHT

Axum, Tigray National State, Ethiopia

HALF AN HOUR later, in the relative quiet of his hotel room, Will connected his laptop computer to the satellite internet setup they'd brought with them for secure communications with Project: RESCUE headquarters in western Massachusetts. The war had severely disrupted Tigray's communication infrastructure, and now, three years later, there was no sign of it being restored. For those who could afford it, satellite phone technology provided the only reliable connection to the outside world. With that connection established, Will sent a request for a video meeting with Scott Devlon at Project: RESCUE headquarters.

After a few seconds, Devlon's face appeared on the screen. A few years Will's senior, Devlon looked enough like Will to be his older brother. Now, gazing across nearly seven-thousand miles, Devlon's expression was calm but concerned. "Will. Good to see you. I heard you ran into some trouble."

Will wondered how his boss had heard that, but for the sake of brevity simply offered a dismissive shrug. "Just another day at the office," he replied. "Nothing we couldn't handle. We got the MSF team to Axum, safe and sound. Unfortunately, it sounds like getting them on a flight out might be a little tricky."

"I'll work it from this end. I'll charter a bird if I have to."

Will took a deep breath, the weight of responsibility pressing down on him. "There's another wrinkle. Dr. Ramirez wants to go back to Adi Gebru. She's adamant about not leaving her patients."

Devlon frowned. "I assume you told her that's not going to happen."

"I told her that it wasn't up to me, and that she should take it up with her own chain of command. My impression is that she intends to make the trip regardless of whether they give her the green light."

Devlon leaned back in his chair, the lines of his face deepening in thought. "I'll reach out to Doctors Without Borders," he said. "It's their call on how to handle this. Dr. Ramirez's visa is contingent on her relationship with them, so she has to fall in line or risk being deported."

"I'd just as soon not be the one to tell her that," said Will.

"You won't have to. I'm retasking you."

Will raised an eyebrow. "Retasking?"

"It seems you've brought us some new business with your heroic rescue of that diplomatic team."

"Ah. You heard about that."

"Amina Nkosi, the director of the Africa in the 21st Century Initiative, called me personally to express her gratitude for your timely intervention." Devlon paused a moment before adding, "Imagine my surprise. I was under the impression that you had your hands full with Dr. Ramirez. I just pretended that I knew what she was talking about."

Will was unapologetic. "They were in a tight spot. We were in a position to help. I knew that Maisy and Sanjeet could handle Elena's group."

Devlon cracked a smile. "Relax, Will. I'd have been worried if you *hadn't* gone to help them out."

Will wasn't at all surprised by his boss's reaction. Devlon had created Project: RESCUE primarily to help people. That the diplomatic team weren't paying clients hardly mattered.

When it became evident that they had left the attackers behind, Taneisha and the rest of her group had gradually risen from their protective huddle on the floor of the Land Cruiser. As a way of mitigating the stress, Deke had drawn them out with questions about their mission in Tigray and the broader goals of the Initiative. Will applauded their dedication to those goals, but knew they would have an uphill battle. The path to progress in Africa was fraught with the complexities of history, a steep ascent against centuries of entrenched struggle, tribal conflicts, and colonial exploitation. The attack they had just escaped was just one example of the obstacles that the Initiative would face.

"The long and short of it," Devlon went on, "Is that the A21I team is going to continue their work in Tigray, and they want you to escort them."

"You mean they want Project: RESCUE to handle their security?"

"I mean *you*, Will. Evidently, the team leader—" Devlon glanced down at his desktop, searching his note, "Ms. Hayes, thinks you're the right man for the job."

Will frowned. "Scott, at the risk of sounding like the guy who says, 'Not my job,' this isn't what we created the FAST Team to do."

Will did not need to offer further explanation. Devlon himself had directed the FAST Team to be "lean and agile" and "able to get in and out before anyone knows you're there." A security escort, of the type Taneisha Hayes seemed to want, was the complete opposite of that, relying on the perception of strength created by superior numbers of armed men to discourage anyone from attacking a convoy. The four-person FAST Team didn't even carry weapons.

Typically, when Project: RESCUE provided security for an expedition, the job was outsourced to reputable local security providers, which was exactly what Devlon ought to have told the director of A21I. While Will was certainly capable of going out and hiring a small army of guards to accompany the diplomats, it wasn't his area of expertise.

"I'm aware," was Devlon's patient reply. "I explained that to Ms. Nkosi, but she said that Taneisha Hayes was quite insistent that you be the one to take her team back up into those villages." Before Will could offer further protest, Devlon added, "Ordinarily, I would be in complete agreement with you, but things are moving quickly there. Tigray is a powder keg, and the attack at that village today just might have lit the fuse. There's a chance that Ms. Hayes and her diplomats can prevent things from blowing up, but if they're going to do it, they have to act quickly. And quick is what you do best."

"I get it, Scott. But you're asking us to take these people *into* harm's way. That's the opposite of what the FAST Team is supposed to do."

Devlon's gaze, transmitted across thousands of miles, bore into him. "Will, sometimes the way to rescue someone is to put the fire out before it even starts. There's a chance to both defuse this situation and save a lot of innocent lives."

Will understood his boss's rationale and even agreed with it, but felt it was his duty to push back against unrealistic expectations. "And if things escalate? We got them out of there today because the bad guys didn't expect us. We might not be that lucky if it happens again."

"What was it you told me on the mountain? 'You make your own luck.'"

Will frowned. "You know this isn't what I meant."

"I do." Devlon paused a beat. "Look, just talk to Ms. Hayes. Find out what she needs, and if you still have concerns, we'll revisit this."

Will nodded in resignation. "I'll talk to her."

"That's all I ask. Let me know what you decide. And I'll see what I can do about the situation with Dr. Ramirez." Devlon threw a half-wave, half-salute toward the camera, then ended the call.

As the screen went black, Will sat back in his chair and stared up at the ceiling.

The FAST Team—lean, agile, and weaponless—was designed for precision, for extraction, for slipping in and out like shadows.

Now they were being tasked with guard duty. It was like asking a scalpel to become a shield. To make matters worse, Elena—brilliant, headstrong Elena—was on the brink of going rogue, and whether or not she had the official backing of Doctors Without Borders, or for that matter, Project: RESCUE, he wasn't going to let her recklessly throw her life away.

You make your own luck.

The words, a mantra Will had drummed into the heads of students in his mountaineering courses, and which had borne him through countless life-and-death situations, echoed in his head. What the phrase literally meant was that success, or for that matter, survival, was *not* a matter of luck at all, but rather the result of good judgment, situational awareness, and adequate preparations. The statement was often accompanied by "Will's Rules."

Always have a plan.

Always have a Plan B.

That was how you made your own luck.

And unless he was very much mistaken, they were going to need a whole lot of that kind of luck.

NINE

THE YEHA HOTEL, where Taneisha and her colleagues were staying, was perched on a hilltop with a commanding view of both the newer city of Axum to the south, and several of the city's landmarks, most notably the enormous stelae which had once marked royal tombs in the days of the Axumite Empire. Most of the larger examples had toppled over the course of the centuries, but the seventy-nine-foot-tall Obelisk of Axum, which had been carried off to Rome by Italian Fascist forces during their brief occupation, had been repatriated and restored to its former glory with a structural upgrade, and now stood outside the city's archaeological museum, just a quarter of a mile from the hotel.

Will Irons had not come to Axum for the purpose of sightseeing, but that didn't lessen his appreciation of the fact that he was getting a rare look at a part of history of which many Westerners were completely unaware. Driving past the domed cathedral of the Church of Saint Mary of Zion, he could not help but wonder if there was any truth to the claim that the actual Ark of the Covenant was secreted inside a small chapel on the church grounds.

He continued up the hill to the hotel where he took a moment to enjoy the sunset view before heading inside. Taneisha was waiting for him there.

"Long time, no see," she remarked as she shook his hand.

"But a lot sooner than I expected," replied Will, forcing a smile.

If she picked up on his reticence, she gave no indication. "Let's talk in the courtyard."

She led him outside and around to the back of the brick building where a semi-maintained topiary garden ringed a stone pavement. It was a peaceful setting, especially in the waning hours of the day, and a stark contrast to the harried escape from Alem Tekle's village.

Will got right to the point. "I understand that it's your intention to go back into the mountains."

"It is." There was more than a little pride in Taneisha's tone. "If anything, what happened today underscores the urgency of resuming the negotiations."

"You're not wrong," said Will. "But given what happened to you today, I hope you can understand the need to proceed cautiously."

Taneisha gave him a sidelong glance. "You didn't strike me as the cautious type."

Will didn't smile. "I'm *very* cautious. If I choose to do something dangerous, it's only because there's not a safer way forward."

Taneisha crossed her arms in a show of defiance. "You think going back out there is reckless."

It was more an accusation than a question, but Will answered honestly. "It's risky," he clarified. "It only becomes reckless if you don't take the appropriate steps to mitigate that risk."

"Well, that's what I've got you for. That is what you do, isn't it?"

Will frowned. "I think you might have gotten the wrong impression about me. The organization I work for, Project: RESCUE, *does* provide security and logistical support for NGOs operating in dangerous environments, but my team is more... reactive. We're like firefighters. I'd be happy to put you in touch with the Project: RESCUE regional coordinator in Addis Ababa. He's far more capable of providing the services you need."

Taneisha's eyes held a spark of determination as she faced him. "I know what you're capable of, Will. *You* got us out of that mess. If something like that happens again, I want you there with us."

"That's not the point, Taneisha. It's about having the right resources. A larger security force could—"

"Draw too much attention," she interjected. "Look, we went up there today with half-a-dozen armed guards in a three-vehicle convoy. All that did was put a target on us. We don't need more guns or a show of force. We need subtlety and speed. That's what you do, right?"

"Subtlety isn't going to stop a bullet."

"No, but it might just keep us from being shot at in the first place."

Will frowned. He had not anticipated her turning the limited focus of the FAST Team's mandate into an argument in favor of using them as a protective detail. Still, he couldn't disagree with her logic. He knew from his years of experience guiding summit expeditions on some of the world's toughest slopes, that the bigger the party, the bigger the problems. Small but skilled climbing teams, moving fast and traveling light, almost always fared better.

But the analogy was far from perfect. Mountains didn't actively target climbers.

"You do understand that this approach increases the risk to your people. And mine."

"We know. And we're all willing to take that risk if it means even a chance of stopping the bloodshed."

"Even Pierre?" Will had not failed to notice that, of Taneisha's colleagues, DuBois seemed to have had the hardest time coping with the events of the day.

Taneisha smiled. "Maybe some of us are a little more willing than others."

Will looked out over the topiary garden, watching as the sun touched the distant mountains to the west. In such a peaceful setting, it was easy to be cavalier about the very real dangers they would face.

"All right," he said finally, turning back to her. "We'll do it. But we're going to do it my way."

Taneisha raised an eyebrow. "Meaning?"

"Meaning we wait until I've assessed every angle. Until I'm convinced we have a plan that minimizes those risks."

Taneisha's expression hardened. "Time isn't a luxury we have. If we don't act quickly, the situation could escalate."

"I'm aware," Will replied, his voice firm. "But rushing in without proper preparation is only going to make a bad situation worse. We're not going back out there until I know who it was that attacked you and why."

"How long will that take?" she asked, her frustration evident.

"It will take as long as it takes," Will said, unyielding. "You hired me to ensure your safety, and that's what I intend to do. If that means we lose a day or two, so be it. Better than losing lives."

Taneisha's shoulders slumped slightly. "All right. We'll do it your way. But make it quick."

Will offered a nod, the closest thing to a promise he could give, and then rose and left her alone with the fading sunset.

TEN

THE SETTING SUN cast long shadows across the sun-bleached tarmac of Axum's Emperor Yohannes IV Airport. The facility, which still bore the scars of battle damage sustained during the civil war, was eerily quiet, owing to the cancellation of regular flights. Except for the Ethiopian National Defense Force soldiers manning the main gate and patrolling the grounds, it might have been something from a post-apocalyptic nightmare, a place inhabited only by ghosts.

"I really thought the next time I came here, I'd be getting on a plane," remarked Deke as he parked the Land Cruiser near the entrance to the main terminal.

"You and me both," agreed Maisy from the shotgun seat.

They made their way inside the empty terminal building to the security office where Colonel Tesfaye, the commander of the ENDF brigade assigned to Axum and the surrounding area, held court. They had briefly met with the colonel upon arriving the previous day to inform him of the reason for their visit and inquire about the security situation. As was often the case with men in positions of power, he had been uncooperative almost to the point of hostility, hinting, without coming right out and saying it, that they were CIA operatives sent by the American government to sow the seeds of chaos in Tigray. Maisy still wasn't sure what exactly Tesfaye thought the American government stood to gain by fomenting instability. But rather than engage with him on the topic, Will, taking the lead, had stuck to their story, which had the benefit of being one hundred percent true, until the colonel sent them on their way. Experience told her this second meeting would follow a similar trajectory.

A soldier escorted them into the colonel's dimly lit office, uttering a few words in Amharic, presumably explaining the presence of the visitors, then exited. Tesfaye, seated at his desk, studying a map of the region, did not look up.

"Colonel Tesfaye," Maisy began, approaching the desk like a supplicant. Tesfaye, like many educated Ethiopians, spoke some English. "We appreciate you taking the time to speak with us again."

The colonel sighed and leaned back in his chair, eyeing them with suspicion. "I was told that you returned with those doctors." His voice was gravelly, edged with suspicion. "And yet, you are still here."

"Guess you didn't hear," said Deke. "We got bumped off our flight. Thought we'd make the best of the situation and see the sights."

Confusion furrowed the colonel's brow, but before he could inquire further, Maisy spoke up. "Actually, we're working with the Africa in the 21st Century Initiative. I guess you know that they were attacked earlier today."

Tesfaye's eyes narrowed suspiciously, then he shook his head. "You Americans. So arrogant. You come here, telling us how we ought to live, promising to help, but only if we fall in line."

It was a variation on one of the diatribes he'd subjected them to the previous day. Maisy considered telling him that A21I was not an American entity—it was actually based in South Africa—but doubted the distinction would make a difference to the officer. "They're trying to negotiate with the former TNF leaders in order to prevent further bloodshed."

Tesfaye made a dismissive wave. "The TNF are terrorists. Bloodshed is their currency. It buys power, loyalty, fear. It is a waste of time to negotiate with them. They will never listen to reason."

Maisy shrugged equivocally. "We're not actually involved in that discussion. Our role is simply to get Taneisha Hayes and her party there and back again."

Tesfaye's expression underwent an abrupt change. "What do you mean?"

"I guess you could say, they're getting back on the horse," intoned Deke.

The colonel's eyes narrowed. "They are going back? When?"

"We're still working out the itinerary," said Maisy, "Possibly as early as tomorrow. The first stop will be the village that was attacked today."

Tesfaye shook his head. "That is unwise."

"I don't disagree," said Maisy. "But they've contracted with our company to get them there and back safely. If we're to do that, it would help to have an idea of who was behind the attack today."

This brought a snort of laughter from the colonel. "Who do you think?"

Maisy tilted her head to the side, prompting him with her silence.

"Isn't it obvious. The Tigrayan National Front."

"The TNF supports the ceasefire."

The colonel chuckled as if amused at her naivete. "That is what they say, but in the shadows, they are already arming themselves for the next fight."

"Even if that's true, what would they stand to gain by attacking a diplomatic mission?"

It was Tesfaye's turn to shrug. "They are terrorists. Animals." His gaze focused on Maisy, a warning etched in his eyes. "Westerners should stay in Axum until a flight out can be arranged. The mountains grow more dangerous by the day. This attack will only inflame the rural villages, leading to more violence."

He then leaned forward. "Tell your..." His eyes narrowed. "*Friends...* That they are wasting their time trying to bring peace to Tigray." He thumped his chest with a fist. "That is my job."

Sensing that they would get nothing of substance from him, Maisy simply nodded. "I will pass that along to our clients. Thank you for your time."

"That went well," remarked Deke as they made their way back through the terminal.

"About as well as I expected it to. He was never going to help us." Then her lips curled into a smile. "Not willingly, at least."

As soon as they were back in the Land Cruiser, Maisy activated her tablet computer connected to the vehicle's satellite antenna, and brought up the app that had been running in the background. The display indicated a sound recording in progress.

"Pay dirt," she announced. "He called someone the minute we left."

Maisy had not expected the Colonel to cooperate, but that wasn't why they had come to see him. The real purpose behind their visit was to surreptitiously clone Tesfaye's satellite phone—a feat easily accomplished with the help of a piece of classified hardware she'd borrowed from her previous employer—and then monitor any subsequent conversations in hopes that the officer might know more about the attack than he had been willing to share with them.

"Let's hear it," said Deke, as he started the engine.

Maisy rolled the recording back to the beginning, and then tapped the 'playback' button. Colonel Tesfaye's voice issued from the speakers, but the words were unintelligible.

"He's speaking Amharic," said Maisy.

"You understand him?"

She wagged her head from side to side. "A little of it. I'm not exactly fluent, but it's similar to Tigrinya, so I think I get the gist."

A moment later, a different voice was heard, a deep but raspy baritone, speaking the same language.

"Well, what are they saying?"

Maisy paused the playback then opened a different application. After a few seconds, the colonel spoke again, only this time, in English. Or at least, that was how it sounded. The voice was actually a nearly perfect electronic reproduction, created by the enhanced AI translation program Maisy was using—another piece of cutting-edge tech that was not yet commercially available.

"General Tadesse. It is Colonel Tesfaye."

"Yes, Tesfaye. What do you want?"

"It's not what I want, General," came the reply. "It's what I can do for you."

The voice reproduction was so perfect, it even captured Tesfaye's servile manner.

"I'm listening," replied Tadesse.

"The negotiators who went to speak with Alem Tekle today."

"Yes. What about them?"

"They escaped the attack on the village."

"Yes. I know this." There was an edge to Tadesse's voice, betraying his impatience. "Why are you calling me about it?"

"They are going back. Tomorrow."

"Are you certain?"

"Yes, General. They seem very determined."

There was a long pause, and then Tadesse spoke again. "This is excellent news, Colonel. It seems we have been given a second chance to finish what we started this morning."

Maisy shot a glance at Deke. The latter shook his head. "I knew there was a reason I didn't like that guy."

ELEVEN

"IT SEEMS WE *have been given a second chance to finish what we started this morning.*"

Maisy tapped the screen of her tablet computer to stop the playback and then looked to her audience to see their reaction.

The four members of the FAST Team were gathered in Will's hotel room for a strategy session to determine how best to accomplish the task they had been given, or if that was even possible, given what they had learned following the conversation with Colonel Tesfaye earlier in the evening.

Deke, who had already heard the phone conversation, sat quietly on a corner of Will's bed, waiting for someone else to weigh in. Sanjeet, sitting statue still, cross-legged on the floor, also seemed to be waiting for someone else to break the silence.

Will leaned against the window, gazing out at the moonlit sky, his rugged features betraying nothing, but Maisy knew him well enough to see the gears turning in his head. "Well," he finally said, "this complicates things."

Deke laughed. "Complicates? That's an understatement. Not only do we know for certain who the target for that attack was, but also that they're still in the crosshairs." He shook his head. "You've got to tell Taneisha that this is a non-starter. There's no way we can guarantee their safety. Not when it looks like the Ethiopian army are the ones trying to kill her."

Will looked to Maisy. "Is that your read on this as well?"

Maisy regarded him for a long moment before answering. "I'm not certain that the attack was sanctioned by the Ethiopian government."

"You think this General Tadesse has gone rogue?"

"That's putting it mildly." She tapped on her tablet, bringing up a dossier filled with notes and photographs. "I reached out to some of my old friends and asked about Tadesse. Turns out, 'General' Tadesse isn't an officer in the Ethiopian National Defense Force. He used to be, but when the war broke out, he fought on the side of the Tigrayan Defense Force."

"He's Tigrayan?" Will shook his head. "That doesn't track. The Tigrayan National Front supports the ceasefire. Why would Tadesse want to sabotage the peace process?"

"I'll go one better," said Deke. "Colonel Tesfaye—the Ethiopian officer we talked to at the airport—flat out accused the TNF of being terrorists, yet he's working with Tadesse." He glanced at Maisy. "How do you explain that?"

Maisy spread her hands. "I can't speak to his motives, but he was obviously trying to misdirect us. But Tadesse is a wildcard."

She scrolled through the dossier, stopping at a black-and-white photo of a young officer. "This is Tadesse, back when he was a captain in the Ethiopian Ground Force. By all reports, a brilliant tactician, but only achieved the rank of Lieutenant Colonel. When the civil war broke out and he sided with the Tigrayan Peoples Liberation Front, they tapped him to lead one of their armies.

"During the war, he was known for using guerrilla tactics. Hit-and-run attacks. He was part of the force that outflanked the Ethiopian army, seizing control of key towns and commandeering armaments from the national military's hardware."

"Sounds like he could have been the Tigrayan George Washington," remarked Deke.

Sanjeet, who had been silent up to that point, spoke up. "A man like that doesn't just fade into obscurity. Perhaps he sees the cease-fire as weakness."

"Do we know what he's been doing since the war ended?" asked Will.

Maisy's fingers danced across the tablet, bringing up more recent intelligence. "At last report, he and a bunch of his former freedom fighters are now doing private security work for foreign investors."

"Mercenaries," muttered Deke, as if the word had left a bad taste in his mouth. "He's been fighting his whole life. For his country, for Tigray, and now... for profit?"

Maisy shrugged. "So, he's a warrior without a war. What else is he supposed to do?"

"Any particular foreign investors?" pressed Will.

Maisy consulted her tablet. "It looks like he's under contract with VEK to provide onsite security at their facility in Tigray."

"VEK?"

"*Volga Energeticheskaya Korporatsiya*—the Volga Energy Corporation. They're a major player in the petroleum industry. Even bigger than Rosneft."

"Petroleum?" said Will. "There's oil in Tigray?"

Maisy glanced down again. "Shale oil, actually."

"What's the difference?" asked Deke.

"Shale oil is oil that's produced from the extraction of a fuel called kerogen from certain sedimentary rock formations—called 'oil shale'," explained Will, drawing on his science background. "Mineral oil has actually been used for centuries, both as a fuel and a lubricant."

"Fuel from rock. So, it's like coal?"

"There are similarities, but coal has a much higher percentage of organic matter, which is why it burns at relatively low temperatures. Oil shale has to be processed extensively for use as fuel. and that process is energy intensive, which means that shale oil production is only profitable if the price of oil stays high. Say above $50 per gallon."

"How much is it now?"

"It fluctuates from day to day, but it's been holding in the eighty-dollar range for the last couple years." He turned to Maisy. "How big are the Tigray reserves?"

Maisy turned the tablet around and began typing the request into a search engine. "There are a few shale fields, but the largest by far is the Naeder Adet shale, about twenty-five miles due south of Axum. The field is about twenty square miles and has an average depth of about 150 feet. Estimates put the total yield in the neighborhood of four-billion tons." She paused a beat, then added, "And VEK has been issued an exploratory permit to begin developing it."

"Four billion." said Deke. "That sounds like a lot." He glanced over at Will. "Is that a lot?"

"Four billion of anything is a lot, but in terms of value, it varies depending on the quality of the shale. If I recall correctly, a ton of shale produces roughly three-quarters of a barrel of oil, so... Three billion barrels of oil. That's about equal to four months of the total global output."

Deke let out a low whistle. "So, Tigray's sitting on a buried treasure. And General Tadesse is guarding it for the Russians."

Will nodded, his mind racing with the implications. "If Tadesse is protecting the shale oil for VEK, then instability in the region could actually work to his advantage."

Maisy leaned in. "Exactly. In a stable region, you have laws, regulations, and government oversight. But in chaos? That's when corporations like VEK can operate under the radar. They can exploit resources with little to no interference."

Deke frowned, trying to keep up. "But wouldn't war be bad for business? Who's going to invest in a warzone?"

"That's the paradox," Will said. "For oil companies, the long-term goal is stability. But short term? Instability can inflate oil prices, and that's when unconventional sources like shale become gold mines. Plus, war is an expensive proposition for all parties involved. A cash-strapped government is likely to give very good terms to foreign investors."

Sanjeet, who had been quietly listening, spoke up. "And if Tadesse can control the chaos, he controls the gold mine."

Deke leaned back, arms crossed. "So, he's gone from a national hero to a mercenary for foreign oil?"

Maisy nodded. "He's not just a mercenary; he's a gatekeeper. If VEK wants to access the Naeder Adet shale, they need Tadesse."

Will's expression grew somber. "So, we have a former freedom fighter turned mercenary, guarding a treasure trove for a foreign power, in a land teetering on the brink of war. Sounds like a perfect storm."

Deke leaned back, his mind clearly troubled. "And the more unstable Tigray becomes, the more indispensable Tadesse is to VEK. It's a vicious cycle."

The room fell silent as the gravity of the situation settled over them. The stakes were even higher than any of them had imagined. It wasn't just a matter of protecting diplomats or even preventing a war—it was about the future of an entire region, and the invisible hands that moved the pieces on the board.

Will finally broke the silence. "We're making some big assumptions here. We need to find out what Tadesse really wants. Is it money? Power? Or something else entirely?"

"How do we do that?" wondered Deke.

Will considered the question for a moment, then his lips curled into a grin. "Maybe we should just ask him."

TWELVE

Belém do Pará, Brazil

PETROV STRODE THROUGH the milling crowd, his sharp gaze scanning the sea of delegates and activists for the one person who could make his bold plan a reality. The opening ceremonies now completed, the real work of the gathering would begin. The air was electric with discourse, debate, and negotiation, a symphony of languages and ideologies clashing and mingling under the high glass ceilings. Petrov, however, was not here to discuss carbon footprints or renewable energy targets; his mission was far more pragmatic.

If they only knew, he thought, *that I am about to solve all their problems.*

At the heart of the convention center, beneath a sprawling banner proclaiming "Sustainable Futures for All," he found his quarry. Dr. Lena Andersdotter, a stern-looking woman in her early sixties, was a prominent climate scientist, but more importantly, she was the chair of the conference's scheduling committee.

Petrov waited patiently as Andersdotter engaged in a heated discussion with a group of young environmentalists. It was plainly evident from the conversation that while the youths were passionate about their cause, they had very little understanding of the science or the broader economic issues beyond their well-rehearsed talking points. They seemed to believe that if all the world's young people would simply "go on strike," the "corrupt governments and corporations" would have no choice but to submit to their demands.

Petrov had to hide his laughter. *Children are so naïve, believing that their tantrums can change the world.*

As the conversation waned and the group dispersed, he seized the opportunity.

"Dr. Andersdotter," he called out, his voice cutting through the residual chatter with practiced ease, commanding her attention.

The scientist turned, her expression one of mild surprise. "Mr. Petrov? Well, this is a good sign."

"A good sign?"

"A senior VP of Volga Energy, slithering out from under your corporate rock to protect your interests in person? You must be quaking in your boots."

Petrov affected a look of mock-hurt as he leaned against a minimalist eco-friendly exhibit, a model of a wind turbine spinning silently beside him. "Lena. You know that VEK is deeply committed to achieving carbon neutrality. We're investing in renewable energy and cutting-edge technologies to reduce our carbon footprint."

Dr. Andersdotter raised an eyebrow, her arms folded. "That's nice copy for your corporate website, but we both know you've actually been *expanding* oil production across the globe."

Petrov's smile didn't waver. "We intend to offset our carbon emissions by investing in projects that reduce greenhouse gases elsewhere. It's a pragmatic approach to a complex problem. A real solution."

"A temporary solution at best," countered Andersdotter. "Offsets don't solve the problem. They're little more than a feel good measure. What is VEK doing to reduce your actual emissions? You could be leading the transition to sustainable energy sources, but instead you're doubling down on fossil fuels. Just like everyone else."

Petrov waved a dismissive hand. "Let's not pretend we're at a gathering of saints, Lena. This conference," he gestured broadly at the bustling hall around them, "is an exercise in hypocrisy."

"Hypocrisy?" she snorted, her eyes flashing with indignation. "Well, you are certainly the expert on that."

"Every delegate here talks a good game about sustainability and green initiatives. But outside these walls? It's business as usual. The oil flows, the coal burns, and the so-called 'green' countries keep buying."

He leaned in, his tone laced with a bitter edge. "You accuse me of hypocrisy? For years, every nation here has made pledge after pledge to cut emissions, yet their economies are still tethered to fossil fuels. They demand change, but balk at the cost."

Andersdotter opened her mouth to protest, but Petrov raised a hand to stop her. "This conference is a feel-good measure, a chance for everyone to pat themselves on the back and say they tried. But we both know that when the lights go out and the cameras are packed away, nothing will have changed."

Andersdotter stared back at him, her breath quickened, visibly rattled by the accusations. Finally, she swallowed, and in a small voice said, "What else can we do?"

Then she stiffened with resolve. "The scientific community has been sounding the alarm for more than fifty years. The world keeps getting hotter, but no one listens because you..." She stabbed a finger at him. "You and all the other oil barons keep drowning out our voices, sowing doubt, buying off the politicians... Lying through your teeth. All we have is the science. The *truth.* All we can do is continue shouting it in the streets until the world stops listening to your lies, and starts believing what's happening right under their noses."

Petrov hid a grin of satisfaction. The scientist had played right into his hands. "Dr. Andersdotter, there's a saying... Perhaps you've heard it... That the definition of insanity is doing the same thing over and over and expecting a different outcome."

Andersdotter's gaze narrowed but she said nothing.

"That is as true for my industry as it is for your efforts," Petrov went on. "We are not fools. We know the world is changing, just as you warned us. But we are like men with a map to buried treasure. If we don't dig it up, someone else will. That is the way of the world."

"It will mean the end of the world," she replied, impassioned. "Don't you see that?"

"I do. We all do." He paused a beat. "It's time to stop the insanity. Time to do something different."

She cocked her head to the side, suspicious. "Go on."

He shook his head. "Let me address the conference. I will tell everyone."

She recoiled. "You? Address the conference? That's preposterous. I would never give you a platform from which to spew your propaganda. Besides, the speaking roster was finalized months ago. I couldn't put you on the stage even if I wanted to."

Petrov smiled patiently. "We both know that you could. If you wanted to."

"Well, I don't." Andersdotter fixed him with an accusing stare and crossed her arms defiantly. "You speak of change, yet you continue to defend the status quo. What could you possibly say to convince me, let alone this conference, that you, of all people, have a real solution?"

Petrov leaned in, his voice a low rumble of confidence. "You know what drives men like me. Profit. You will never... Not ever, convince us to simply give up our wealth. Our power. No, what you must do is make a better offer."

"Saving the world isn't incentive enough for you?"

Petrov smiled patiently and went on. "What if we could make it more profitable for men like me to simply leave the treasure where it is?"

"Profitable? How?" Andersdotter asked, her arms uncrossing, a sign that her curiosity had overtaken her doubt.

"Let me address the conference. Thirty minutes is all I ask. That is all the time I need to unveil a strategy—bold, but elegant in its simplicity—that will revolutionize our approach to the climate crisis."

Andersdotter considered him for a moment, the gears turning in her head. "You have to give me something more."

"A plan so bold as this..." Petrov shook his head. "No. I must share it with everyone."

"Something tells me I'm not going to like your plan."

Petrov spread his hands. "Perhaps not. But shouldn't we let the world decide?"

She narrowed her eyes. "I'll give you twenty minutes."

Petrov smiled and inclined his head in what he hoped looked like a gracious bow. "Twenty minutes. Better than a TED Talk, no?"

"Tomorrow afternoon. Thirteen hundred. But I promise you, if this is a ruse to give you a platform to spread your anti-climate propaganda, I will pull the plug and yank you off the stage myself."

THIRTEEN
Tigray National State, Ethiopia

WILL AND DEKE were up with the sun, driving their Land Cruiser through the streets of Axum as the city came bustling to life around them.

Colorful awnings stretched out from the buildings lining the street, fabric billowing like sails caught in a gentle breeze, beneath which vendors peddled food—mostly fresh bread and produce— along with bottled water and soft drinks. A few hawked handwoven baskets, textiles, and handcarved trinkets, as well as bootleg DVDs, watches, and jewelry. Locals bartered with animated gestures, their laughter punctuating the rhythm of commerce.

As the Cruiser crept along, sharing the streets with pedestrians and donkey carts, a group of children darted alongside the vehicle, their bare feet kicking up dust, their laughter a chorus of innocence. Deke, taking note of a boy balancing a wooden hoop on a stick, rolled down his window and tossed a shiny bi-metallic coin to the boy. The coin, a one Birr piece, was worth about two American cents.

The boy grinned in triumph, holding up his prize for the inspection of his peers.

"Now you've done it," remarked Will. "They'll be swarming all over us in a minute."

Deke laughed. "Ah, let them come. I got plenty more."

Will shook his head, the corners of his mouth turning up despite his feigned exasperation. "You're a soft touch, Deke. You know that?"

Deke shrugged, his gaze following the boy who was now darting away, victorious. "Maybe. But these kids have it tough. If a coin can bring that much joy, I say it's worth every cent."

The expected juvenile swarm was averted, however, when a procession of Ethiopian Orthodox priests, white robes flowing like prayers set in motion, crossed the dusty street in front of them, their chants resonating through the air. Behind them, a group of monks in faded saffron robes moved with quiet purpose, their eyes downcast.

The locals—men, women, and children alike—paused as the holy men passed. Some crossed themselves, others bowed their heads. The priests and monks were the guardians of faith. The keepers of an unbroken lineage that stretched back to the days when Axum was a beacon of Christianity in Africa, and their presence was woven into the fabric of daily life. Serving as a reminder that Axum's sacred pulse beat stronger than ever.

As they waited for the road ahead to clear, the mingling scents of frankincense and roasted coffee wafted in through the Cruiser's open window, filling the vehicle's interior with a heady aroma, tempting them to delay their departure to enjoy a cup or three. On any other morning, Will would not have passed up a chance to enjoy the ritual coffee service, but today he had more pressing concerns.

One way or another, the meeting with General Tadesse would determine whether Taneisha and the diplomats would be able to continue their mission.

He recalled Maisy's reaction to his declaration the previous night. "Will, that's just about the stupidest idea you've ever had. Tadesse tried to kill those diplomats yesterday, and now that he knows that we're working for them, we'll be on the target list, too."

Will's confidence in the plan had remained unshaken. "Tadesse is a mercenary. That means he can be bought. Or at the very least," he added, with a knowing glance at Deke, "that he might be willing to negotiate."

Deke raised an eyebrow. "I guess that means I'm going with you, then?"

"Wouldn't trust anyone else with the job," replied Will, grinning.

It would not be the first time the two of them had stepped into the figurative lion's den. Sitting down and talking to unsavory individuals was often a very necessary part of what they did, and at the end of the day, got results.

Earlier that year in Peru, when they'd gone in to rescue the scientists stranded in the Andes, Deke's skillful negotiations with a local *narcotrafficante*—a man who would have not hesitated to personally shoot both of them in the back of the head—had turned a potentially dire situation into a blessing.

Deke's methods were as much about intuition as they were about strategy. He began by figuring out the power dynamics in play, recognizing that in such a lawless region, the trafficker's authority was absolute. Threats of bringing down the wrath of the US government—as if that was even something they could have done—would have been futile and dangerous. Instead, he sought common ground, connecting with the man on a human level.

As Deke was fond of saying, "Nobody is just one thing. Find that part of them that cares about something you care about, and then you can have a conversation."

Deke always remained calm and composed, his demeanor unflappable even in the face of threats. He used the universal language of respect, carefully choosing his words to de-escalate tension and build a bridge of mutual understanding.

Will might have had absolute confidence in Deke's abilities, but Maisy remained less than enthusiastic about the plan.

"You're going all in on a weak hand, Will," she said. "He knows that we're working with A21I. What's to stop him from just shooting first, no questions asked?"

"I don't think he will. He doesn't know that we know he was involved in the attack. As far as we know, he's a hired gun. We'll approach him with an offer to provide security for Taneisha's next visit to the mountains and see how he reacts."

"Oh, that's a wonderful idea. You're going to hire the fox to escort the chickens into his den."

Will laughed. "I didn't say that we'd hire him. But if money is his primary motivation and we make a better offer, then problem solved."

Maisy narrowed her eyes at him. "Something tells me it's not about the money. Or if it is, it's a hell of a lot of money."

Will just nodded. "That's what I want to ask him about."

ONCE BEYOND AXUM'S rustic environs, the main highway stretched before them, a ribbon of asphalt that cut through the city's outskirts. The pavement beneath them was smooth, a stark contrast to the rugged terrain that lay just beyond the road's edge. The highway was an anachronism, out of place in the timeless landscape that surrounded as they ventured westward, a declaration of the present, boldly asserting itself amidthe echoes of antiquity that whispered from the mountains and valleys. It was a symbol of progress, a path that connected the past to the present, and yet it stood in stark contrast to the ageless rhythm of life that pulsed in the heart of Tigray. It was this juxtaposition—the old and the new—that often struck Will when he traveled.

This journey, like many before, was a reminder of the delicate balance between preserving the essence of what was, and embracing the promise of what could be. Will felt a kinship with the road, understanding that his own life was a similar blend of history and modernity, of experiences etched into his being like the countless footsteps on ancient trails.

He considered the layers of history unfurling beneath the tires—the ancient kingdoms that once ruled, the traders who had traversed these lands, and now, the two of them, modern-day sentinels straddling past and present. He mused on the resilience of the land and its people, how they adapted to the new while honoring the old.

He kept his eyes on the horizon, while Deke monitored their progress on the GPS unit. It was only about thirty miles from Axum to the approximate location of the oil shale field in Naeder Adet, but only a small portion of that would be on the paved highway. Five miles west of Axum, they turned onto an unpaved road which, while well-maintained, obliged them to reduce their speed by more than half.

The track wound its way through this canvas of ochre and sage, a serpent navigating an ancient world. Fields of crops stood in neat rows, a checkerboard of greens and browns that spoke of the region's agricultural backbone. Thorn trees dotted the landscape, their silhouettes stark against the sun-baked earth, while acacia trees reached skyward, their branches a haven for the birds that flitted between them. The Simien Mountains loomed in the distance, their peaks bathed in the soft morning light, a reminder of the natural majesty that had watched over this land for millennia.

The unpaved road gave way to a rugged track that snaked through the increasingly arid landscape. The lush fields of crops thinned out, replaced by hardy shrubs and the occasional burst of color from resilient late-season flowers—blooms of lantana, golden dewdrops, and Jimson weed.

According to the GPS, it would take another hour to travel the remaining distance.

The track reminded him of the mountain road from Adi Gebru to the rural village where Elena and her team from MSF had set up shop. The thought of the stubborn doctor brought an unexpected smile to his face. He admired her obstinate resolve and her willingness to sacrifice everything to help others.

As if reading his thoughts, Deke said, "Elena's got guts. I'll give her that. Setting up shop in the middle of nowhere,"

Will quickly hid his smile, focusing on the road ahead. "She's determined to make a difference."

"You think she's gonna do what she said? Go back, with or without our say so?"

"I'm sure she'll come to her senses. She can't very well run the clinic without support from MSF. She knows that better than anyone."

"I don't know. She seemed pretty fired up."

"That's why I told Sanjeet to make sure they get on the first flight out."

"You really think he's gonna get her on a plane if she doesn't want to go?"

Will gave an equivocal shrug.

Deke chuckled. "Stubborn as they come. But you gotta admit, there's something about her, eh?"

"I don't know what you're talking about."

"Aw, come on. You two have a... how should I put it... a certain chemistry."

Will's grip on the steering wheel tightened, and he kept his gaze fixed on the road ahead. "We're here to do a job, Deke. That's all that matters."

Deke raised his hands in mock surrender. "All right, all right. No need to get tense. Just making an observation."

The conversation fell fallow as they continued their journey, the Land Cruiser's engine revving higher as they began the slow crawl up the mountain road toward their destination. As they ascended, the terrain became more challenging, the road a test of the resilience required to traverse this part of Tigray. The occasional herdsman could be seen in the distance, guiding flocks along the sparse grasses that clung to the earth. The air grew cooler, a welcome respite from the heat that had begun to settle in the lower valleys.

Naeder Adet was not a specific location, but a *woreda*—an administrative region similar to a county or parish. Prior to the war, the region had boasted a population of well over a hundred thousand, with only a small fraction of them living in towns. Most were scattered throughout the countryside, living in small communal settlements with few modern conveniences. How many of them remained following the cessation of hostilities was anyone's guess.

There had been little in the way of detailed information about the oil shale field, but after some digging, Maisy had located a scan of a geological survey map which would at least put them in the ballpark.

After another half-hour of slow progress, Deke asked, "So what does a shale oil field look like, anyway?"

"Technically, it's an 'oil shale' field. Shale oil is the name for the refined product. Oil shale is the rock."

Deke brushed the distinction aside. "Great. I hope I remember that if it ever comes up on Final Jeopardy."

"To answer your question," Will went on, his eyes still on the winding road, "Oil shale just looks like ordinary rock. But you aren't going to find it laying around on the ground."

Deke raised an eyebrow. "So it's not like a tar pit or anything? I figured the rocks would be oozing oil or something."

"Nope. The shale is formed of decomposed plant matter, sandwiched inside layers of sedimentary rock. Think of it like a layer cake, but instead of frosting, the layers are rich in organic matter—mostly decomposed plants. It's not the liquid black gold that spurts out in a gusher; it's more like a solid stone that needs to be cooked to give up its treasures."

"Cooked?" Deke visualized a stock pot, filled with chunks of shale, slowly simmering on a stove top.

"Oil shale contains kerogen—a precursor to oil. It's extracted by mining the rock and then heating it in a process called pyrolysis. The heat breaks down the kerogen, releasing oil. Shale oil." Will paused as he negotiated a particularly sharp turn.

"So, you have to bake the rocks to get oil?" Deke prompted, changing his mental picture to a sheet pan with the same chunks of rock arranged like pieces of cookie dough.

"Exactly. But it's not your average kitchen oven. We're talking temperatures between 650 to 700 degrees Fahrenheit, at a minimum. That's the real problem with processing oil shale. Like I said before, you end up using almost as much energy as you produce. And the extraction process uses a lot of water and leaves behind a significant amount of waste rock."

Deke had no mental image for that. "Sounds like a messy business."

"It can be, but if they use in-situ processing... That's where they heat the rock underground and pump the oil out, it's less destructive. No massive open pits or mountains of discarded tailings to deal with."

Deke gazed out the window. "So are we looking for a mine or an oil well, or what exactly?"

Will shrugged. "Hard to say. I guess we'll know when we get there."

"'That's the thing, though. If the GPS is right, we've been smack dab in the middle of the field for about ten minutes now and not a mine or oil well in sight."

FOURTEEN

WILL BROUGHT THE Land Cruiser to a gentle stop, the gravel crunching softly under the tires. When he killed the engine, the sudden silence was profound. Deke looked at him, a question in his eyes, but Will was already opening the door, stepping out into the crisp mountain air.

The landscape was stark, beautiful in its desolation. The ground was a mosaic of rock and hardy shrubs, the vegetation clinging to life in the harsh environment.

Deke joined Will, his gaze sweeping the horizon. "Not much going on here."

Will shook his head, his eyes scanning the ground. "There's no fence, no signage. No indication that this road is in regular use by tanker trucks coming and going. If there's an oil shale operation out here, it doesn't look like it's ever been active."

Deke frowned, his brow furrowing. "Then why did that Russian oil company hire Tadesse to guard it?"

"That's a very good question," replied Will, gazing down the road yet ahead of them. "Let's keep going."

They got back in and continued along the rugged track, scanning the horizon in every direction until, a few minutes later, a glint of metal caught Will's eye. He pointed. "Do you see that?"

Deke followed his line of sight. "Yeah, I see it. Some sort of building?"

"Let's check it out." Will steered off the track and made a beeline for the distant shape. The structure grew larger as they approached, an imposing edifice of corrugated metal, three-stories high and big enough to cover a football field, rising like some forgotten temple from the midst of the barren landscape. As they neared it, their path crossed an overgrown dirt road which led the rest of the way to their destination.

"Looks like a pole barn," remarked Deke. "Maybe they're using it for a garage or equipment shed."

Will drove right up to the structure, stopping a car length away from the large swing doors. When he shut off the Land Cruiser, the silence was eerie. The only sound was the persistent ticking of the cooling engine.

"No lock," said Will as they approached the door which was held shut by weathered hasp latch.

"Not much need for one out here," observed Deke. "We're miles from the nearest neighbor."

Will acknowledged the observation with a nod, then flipped open the latch and slid the door open. The rollers squealed in protest, shattering the ominous silence.

"Open sesame," murmured Deke.

The interior was dim, illuminated only by the light filtering in through the partially open entrance. Will took out his phone and activated the flashlight, shining it into the gloom as they ventured inside.

The vast space inside was surprisingly empty. The only piece of heavy equipment was a large, tracked Caterpillar excavator, its yellow paint dulled by dust, its backhoe arm extended with the bucket resting on the ground.

"Now that's more like what I was expecting," said Deke.

Will gave a thoughtful hum. "It's something. You'd need a lot more than just an excavator to run an oil shale operation, though."

"Maybe they're using it for construction? If this place isn't up and running yet, it would explain why we haven't seen any signs of activity."

Will didn't reply, but ventured inside the structure, approaching the excavator and shining the light up into the cab. "It's been sitting here for a while."

Deke, who had circled around the excavator now called out, "Will, take a look at this."

Will turned and moved alongside the industrial behemoth to where his friend stood, shining his phone's light down into a large trench, cut into the earthen floor beneath the structure. The cut was about fifteen feet across, fifty feet long, sloping down to a depth that lay beyond the reach of their lights. Great mounds of dirt and rock were piled up to either side of the trench, creating the impression of even greater depth.

"Some kind of test hole?" wondered Deke.

Will continued to appraise it thoughtfully. "Oil shale lies below bedrock, so it's possible that's what this is. I don't know why they would dig it up, though. Drilling core samples would have been more efficient."

"Swimming pool?"

Will chuckled. "Or some kind of underground storage facility." He shone his light down the ramp-like slope leading to the bottom of the trench. "Let's have a look."

Deke hesitated at the edge of the trench, his gaze flickering between the dark opening and Will's back as he strode determinedly down into the cut. "You sure about this, Will?" he asked, his voice carrying an edge of unease. "Now that I'm looking at it, I think it looks more like an open grave, and I'd rather it not be mine."

Will paused, turning to face his friend. "You can stay up here if you want."

Deke brightened visibly at the offer, but then just as quickly frowned in chagrin and started forward. "Nah. I'm not going to let you go down there alone. Someone's gotta hold your hand."

They descended, the silence of the vast space swallowing their cautious steps. To either side, the cut walls of the trench exposed the geological history of the region—layers of sediment, representing millions of years. At the bottom, at least fifty feet below ground level, the slope flattened out, and there they discovered the secret hidden in the depths of the excavation. Revealed in the beam of Will's phone light was a line of pallets, all loaded chest high with large paper sacks as might be used to ship cement or sand for use in a construction project. The block printing on the sacks likely would have revealed their contents, but the Cyrillic letters were as incomprehensible to the two men as Egyptian hieroglyphs.

Will approached the nearest pallet, his fingers tracing the letters. "Russian."

"That tracks," said Deke. "VEK is a Russian outfit."

"I'll see if I can get a translation," Will said, but then after checking his phone display, said, "No signal down here." He took a moment to photograph the label, then moved down the line, checking the contents of each pallet in turn. He stopped at the third. "This one says something different. And there's a GHS warning label."

GHS—the Globally Harmonized System of Classification and Labelling of Chemicals—was an international protocol used for the trade and transportation of potentially hazardous materials across borders. While not as detailed as the OSHA hazardous materials scheme used in the United States, the simple pictograms of the GHS transcended language differences.

Deke advanced to peer over his friend's shoulder. Although the writing remained indecipherable, the small, diamond-shaped label affixed to the bag was almost self-explanatory. Inside the placard's red border was a picture of a flaming circle.

"Flammable," said a wide-eyed Deke. He glanced at the cut walls of the trench. "Uh, this shale oil... It *can* burn, right?"

"Only at very high temperatures," replied Will. He tapped the label. "And this isn't the symbol for 'flammable.' This circle means that it's an oxidizing agent. It won't ignite on its own, but it can make a fire burn hotter."

"Is that supposed to make me feel better?"

"These pallets usually hold about 4,500 pounds," mused Will, ignoring the question. "So we're looking at two-and-a-half tons of the stuff. I wonder what they plan to do with it,"

"You said they have to heat the rock up to extract the oil," speculated Deke. "Maybe that stuff is part of the process."

"Maybe," replied Will, unconvinced. He captured the text with his phone, and then kept moving.

The next pallet also contained the oxidizing agent. The four that remained held something else entirely. Revealed in the light of Will's phone was a different GHS warning label. It showed a spherical object—like a bomb or cannonball from an old cartoon—in the process of exploding.

The placard wasn't the only difference, however. Unlike the contents of the other pallets, the bags loaded on the last four were labeled in English and French, with the manufacturer's name in large, bold blue letters.

Dyno Nobel.

The company took its name from the scientist and inventor who also gave his name to what was arguably the most prestigious award on Earth celebrating scientific and humanitarian pursuits—the Nobel Prize—and the invention that not only made him one of the wealthiest men of his time, but also funded the million-dollar award that accompanied his namesake prize more than a hundred years later—dynamite. Dyno Nobel, not surprisingly, was one of the world's leading suppliers of industrial explosives for use in mining and engineering endeavors, which meant there was little question regarding the contents of the bags on the remaining pallets.

For an ominously long moment, neither man said a word.

Deke finally broke the silence. "I think I'd like to go home now."

Will continued examining the label on the bag. "Ammonium nitrate," he murmured.

"That's an explosive, right?" said Deke. "People make bombs with it?"

"It can be used for that. It's also used for fertilizer."

Deke made a show of looking around. "So, you're telling me their gonna turn this place into a farm?"

Will allowed himself a small smile. "Explosives are sometimes used in the in-situ extraction process," he explained. "Blasting agents break up the shale and make it easier to get the oil out."

"Won't that set the oil on fire?"

Will shook his head. "Not if it's done right. In order for the oil to ignite, it has to vaporize in the presence of oxygen."

"So this—" Deke gestured to the pallets. "This is normal? To have this much explosive material laying around"

Will spread his hands. "Mind you, I'm not a mining engineer, but it's consistent with what I've read about the industry."

"Well, okay, then." Deke shuffled his feet. "Mystery solved. We can go now."

Will nodded, but despite having a rational explanation for the presence of such a large quantity of high explosives, a sliver of doubt remained. He took one last picture, and then indicated that they could make their way back to the surface.

As they ascended the dimly lit slope, the discovery continued to weigh heavily on them. The silence was oppressive, punctuated only by the echo of their footsteps. After several minutes spent in the near total darkness of the trench, the sunlight pouring in through the slightly ajar door was almost blinding.

As he stepped out into the open, one hand raised to shade his eyes, it took Will a moment to realize that they were no longer alone.

Standing directly before them, attired in mismatched camouflage fatigues, were a dozen men, all armed with AKS-74 carbines, all of which were pointed directly at Will and Deke.

Deke tensed, a reflex from his gridiron days, but immediately caught himself. Because this was no game, and there were no referees here.

Will raised his hands slowly, studying the faces. All of them had the lighter, mocha-colored skin and sharp features of Tigrayans. Not surprisingly, he immediately recognized one of them from the photographs Maisy had shown him the previous night.

Will inclined his head toward the man, and in a steady voice said, "General Tadesse, I presume."

FIFTEEN

MAISY COLE SIPPED from the mug of herbal tea and then resumed reading the information displayed on the screen of her tablet. In order to keep from worrying about Will and Deke's safety—and what she still maintained was a foolhardy mission to negotiate with General Tadesse, she had decided to do a deep dive into the Volga Energy Corporation hoping to learn more about their operation in Tigray.

She had been surprised to learn that Tigray was not the only remote place wrapped up in VEK's tentacles. Although the Russian company already had access to decades' worth of petroleum reserves in their own backyard, they had secured exploratory rights for untapped oil shale fields in the Congo, Morocco, Algeria, and Jordan, as well as entering into a partnership with the governments of Venezuela and China to develop infrastructure for mining the oil shale and tar sands in those countries.

The easy explanation was simple greed. By snatching up the rights to reserves in under-developed nations, VEK would keep those treasures out of the hands of their competitors.

But what did VEK gain by adding political instability to the mix? Maisy's instincts told her there was more going on than met the eye.

As she continued reading archived news articles about the company, an alert popped up on her screen. She'd set up a keyword filter to check for any news stories concerning the situation in Tigray, General Tadesse, and anything relating to VEK, and it seemed something had fallen into her net.

The banner displayed a headline from the Huffington Post:

OIL EXEC ADDED TO COP 30 ROSTER: A GAME-CHANGER?

Curious, she clicked on the link and began reading:

Belem—In a surprising turn of events, the organizing committee of the 30th UN Conference on Climate Change (COP 30), currently underway in Brazil, announced the addition of a high-profile oil executive to its roster of speakers. Boris Petrov, Senior Vice President of Global Operations for Russia's Volga Energy Corporation is slated to address global leaders and environmental experts at today's session of the environmental conference.

Petrov, whose career spans over two decades, is known for his shrewd business acumen and influential role in shaping Russia's energy policy. His inclusion in the COP 30 lineup has sparked a flurry of speculation and anticipation. He is expected to present VEK's vision for the future of energy, with rumors suggesting a groundbreaking approach that could redefine industry standards. Leading environmental groups have expressed skepticism, questioning the sincerity of an oil executive's commitment to environmental causes, and are bracing for potential surprises.

The decision to add an oil executive to a predominantly environmental conference has raised eyebrows. Howev-

er, insiders suggest that Petrov's message may align more closely with environmental concerns than one might expect from an industry leader. His presence signals a potential shift in the dialogue between the energy sector and environmental policymakers. Could this be the moment when the oil industry and environmental interests find common ground? Only time will tell, but the stage is set for what could be a pivotal moment in the history of climate negotiations.

Maisy read the article, then read it again. She had seen Petrov's name several times during her research. He was a recurring character in the drama of recent foreign shale acquisitions. He also had a reputation for being a figurative 'chess master', always several moves ahead of both his competitors and industry analysts. Under his guidance, VEK's new business model was characterized as 'always expanding, always extracting'.

And now, here he was, to all appearances, stepping onto the environmental stage in the eleventh hour with the confidence of a man who believed he could rewrite the script.

It was ironic, almost laughably so. Petrov, the oil magnate, positioning himself as a champion of the green revolution while his company continued to drill and develop new fossil fuel projects. What game was he playing? More importantly, was there a connection between Petrov's sudden environmental evangelism and the situation unfolding in Tigray? Somehow it was all tied together; one just had to wonder how intricate those knots were.

Petrov's big speech at COP 30 might very well be a smokescreen, a diversion from activities that were anything but environmentally friendly. And what of Tigray? Was VEK's presence there part of a larger strategy, or merely another entry in Petrov's ledger of assets?

The timing was more than just a little suspicious. Surely those in attendance had to be thinking the same thing.

Maisy knew that the answers wouldn't come from speculation alone. She needed more information, more context. But unfortunately, she, like everyone else, would have to wait for Petrov to make his speech. There was a six-hour time difference between Ethiopia and Brazil, and given that the sun wasn't even up in Belem, it would probably be at least eight more hours before Petrov took the stage.

An insistent knock at the door disrupted her musings. Maisy had a feeling she knew who would be waiting on the other side of the door, and wasn't looking forward to the conversation that she knew would follow. With a sigh, she set the tablet aside and rose, crossing the room to open the door.

She had expected to see a defiant Dr. Elena Ramirez, and so was a little surprised to find someone else standing outside her room. It was someone Maisy would have recognized even if she hadn't seen a picture of the woman on the A21I website the previous night.

"You must be Taneisha Hayes," Maisy said, extending her hand.

Taneisha, looking only a little surprised at being recognized, accepted the handshake. "I am. And you are Ms. Cole, from Project: RESCUE?"

"Call me Maisy. Please, won't you come in?"

As Taneisha stepped into the room, Maisy took a moment to study her. Taneisha was African-American, full-figured, but with an almost regal bearing. She was poised, her intense, purposeful eyes reflecting a mind that was constantly analyzing, calculating. This was a woman who was used to getting things done.

Taneisha's gaze swept the room before settling back on Maisy. "I was hoping to speak with Will Irons, but the desk clerk told me he left early and that I should talk to you instead."

"That's right. Will and Deke went on a little scouting trip to determine whether it's safe to take you and your team back up into the mountains."

"Do you have any idea when they'll be back? I need to get back up there as soon as possible."

Maisy regarded her guest for a moment before answering. "All I can tell you is that they're following up on a lead that might reveal who was targeting you," Maisy said, her voice measured. "As for their return, I can't say for certain. These things can be unpredictable."

"A lead?"

Maisy weighed the question of how much she ought to reveal and decided to take a chance. "There are rumors that someone named Tadesse was behind the attack."

"Tadesse? General Tadesse?"

Maisy nodded but said nothing, using her silence to prompt Taneisha to go on.

"He's Tigrayan. Why would he want to disrupt the peace process?"

Maisy waited a moment longer to see if Taneisha would answer her own question. She debated whether to mention the oil shale field, but decided it was too soon to reveal that bit of information. "That's what Will is trying to sort out," she said. "But there's no question that Tadesse was behind the attack on you. I've got a recording of a phone call in which he as much as admits to it."

Taneisha's expression tightened, a mix of frustration and concern. "I understand the need for caution, but every moment we're not there is a moment lost in our efforts to stabilize the region. My colleagues and I knew the risks when we came here."

Lord, spare me another crusader, thought Maisy. Elena Ramirez had said almost exactly the same thing.

"I get it," said Maisy. "Really, I do. But how much good can you do if you get yourself killed?" She paused a beat to let that settle in, then went on. "Will and Deke are good at this. The best, in fact. Let them do their job."

Taneisha's eyes held a steely resolve, but the edges softened just enough to show she understood. "Please let me know as soon as you hear from Will."

Maisy nodded. "You'll be the first to know when they're back and what they find out. We all want the same thing."

Taneisha gave a curt nod, accepting the situation for what it was, and turned for the door. Just then, another knock sounded. Once more dreading the prospect of a visit from Elena, Maisy called out a "Just a moment!" and then opened the door to reveal Sanjeet looking uncharacteristically miserable.

"Sanjeet," said Maisy, surprised. She saw his eyes flit to Taneisha and decided to make introductions. "Taneisha, this is Dr. Sanjeet Singh, our chief medical officer. Sanjeet, this is Taneisha Cole from A21I."

Sanjeet's face registered recognition. "Ah, yes. Will told us about you." He extended a hand which Taneisha politely took. Then his gaze came back to Maisy. "I need to speak with you privately."

Taneisha, who had been about to leave, paused at his words, her brow furrowing slightly. "Is this about Will?" she asked, a hint of concern lacing her tone. "Have you heard something?"

Sanjeet glanced at Taneisha, offering a polite but firm shake of his head. "No, Ms. Hayes, it's an unrelated matter."

Maisy saw Taneisha's shoulders bunching and expected the woman to demand that Sanjeet share his revelation, but then she seemed to deflate. Facing Maisy, she simply said, "Thank you for your time." Then she turned to Sanjeet. "A pleasure meeting you, Doctor. I wish the circumstances were better."

"As do I," replied Sanjeet.

Taneisha let her gaze linger on him a moment longer, clearly curious about the urgent matter, then she left the room, closing the door behind her.

Once she was gone, Sanjeet turned to Maisy, his voice low. "Elena hired a local driver to take her back to Adi Gebru."

"What? When?"

"They left a few minutes ago. I tried to dissuade her, but you know—"

"I know," Maisy groaned, and then sighed. "That's... not ideal."

"We need to go after her."

He spoke the words as if delivering a terminal diagnosis, which Maisy supposed, in a way, he was. She paced the room, weighing their options. While it was true that she and Sanjeet had stepped up the previous day, taking charge of the MSF convoy when Will and Deke had gone off to rescue Taneisha and her people, the biggest difference was that they had been moving away from danger and toward safety.

This situation would require them to do the exact opposite.

She was no stranger to danger. She'd faced more than her share of it, both in her past life as an intelligence officer and in her present role with the FAST Team. But she did her best work behind the scenes, in the shadows.

And Sanjeet? He was a doctor, a healer. Calm and steady in a crisis, but not necessarily adept at dealing with the sort of dynamic situations that they might encounter.

Taking point on a rescue mission was usually Will and Deke's contribution to the team. As she thought about Elena, alone and vulnerable, she questioned whether they could fill the void left by Will and Deke's absence.

"We can't just chase after her," she said finally. "But we can't just abandon her to her fate."

Beneath the cobalt blue of his turban, Sanjeet's brows drew together in a look of consternation. "Elena is tough, but I don't think she has a realistic grasp of how dangerous the situation is."

Maisy pursed her lips in thought, then came to a conclusion. "I'll give Will a call. See what he wants me to do."

Sanjeet accepted this with a nod. Maisy took out her sat-phone and dialed Will's number, her fingers tapping impatiently as the call went out. After several rings, the call connected and she heard Will's familiar voice.

"You've reached Will Irons with Project: RESCUE..."

Maisy held the phone at arm's length, staring at it in disbelief as the recorded voicemail greeting played.

It wasn't like Will to let a call go to voicemail. The fact that he had not answered meant that either the call hadn't gone through—which was entirely possible since it relied on line-of-sight with a satellite, and even dense cloud cover could block the signal—or he was otherwise occupied and unable to pick up.

Either way, she wasn't going to be able to rely on him for guidance. At the tone, she said, "Will, it's Maisy. It looks like Elena wasn't bluffing. She hired a local to drive her back to Adi Gebru."

She paused, considering what to say next. The words, *call me when you get this,* were on her lips, but unexpectedly a silent resolve overcame her.

They had to be enough. Elena was still their client. Their responsibility. Whatever happened, she and Sanjeet would rise to the challenge. Because that's what they did—they adapted, they overcame, and above all, they never left anyone behind.

"We're going after her," she finished. Then, she ended the call and faced Sanjeet. "All right. Let's do this."

Sanjeet gave a firm nod, his face set with determination, and then followed her out to the small lot where the second forest green Project: RESCUE Land Cruiser was parked. Maisy took the driver's seat, her hands gripping the wheel to steady her nerves as Sanjeet retrieved the coordinates of Elena's clinic from the GPS.

A sudden movement from behind Maisy startled her. She half-turned in her seat, just in time to see the back door of the vehicle swinging open and then Taneisha Hayes, her face set with resolve, climbed into the back seat.

"What are you doing?" blurted Maisy.

"I could ask you the same thing," replied Taneisha, defiantly.

Maisy frowned. "It's nothing that concerns you. Another client of ours has..." She hesitated, searching for the right words. "Ignored our advice."

"You're talking about one of the doctors from the medical mission. Will told me about them."

"Dr. Elena Ramirez," supplied Sanjeet.

Maisy frowned at her counterpart. Taneisha didn't need to know the details.

"Let me guess," Taneisha went on. "She's gone back to her clinic. And you're going after her." She didn't wait for Maisy's answer. "I'm coming with you."

"Absolutely not. It's too dangerous. When you contracted with Project: RESCUE to provide for your security, you agreed to follow our lead. And right now, that means staying put."

"It's only going to get more dangerous the longer we wait," Taneisha countered. "You're heading back into the mountains, right? You'll be passing close to where I want to go. You can kill two birds with one stone."

"Probably not the best choice of metaphor," remarked Sanjeet, though Maisy detected a rare note of humor in his tone.

"What I mean is, it's efficient. We both get what we want, and in one trip. The situation is only going to get worse. We may not even get another chance."

Maisy sighed. "This isn't about efficiency, Taneisha. It's about safety—yours and ours."

Taneisha narrowed her eyes. "Maybe I should borrow a page from Dr. Ramirez's playbook. If you won't take me along, maybe I'll just have to find my own way back."

Sanjeet looked to Maisy. "This might be the best way to keep track of both our clients," he said. "Kill two birds... So to speak."

With Sanjeet's defection, Maisy saw that any further argument would be futile. "I'm sure I'm going to regret going along with this," she muttered. Fixing her stare on Taneisha, she said, "From here on out, you do exactly as we say, when we say it. Understood?"

"Understood," said Taneisha. Then, with a triumphant grin, she pulled her seatbelt across her body and secured it in place. "What are you waiting for? We're burning daylight."

SIXTEEN

Belém do Pará, Brazil

BORIS PETROV LEANED back in the plush armchair, gazing absently out the floor-to-ceiling windows at the black mirror of the Amazon flowing serenely past the city, and thought about the future—specifically, the very new future. Tomorrow would be a day to remember, and the anticipation was almost intoxicating.

Almost as intoxicating as the chilled Russo-Baltique vodka in the crystal shot glass resting on the mahogany side table.

The breathtaking view was just one of the amenities provided to those who could afford to book the Royal Suite of the Grand Hyatt Belém. The room was a blend of modern elegance and tropical splendor, with rich wooden floors, opulent furnishings, and vibrant artwork adorning the walls. A crystal chandelier cast a soft glow over the room, reflecting off the polished mahogany of the side table. The living area boasted a grand piano, plush sofas, and a dining table set for twelve—none of which he had any intention of using. Fresh orchids adorned the tables, their delicate fragrance mingling with the scent of high-end leather and polished wood. The bathroom, larger than most apartments, featured a jacuzzi tub and a rain shower, all inlaid with marble.

The Russo-Baltique, however, was not one of the luxuries that came with the room. Petrov had brought that with him. At just over 110 million rubles—about $1.3 million US—it wasn't the sort of spirit that could be purchased on the retail market.

The vodka was excellent, smooth as glass, twice-filtered through quartz sand and then once more through a silver filter, with notes of vanilla, sage, white pepper, and cream, but those qualities alone did not justify its exorbitant price tag. That had more to do with the packaging. The bottle, sheathed in gold and silver taken from antique coins minted between 1908 and 1912 with a diamond-encrusted cap inspired by the radiator guard of the legendary Russo-Baltique car company, was a work of art.

There was also the fact that the production run was limited to just 625 bottles. Petrov had managed to acquire two of them. Tonight, in anticipation of his speech to the COP 30 climate conference, he had broken the seal on one of them.

What he liked most about the Russo-Baltique, even more than its value as a status symbol, was the bottle. Not the sheath or the stopper, but the glass itself.

It was bulletproof. Unbreakable. Made to survive any misfortune so that not a drop of the liquor would ever go to waste.

As he contemplated what the next day would bring, he hoped that some of that invulnerability would transfer to him.

He tossed back the contents of the shot glass in a single swallow, then slammed it down on the table and reached for the bottle. As he did, he glanced at his tablet computer which also rested on the table. The screen still displayed a list of news articles reporting on his addition to the COP 30 roster and speculating on what he might say. The media was buzzing over the announcement. The world, it seemed, was hanging on his every word, waiting for the bombshell he would drop the next day.

They have no idea, he thought, as he decanted another portion of liquid invincibility.

Before he could raise the glass to take another sip, however, the buzz of an incoming phone call disrupted his reverie. His heart skipped a beat as he saw the caller ID. Sergei Ivanov, the Russian Minister of Energy.

Because so much of Russia's wealth and influence was tied to oil, the Minister of Energy was one of the most powerful men in the country after the President. As such, it was a coveted, hard-won position, and Sergei Ivanov was fiercely protective of it. Born in a small Siberian town, Ivanov had risen from humble beginnings, his ascent marked by calculated moves and a keen understanding of power dynamics. He had clawed his way to the top of Russia's energy sector through a combination of shrewd intelligence and unrelenting ruthlessness, crushing his foes and rivals without mercy, sometimes literally. Many an opponent of his policies had met with an untimely accident.

As the Russian Minister of Energy, Ivanov wielded his influence with an iron fist, shaping policies and dictating terms with an authority that few dared to challenge. Petrov had once served as his deputy, a position that had offered him a close view of Ivanov's formidable leadership. Petrov had idolized Ivanov, admiring his strategic brilliance and unyielding resolve. Yet, that admiration was always tinged with fear, for he had witnessed firsthand the swift and often brutal consequences of failing to meet Ivanov's exacting standards. Even now, Petrov could feel the shadow of his former mentor looming over him, a constant reminder of the high stakes and the unforgiving nature of the man who held so much power over his fate.

With a deep breath, Petrov answered. "Minister Ivanov," he said, forcing a note of casual confidence into his voice. "To what do I owe the pleasure?"

"Petrov," Ivanov's voice was cold, each word measured. "I see that you have made the news. Addressing the UN climate conference. Do I understand that correctly?"

Petrov took a breath before answering. "Yes, Minister."

"Why?" The word was a flat, discordant note, full of menace.

Petrov weighed his answer carefully. He couldn't risk revealing his plan to Ivanov—the man could, and probably *would,* forbid him to make the speech, utterly.

But he had to tell Ivanov something. "These climate activists keep calling for change, demanding an end to fossil fuel consumption. Clearly, that's not something we can afford to do, but sometimes, it helps to make them think we are taking them seriously. To placate them."

Ivanov made a sound that was the auditory equivalent of a scowl. "These reports say that you have some sort of revolutionary proposal."

"I have a proposal, yes. If they embrace it... Well, then we stand to—" He was about to say *reap immeasurable profit,* but decided it might be better to manage the Minister's expectations. "—make a great deal of money. If they do not, the public perception will be that we are willing to deal, and it is the activists who stand in the way of a solution. Think of it as a way to cover our bets. Either way, we win."

There was a pause, the silence heavy with unspoken threats. "I dislike these schemes, Boris. Ours is a straightforward business. We take the oil out of the ground. We sell it. That makes us a great deal of money."

Petrov swallowed, choosing his words carefully. "I understand, Minister. But if they accept my proposal—and I think in the long term, they will—the reward will be well worth the risk."

Ivanov's voice hardened. "And if they do not?"

Petrov's pulse quickened. "I believe they will. The world is ready for this change, and we will be at the forefront."

Another long, dangerous silence followed. "Very well, Boris. I am willing to let you take this chance. Just remember, there is a high price to be paid for failure."

The line went dead, the weight of the conversation settling heavily on Petrov's shoulders. He poured another shot of the vodka and downed it in a gulp, the liquid burning a path down his throat.

"Bulletproof," he murmured. "I am bulletproof."

If only saying it could make it so.

He poured another shot and then picked up the tablet and began reviewing the text of his speech.

He would only get this one chance. There was no room for error. Tomorrow, he would either rise to unprecedented heights, or fall into the abyss.

SEVENTEEN
Tigray National State, Ethiopia

TADESSE'S EYES NARROWED, a flicker of surprise passing over his sharp features, likely a reaction to hearing a stranger speak his name. He spoke a few words, his voice calm but with an edge of authority, but his utterance—likely in Tigrinya—was completely incomprehensible to Will and Deke.

Will didn't even know how to say 'hello' in Tigrinya, but he had a pretty good idea what the man wanted to know. Keeping his hands raised, his expression open and non-threatening, he said, "I'm Will. This—" He made a cautious half-turn gesturing to Deke. "Is Deke. We're not your enemy."

He used English, hoping that Tadesse might be one of the educated upper-class Ethiopians who had learned the language. Tadesse's blank expression suggested otherwise.

"Well, it was worth a shot," he murmured. With his eyes locked with Tadesse's, he began lowering his hand, moving it with deliberate slowness toward his pocket,

The gunmen reacted to even this slight provocation, jabbing the muzzles of their weapons at him, shouting warnings that required no translation.

"I'm just going to get my phone," Will said, his voice steady. He moved his hand up, pantomiming making a call, and repeated. "Phone."

Tadesse regarded him with an almost curious expression, then gave a subtle nod. Will resumed the slow reach into his pocket. He found the sat-phone, gripped it between thumb and forefingers and drew it out. With the phone now in hand, Will thumbed the screen to life. His heart skipped a beat when he saw that he had a missed call from Maisy, probably while he and Deke had been inside the storage building. Maisy wouldn't call without good reason, and unfortunately 'good reason' almost always meant 'bad news'. He desperately wanted to call her back, but knew he was already on thin ice with Tadesse as it was. Whatever it was, it would have to wait.

Still moving with glacial slowness, he tapped on the icon for the real-time AI translation app—the same one Maisy had used to decipher Tadesse's phone conversation with Colonel Tesfaye—and selected 'Tigrinya.'

Hope this works as advertised, he thought, and then, speaking in a low voice, repeated his earlier introduction.

A moment after he stopped speaking, his own voice—or rather, a near-perfect electronic reproduction of it—issued from the device, but speaking words he did not comprehend.

Tadesse's eyes widened at the sound of his language coming from the small device in Will's hand, but the surprise was quickly replaced by a calculating look as he understood the purpose of the phone. A murmur rippled through his men, a mix of confusion and curiosity.

Tadesse spoke again, his voice firm. The translation app relayed his words into English, and in his own voice. "Why are you here?"

Will took a deep breath, choosing his words with care. "We're with an organization called Project: RESCUE." he began, speaking slowly to give the app time to translate. "Our goal is to ensure the safety of those working toward a stable future for Tigray."

Tadesse listened to the translation, his expression unreadable. The gunmen remained still, their attention fixed on the exchange.

"We have a client who needs protection while operating in the area," Will continued, "and we've heard that you can provide that for the right price."

Tadesse's suspicion only seemed to deepen, his eyes narrowing into slits as he processed Will's words. "Spies," he spat out the accusation, the word slicing through the tension in the air. "You are spies sent by my enemies."

Will kept his composure. "We are not spies," he insisted, his voice firm. The translation app dutifully echoed his denial in Tigrinya.

Tadesse scoffed, a harsh sound that needed no translation. "You expect me to believe that? You, with your technology and your soft words, come here uninvited and speak of peace?"

Will could see his grasp on the situation slipping away, the fragile thread of understanding unravelling fast. Glancing back, he murmured, "Deke, feel free to jump in."

But before Deke could say a word, Tadesse took a step forward and snatched the phone from Will's hand. He then barked an order to his men, which the phone dutifully translated. "Bring them!"

Following Tadesse's lead, and with most of the gunmen walking behind them, occasionally prodding them with the muzzles of their Kalashnikovs, Will and Deke trudged across the rocky terrain, moving away from both the metal building and the mountain road they'd driven in on.

"They're on foot," he remarked. "That must mean that their base of operations is close by."

The translation app on his phone, still active in Tadesse's hand, picked up the comment and translated it into Tigrinya. The general glanced back but said nothing.

"I have to ask," said Deke in a faintly sardonic tone. "Is this all going according to your plan?"

"Well, we did come here to talk to Tadesse, so that's a qualified 'yes.'"

"He doesn't seem too interested in talking."

Will shrugged. "Well, we're still alive. I choose to take that as a good sign."

With the uneven terrain stretching out before them, Will lifted his gaze to the horizon, searching for some sign of their destination. After a couple hundred yards, he spied a dun-colored, medium-sized, military-style tent, and then another and another, for a total of five, all arranged in a neat row, like soldiers lined up for inspection. As they drew nearer, he saw that the tents were badly worn, the patched and poorly repaired canvas telling a tale of years of constant use in this unforgiving environment.

His eyes narrowed as he spotted a familiar-looking pickup truck parked near the edge of the camp. Its silhouette was unmistakable. It was, he knew, one of the vehicle's that had given chase after the attack on Alem Tekle's village—the one that hadn't been destroyed in the landslide.

The sight of it, and the memory it stirred, sent a chill down his spine, but he kept the discovery to himself, knowing that any outward reaction could unbalance their already precarious position.

Deke, sensing Will's tension, leaned in slightly. "You see something?" he whispered, his voice barely audible.

"Just taking in the view," Will replied with a forced casualness. He couldn't risk drawing attention to his discovery, not with Tadesse listening to their every word.

Recognizing Will's attempt to shift attention away from the pickup, Deke pitched his voice a little higher. "You know, this place looks nothing like the brochure. I may have to post a review on Yelp."

Will smiled. "Nothing says 'luxury' like a canvas cot with a rock for a pillow."

"Think they have a spa?"

"Hot stone massages using actual hot stones."

Will could hear the translation app—his voice and Deke's, rattling off the banter in rapid-fire Tigrinya—and couldn't help but wonder how accurate the translation was, or what Tadesse might be thinking as he listened to it.

They stopped in front of the middle tent, whereupon Tadesse barked an order to his men, which the app dutifully rendered into English. "Put them inside. Tie them up."

"Guess the massage will have to wait," remarked Deke.

One of the armed men threw back the tent flap and motioned for them to enter. Will obeyed, stepping into the dark interior. The air was stale, heavy with the scent of dust and sweat. The transition from daylight left him nearly blind, but he groped his way forward until one of their captors barked a command, which Will could only assume meant that they should stop. There was no automatic translation; Tadesse evidently had chosen to remain outside.

"I specifically asked for a room with a view," remarked Deke, his tone still upbeat despite their situation. "This is definitely going in my review."

Their captors were not amused. Will felt rough hands grab his shoulders, forcing him to his knees. His arms were pulled back, his hands brought together behind his back, and then a loop of something—coarse twine, perhaps—encircled his wrists and was pulled tight enough to make him wince. Then, he was shoved forward, falling face down on the canvas floor of the tent, while his ankles were lashed together. Hands groped him, searching for weapons. His pockets were turned out, his Leatherman Rebar multi-tool taken, along with the key to the Land Cruiser. His watch, an inexpensive Timex—he knew better than to wear an expensive watch when traveling abroad—was torn from his wrist.

Their captors worked silently, efficient in their task. Once satisfied that Will and Deke were securely bound, they stepped back, leaving the two men kneeling on the tent floor. The flap closed behind them with a snap, plunging the interior into near-total darkness.

Deke finally broke the silence. "So, about that plan...."

EIGHTEEN

BEFORE WILL COULD answer, the tent flap was thrown back again to reveal the figure of General Tadesse, silhouetted in the opening. In one hand, he held Will's sat-phone. In the other was an electric lantern which he switched on and shone directly into Will's face. The harsh light forced Will to squint as he tried to adjust to the sudden brightness. General Tadesse stepped inside and hung the lantern from a hook that dangled from the ceiling. Its glow filled the tent. revealing stacks of wooden crates and ammunition cans lining the walls. Tadesse squatted down beside Will and held up the phone. "This is a clever device. Do you still deny that you are spies? Working for the American Central Intelligence Agency?"

Deke chose this moment to begin working his magic. "General Tadesse," he began. "You're obviously a very intelligent man. Do you really think that if we were working for the CIA, we'd just come out here, completely unarmed, with nobody watching over us? Say maybe with a drone, flying over us right now?"

As the app translated Deke's words, Tadesse's eyes widened, and he began looking around nervously.

"Relax," Deke went on. "There's no drone, because we aren't spies. We're exactly who we said we are. I'm Deacon Jones. I used to play football. Now I work for Project: RESCUE. My friend Will and I just want to talk to you about a job. A job that pays very well."

Tadesse continued to regard them with suspicion. "What is this job you speak of?"

Deke smiled and nodded, as if to say, *now we're getting somewhere.* "Our client, the Africa in the 21st Century Initiative, is trying to work out a long-term solution to the conflict here. They're trying to prevent the war from starting up again by negotiating directly with the elders of the villages in the mountains west of here." He paused, allowing the app to catch up. "Now, as you've probably heard, Tigray can be a pretty dangerous place. In fact, our clients were attacked yesterday. Almost killed."

He stopped again, not only to wait for the translation, but also to watch Tadesse's reaction. To his credit, the general's face remained impassive throughout.

"Before we let them go back up there, we want to make sure that they have a reliable security detail." Deke's voice was steady, his eyes holding Tadesse's stare. "We need someone who knows the land, the people, and the dangers. Someone with influence and the capability to ensure our safety. From everything we've heard, you're that person, General."

Tadesse's posture stiffened, the suspicion in his eyes giving way to a flicker of interest. "And what makes you think I would assist you?" he asked, the translation app echoing his words in English.

"Peace in Tigray means stability, and stability is good for business, isn't it? Especially for someone with your... connections."

Will watched the exchange, impressed by Deke's approach. The former NFL player had a way with words, and his psychology education not only gave him the uncanny ability to read people—even someone as unreadable as Tadesse—but also to get them to say 'yes', even when their first instinct was to refuse.

Tadesse considered Deke's words, his gaze shifting between the two captives. "You speak of payment. How much are you offering?"

Deke's smile didn't waver. "Enough to make it worth your while. Plus, consider the goodwill you'd earn by helping to stabilize the region. Goodwill is a currency in itself, wouldn't you agree?"

The general's eyes narrowed, not with suspicion, but with calculation. Will could almost see the wheels turning in his head. Tadesse had been the one targeting Taneisha and her team, and now her representatives were asking *him* to give her safe conduct. For a fleeting moment, Will thought the general was on the hook, that he would take the job, if only to have his quarry delivered into his hands. But then Tadesse's expression hardened.

"I think you are lying to me," he said. "And I think that you are spies.

As the translation played, Tadesse stood up abruptly, and without any sort of warning, drew back his foot and drove a hard kick into Will's hip. Pain radiated from the impact, but Will managed to stifle any reaction. Nevertheless, Tadesse's kick sent a clear message—this was no longer a negotiation; it was an interrogation.

"You were caught coming out of our equipment shed," he growled, his voice low and menacing. "What we're you doing there?"

"We were looking for you," replied Deke in his most placating voice. "There weren't any 'no trespassing' signs, and the door was unlocked, so we just—"

Tadesse shouted something and then delivered another kick, eliciting a grunt from Will. Belatedly, the app provided a translation. "Liar."

Tadesse was already speaking again. "You have one chance. Tell me the truth, or you will both suffer."

Deke's eyes met Will's, a silent conversation passing between them. They were trained to handle stress, to remain calm under pressure, but the threat of physical harm added a new layer of urgency to their predicament.

"We've told you the truth," Will said, his voice steady despite the throbbing pain. "We're not spies. We're here to help the people of Tigray."

"You expect me to believe that? You, who appear out of no-where, speaking of peace and goodwill?" Tadesse sneered. He shook his head. "I will let you think on this for a time, and then we will speak again. Either you confess, or I will extract the truth myself."

With that, Tadesse turned on his heel and exited the tent, the flap falling shut behind him. The light from the lantern flickered, casting dancing shadows across the tent walls.

"Well," said Deke. "That could have gone better."

NINETEEN

IN THE COOL shelter of another tent, Mikhail Andreyevich Sokolov sat in a foldable camp chair and listened as General Tadesse related the gist of his conversation with the two men they'd caught snooping around the equipment shed. He was a large man, almost as big as the black man Tadesse had brought back as a prisoner, which only made the tent seem that much more confined.

Tadesse was speaking in Amharic, a language that Sokolov had learned more than a decade before when he'd served with the GRU Spetsnaz, conducting covert missions in the Horn of Africa, so there was no need for a translator.

"They say they work for an organization called Project: RES-CUE," Tadesse was saying, his brow creased with uncertainty.

Sokolov's eyes narrowed slightly. "Project: RESCUE," he repeated with a sniff of disapproval. "A well-known front for the American intelligence service." Sokolov had no idea if this was true, but felt it was important that Tadesse believe it. "And what is it they say they are doing here?"

Tadesse shifted uncomfortably. "They want me to work for them. They say they want safe conduct for their clients—the very people you sent us to eliminate."

Sokolov laughed. "There, you see? They knew that you were the one who attacked them, and came here to prove it."

Tadesse nodded, his expression grim. "I sensed deception. They knew my name, my role here."

Sokolov leaned forward, his hands clasped together. "You see? They are spies, Tadesse. It's the only explanation. You said you caught them in the equipment shed. What more proof do you need? They are here to disrupt our operations, to thwart the plan."

Tadesse's fists clenched at his sides. "What would you have me do?"

"Take the gloves off, Tadesse. It's time to show them you mean business. We can't afford to be gentle."

Tadesse's hand clenched into a fist. "Torture, you mean?"

Sokolov leaned forward, his voice a whisper of steel. "Make them talk. Find out who sent them, what they know, and then dispose of them. We can't afford loose ends."

Tadesse hesitated.

"Is there something else?"

"They said... The big man said that if they really were CIA spies, they would have a drone over us. Watching us."

"A drone?" A nerve in Sokolov's cheek twitched involuntarily. Then, he shook his head. "An interesting bluff. But that's all it is—a bluff."

Tadesse's eyes were searching, imploring. "But what if it's not? What if they do have eyes in the sky? Or missiles to shoot at us?"

"They don't. If they had a drone, they would not have told you. They were just trying to save their own skins." Sokolov said, with far more confidence than he felt. He stood, his bulk filling the space. "We are too close to the end to lose heart, Tadesse. Break them. Find out how much they know."

Tadesse, still looking uncertain, nodded, and then turned for the exit. Sokolov watched as the flap fell shut, and then closed his eyes and let out an anxious sigh. Despite his words of assurance, the unexpected intrusion by the American agents was an ominous development, especially coming on the heels of Tadesse's failure to kill the foreign diplomats.

Like it or not, he had to tell Petrov.

He retrieved his satellite phone from his rucksack and then exited the tent to get a better signal. The satellite phone heavy in his hand, he dialed the secure number that connected directly to Petrov in Brazil. With the time difference, it would be very early in Belém. He dreaded the thought of waking Petrov up with more bad news.

The line crackled as the connection was established across continents. "Yes, Mikhail."

Petrov's voice was slow and thick.

"Boris Ivanovich" Sokolov began without preamble, his voice low and urgent. "Something has happened."

There was a pause on the other end, and then Petrov's voice came through, tinged with annoyance. "I'm listening."

"Two Americans were caught sneaking into the equipment shed," Sokolov replied. "They claim to be with an organization called Project: RESCUE, but I don't believe them."

Petrov's annoyance shifted to concern. "Spies?"

"It would seem so," Sokolov confirmed. "Tadesse is questioning them. We will get at the truth. But if the Americans are sniffing around, it can only mean that they know what we're doing here."

"Impossible."

"Then why are they here? They must have their suspicions. Especially after what happened yesterday."

Petrov was silent for a long moment. Finally, he spoke, his voice now laced with a cold determination. "Mikhail, we cannot afford any disruptions. Failure is unacceptable. The stakes are too high. You must ensure that we are not compromised."

Sokolov's jaw set firmly. "I understand. Tadesse will extract the information we need from them. Then we will dispose of them."

"No. You must do it, Mikhail. The general is too unpredictable. If he learns what we're really doing..."

Petrov did not finish the sentence. He didn't need to.

"I understand," said Sokolov. "I'll take care of it. Personally." He ended the call, shoved the phone into a cargo pocket, and strode purposefully toward the tent where Tadesse was probably already beating the two American agents senseless. When he reached it, he pulled back the flap, stepping into the dimly lit interior. "Tadesse..."

The shout died on his lips. The sight that greeted him was not what he expected. General Tadesse lay sprawled on the floor, unmoving. The two captives were nowhere to be seen.

For a moment, Sokolov stood frozen, taking in the scene. The bindings that had held the Americans lay in pieces on the floor, but aside from Tadesse's still form, there was no sign of struggle. It was as if the prisoners had simply vanished into thin air.

TWENTY

YOU MAKE YOUR *own luck.*

Will's mantra was as true when visiting a ruthless revolutionary general-turned-mercenary as it was in the mountains. But that kind of luck, as he had explained to Scott Devlon, was all about preparation—the foresight to expect the unexpected, and plan accordingly. It was a mindset that had kept him alive in the most treacherous of climbs and the most volatile of conflicts.

As soon as Tadesse's footsteps had faded, Will and Deke had gone to work. The razor blades, taped discreetly to their forearms with flesh-colored bandages were a standard precaution for the FAST Team, as were similarly concealed handcuff keys and the diamond-studded cable saw threaded into their bootlaces—precautions taken for situations exactly like this. With swift, practiced movements, they cut through their bindings, freeing themselves to make their escape.

Of course, real luck played a role as well. When Will had decided to venture into Tadesse's territory, he had gambled on the fact that the mercenary general would do nothing worse than simply hold them captive, perhaps with a view to demanding a ransom. Had Tadesse simply decided to shoot them both on the spot, no amount of preparation would have saved them. But that was what making your own luck meant—you assessed the risk and acted accordingly. In this case, he had judged the risk that Tadesse would summarily execute them to be relatively low, and he'd been right

Whether that would continue to hold true was another matter entirely.

The first test came, moments later, when, just as Will was about to slice through the canvas at the back of the tent to provide a discreet exit, the flap was thrown open and Tadesse stepped in.

Deke sprang into action before Tadesse could even register what was happening, seizing the general by the arm and yanking him inside, simultaneously covering the man's mouth with one massive hand and wrapping the other arm around Tadesse's neck. While the FAST Team preferred to avoid using violence, there was a time and place for physical aggression.

Once more, luck played a decisive role. Had Tadesse been accompanied by one of his men, or if he'd managed to cry out in alarm before Deke subdued him, or if he'd come in carrying a gun... If any of a dozen different things had happened...

But they didn't.

The Tigrayan was no match for someone of Deke's size and strength. The latter's biceps squeezed against Tadesse's carotid arteries, blocking the flow of blood to his brain, and in less than thirty seconds, the mercenary's struggles ceased.

Deke retrieved Will's sat-phone from where Tadesse had dropped it, while Will continued cutting through the tent fabric, creating an exit that would hopefully allow them to bypass the camp's main thoroughfare. After a cautious look to ensure that there was nobody lurking about to observe their exit, he stepped through into daylight.

Another bit of oft-quoted wisdom Will conveyed to students in his climbing classes was from Ralph Waldo Emerson's essay *Prudence*.

In skating over thin ice, our safety is in our speed.

Sometimes, when faced with a tricky situation, the best course of action was to simply *move.* Veteran soldiers he had talked to called it 'getting off the X'.

In this instance, getting off the X meant getting away from Tadesse's camp and his mercenaries as quickly as possible, even if it meant a dash across open terrain. Still, there were ways to minimize the risk.

Carefully checking the blind corners, they leap-frogged from tent to tent until they reached the end of the row. From here, they could see some of Tadesse's men loitering in the open, smoking cigarettes as they idly conversed. They also saw the battered old pickup they'd passed on the way in, just a short hop away. When he was certain that the mercenaries were all looking the other way, Will broke from cover and made the short dash to the truck. A few seconds later, Deke did the same, moving with surprising stealth for someone so big.

From this new vantage, Will saw one other figure moving about the camp—a white man, speaking into a satellite phone. Like Tadesse and his mercenaries, the man wore camouflage trousers but only a grimy T-shirt covered his well-muscled upper body. Will couldn't make out what was being said, but he was pretty sure the man was not speaking English.

Russian, he guessed. *No doubt the local representative of VEK.*

He considered trying to use his phone, both as a listening aid and to translate the conversation, but decided there was a better use for the device. He opened the camera feature and started recording video of the man.

No sooner had he started doing this when the Russian put the phone away and began stalking toward the tent where he and Deke had been held captive only minutes before.

"Uh-oh," murmured Deke. "Looks like it's go time."

"Yep," Will agreed. "No time like now."

As one, they darted from behind the truck, keeping their bodies low at first in hopes of further minimizing exposure long enough to put a little distance between themselves and the men with guns.

The equipment shed where they'd left the Land Cruiser was about five-hundred yards away—not a significant distance for the two men, even in the rarefied high-altitude atmosphere—but given that they would be moving in a free fire zone, it felt like miles. They hadn't gone fifty yards when a shout went up behind them, a harsh command that sent a jolt of adrenaline surging through Will's veins.

The Russian had just discovered their escape.

Pouring on the speed, their boots pounding the earth, they made it another fifty yards before they heard the unmistakable crack of gunfire. Bullets sizzled through the air around them, close enough to hear the weird *zip* of the 5.45-millimeter projectiles breaking the sound barrier.

Will and Deke zigzagged, moving away from each other in an evasive pattern they'd drilled countless times, but kept moving in the general direction of their goal, now just a little more than three-hundred yards away.

Each step forward further increased the odds of survival, but luck, as Will always told his students, could be fickle.

Our salvation is in our speed.

"Keep moving!" he shouted, as the large rectangular shape of the storage shed came into view.

Deke, focused on making himself less of a target, didn't answer.

They kept up their pace, moving as surefootedly as mountain goats across the uneven terrain. Will allowed himself a mental sigh of relief—despite his level of aerobic fitness, he was starting to feel a little winded—when he caught sight of the Land Cruiser, still sitting exactly where they'd left it. Until that moment, he'd worried that Tadesse might have had his men move the vehicle, but once more, their luck held.

Bullets gouged divots in the armored exterior of the vehicle as the two men circled around it, putting it between them and the gunmen. Tadesse had taken Will's key, but there was a spare in a magnetic key keeper concealed up under the driver's side front tire well.

You make your own luck.

Will retrieved the key and used it to manually unlock the Cruiser, and then climbed in, hitting the unlock button so that Deke could get in behind him. Bullets continued to hammer against the far side of the vehicle, the repeated impacts sending spiderweb fractures through the laminated glass of the windows, breaking down what little protection they provided.

Will fired up the engine, put the SUV in gear and peeled away from the shed, only taking the time to check the status of the pursuit in the rearview mirror once they were underway. He could see Tadesse's men, moving in a line, firing their carbines on the go as they ran after the departing fugitives. On the uneven terrain, the Cruiser was only slightly faster than a running pace, but that slight difference quickly added up. After a couple minutes, the intensity of incoming fire slackened and then fell off altogether.

Deke took advantage of the lull to squirm through the gap between the front seats and settled into the front passenger seat.

"Well, that was fun," he remarked.

"Do we need to worry about them coming after us in the truck?"

Deke gave an equivocal shrug. "Depends on how long it takes them to change that tire."

"Wasn't sure you'd be able to cut through the sidewall with a razor blade."

Deke chuckled. "I went for the valve stem."

"Even better."

Deke glanced back. There was no sign of pursuit. Even the massive equipment shed had shrunk to a mere speck in the distance. "You know Tadesse isn't going to just let this go."

Will kept his eyes on the terrain ahead. "No, he won't. If he's secretly working with Colonel Tesfaye, then there's a chance we'll find a less-than-friendly reception waiting for us when we get back to Axum." He paused a beat before adding, "*If* we make it back to Axum."

"So, what are we going to do about it?"

Will had been considering this question. His instincts told him that this was more than just a matter of greed and exploitation. Tadesse and the Russians were up to something, something that was worth plunging Tigray back into civil war, and every fiber of his being wanted to know what that something was.

"The safe play would be to get out of Tigray," he finally said. "Head south. Gondar, maybe."

Gondar, about a hundred-and-fifty miles away, just north of Lake Tana, lay to the southwest of the mountains in the Amhara Region—well beyond the borders of the Tigray National State—and had been chosen as one of their backup departure points in the event that the situation in Tigray became too volatile for planes to land. From Gondar, they could arrange air travel to Addis Ababa, and from there, find a way out of Africa.

"Tell Maisy and Sanjeet to meet us there with the clients," he went on, "and then get out of the country before this place blows up."

"Uh-huh. That would be the safe play. Why do I have a feeling you've got something else in mind?"

Will took a moment to think about how to answer the question. "Scott told me something... When he was trying to convince me to take the job of looking after the diplomatic team... He said, 'sometimes the way to rescue someone is to put the fire out before it even starts.'"

"Our first obligation is to our clients," Deke pointed out.

"Our clients came here to save lives. Taneisha's trying to stop a war."

Deke pondered this for a moment. "So, how do we put out the fire?"

Will thought about the video he'd recorded of the Russian, and the other pictures on his phone, of the chemicals in the trench inside the equipment shed. "We figure out what the spark is that's going to start it."

TWENTY-ONE

MAISY COLE STARED intently out the windshield of the Land Cruiser as it rolled down the B30, one of the few asphalted highways in this part of Tigray, connecting Adwa—by way of Axum—to the city of Gondar in the Amhara Region. Originally built by the invading Italian army in the 1930s, the highway meandered back and forth, following the lay of the land. It was a scenic, if challenging route, but Maisy paid little attention to the landscape. Her mind was elsewhere, or more precisely, randomly flipping between several elsewheres. One moment, she was thinking about Will and Deke. Then her thoughts shifted to Elena, wondering how she would convince the headstrong doctor to come back. She worried that she'd made a huge mistake in letting Taneisha accompany them. And perhaps strangest of all, she wondered what Boris Petrov was going to say when he spoke to the attendees at COP 30.

When her thoughts touched on that subject, it was like stumbling across a beloved song on the radio while flipping randomly through the channels. The news out of Brazil had aroused her curiosity—what was the VEK executive up to? More importantly, did it have any bearing on what was happening in Tigray?

A chirp from her sat-phone startled her out of her ruminations. When she glanced at the caller ID and saw that the incoming call was from Will, her heart skipped a beat. She answered immediately.

"Will? Is that you? We've been trying to reach you!" Concern and relief almost caused her voice to crack.

"We've had a bit of a situation," came Will's strained reply. "Tadesse caught us. We managed to escape, but they're not going to be happy about it."

Maisy's relief at hearing from him was replaced by a growing sense of dread as she processed the news.

"Are you both alright?" she finally managed to ask, her voice steady despite the worry clawing at her insides.

"We're fine for the moment. Listen, I think we may have stumbled onto something big. Tadesse isn't just guarding the oil shale operation. He's taking orders from the Russians. I'm not certain what they're planning, but reigniting the Tigray War is part of it. I've got a video of someone I'm going to send you. I think he's the one calling the shots. See if you can identify him."

Maisy glanced at Sanjeet and then in the mirror at Taneisha. Both were watching her intently. "Uh, I may have to get back to you on that. We've had a little situation of our own here."

"What's happened?" Will's voice was tight, bracing for more bad news.

"Elena took off on her own," Maisy admitted, and she could almost hear Will's frustration through the static.

"Damn it," he growled.

Maisy winced, knowing full well the protective instincts that drove their leader.

"Well, I guess that's not a surprise," Will went on. "She did say that she was going to do it."

"We're going after her."

There was an odd noise across the line. Maisy braced herself for further imprecations, but after a moment, Will replied in a voice that was just barely controlled. "If you believe that's the right thing to do, I support you. I know you guys are more than capable of handling the situation."

"Taneisha insisted on coming with us."

There was a sharp intake of breath on the other end. "Damn it!" Will's curse was louder this time, more forceful. "Anything else I should know about?"

"No, that's pretty much it," Maisy replied, though the weight of 'pretty much' felt like a boulder on her chest.

After a tense pause, Will's voice came through again, a touch calmer but still laced with urgency. "All right, this could work out. Take Taneisha back to the village where we found her. I assume that's where she wants to go."

Maisy found Taneisha's reflection in the mirror. "It is."

"It should be safe for now. Tadesse's too busy chasing us to bother with the village. Maybe she can do some good there. When you're done, don't return to Axum. Head south to Gondar. We'll rendezvous there."

"What about the rest of Taneisha's diplomatic team?"

"I'll have Scott make arrangements to fly them out. They should be safe as long as they don't try to leave the city."

Maisy nodded, though Will couldn't see it. "And Elena? What about her?"

There was a sigh on the other end. "She should be safe, too. At least for the moment. Tadesse's focus is on us, and that gives us a window of opportunity. Use it. Get Taneisha to the village. She's the key to preventing war. Tell her about Tadesse's connection with VEK. She needs to make sure that the people in that village know who the bad guys really are, and that the only way to beat them is to keep the peace."

"Understood," Maisy replied, feeling relieved that Will had found a silver lining.

"I'm going to send you the video I told you about," Will went on. "And some other stuff, too. Take a look at it when you get a chance and see what you can dig up."

"Got it," she said. Then, almost as an afterthought, she added, "You two be careful."

Will's chuckle burbled from the phone's speaker, then was cut off as the call ended.

TWENTY-TWO

THE CRUISER'S SUSPENSION worked overtime as Will maneuvered through the labyrinth of boulders and ravines that dotted the landscape. Deke kept his eyes peeled, not just for the threat of pursuit, but for hidden dangers in the environment that demanded their attention. The terrain was unforgiving, a relentless expanse of rocky outcrops dotted with sparse vegetation that had adapted to the harshness of the highlands.

The GPS was of limited usefulness, insisting that the only viable route to take was the same road they'd come in on, backtracking almost all the way to Axum to get on the B30 highway south—a route which would take several hours, hours in which Tadesse would be hunting them every step of the way. Instead, they sought out back roads and mountain trails, heading due west, through the back country to reach the highway. On the map, it was a distance of only about twenty miles, but it would be a long, hard, slow twenty miles.

As the miles and hours ticked by, with the sun crawling across the sky, they found their way out of the mountain maze and descended toward the Tekezé River valley, where the terrain became increasingly more welcoming. They found a primitive road that took them past cultivated fields and villages, and if the GPS was to be believed, would eventually bring them to a bridge across the Tekezé River.

The Tekezé was a vital artery in the region, carving its way through the landscape. A major tributary of the Atbarah River, which in turn joined the Nile, the river began its journey near Lalibela in the Ethiopian Highlands, and carved a path through deep ravines, flowing northward and then westward, delineating the border between Ethiopia and Eritrea before entering Sudan below Omhajer. More importantly for Will and Deke, once across it, they would have only another twenty or so miles to travel to reach the border between Tigray and Amhara, beyond which they would be, if not completely beyond Tadesse's reach, then at least at enough of a remove to give them some breathing room.

As they approached the supposed location of the bridge, however, their hopes of a relatively quick exit from Tigray were dashed. Where the sturdy structure should have stood, there were only isolated pylons jutting up from the violent rush of water. The span was gone, a casualty of the war.

Will brought the Cruiser to a stop, the engine idling as both men took in the scene.

"Well, that's not good," remarked Deke.

"Looks like the river has other plans for us," agreed Will. "We'll have to find another way."

Deke took up the GPS, scrolling along the displayed map of the river valley, looking for other marked crossings. "We might have to look for a spot to ford," he said after several minutes of futile searching.

Will eyed the river surging past the remnants of the bridge. The force of the current was a product of both the rate of flow and the width and depth of the river. Bridges usually crossed at the narrowest places, where the river was deep and the current strongest, but where the banks were farther apart, the water might only be a foot or two deep—well within the Cruiser's capabilities.

The only question was whether to look upstream or down.

Deke continued to study the satellite map on the GPS, entering waypoints as he did. "All right, I've plotted a route that should keep us close to the river so we can look for a better place to cross. If that doesn't work, eventually we'll reach the highway bridge crossing."

"If it's still there. How far is it?"

Deke tapped out a rough course through the mountains, following the course of the river. "Fifteen miles, more or less. But it will be pretty much like the last fifteen miles. We can cut some of that if we head due west toward Adi Gebru. From there, it's just ten miles on paved road to the bridge."

"At least we'll be moving in the right direction," allowed Will.

With a new plan in place, Will brought the Cruiser around, and began backtracking until Deke directed him to turn onto a primitive track heading north.

The Cruiser's engine hummed a steady rhythm as they rolled along the serpentine path etched across the highland hills. Deke's eyes remained glued to the GPS, the waypoints a digital breadcrumb trail guiding them back into the embrace of the mountains.

Half an hour into this new phase of the journey, Will heard the faint but distinctive sound of a helicopter's rotor blades thrashing the air, a sound that was growing louder by the second. Without a word, he stopped the Cruiser and shut off the engine.

Back home in America, the sight and sound of a helicopter would have hardly been remarkable, but here in the skies above Tigray, where air travel was a rare luxury, it was portentous.

Deke rolled down his window, leaning out to scan the horizon. "There it is," he said as the aircraft emerged from behind a mountain peak to the east. At first it seemed to be moving almost parallel to their direction of travel, but then it changed course, and began moving directly toward them. "Think it's looking for us?"

"I wouldn't bet against it," replied Will, grimly.

As the rhythmic thump grew louder, Will activated his phone's video camera and pointed it skyward, recording the aircraft's approach.

The helicopter had a long cabin with several windows, which made it look a little like a bus with rotors. Its blue and white paint scheme suggested that it was a commercial aircraft, not a military one. He couldn't make out the markings, the details obscured by the glare of the sun on its fuselage, but its presence here, in this remote part of the world, was no coincidence. It had an aura of corporate power, the kind that came with resources and reach. The kind that a Russian oil company might command.

The aircraft soared over them, then descended until it was barely higher than the treetops and came around for another pass. As it drew near, it slowed, hovering over them for a moment, a dragonfly looking for mosquitos to devour, its downdraft stirring up a cloud of dust around the Cruiser.

Will lowered the phone and reached for the key. He expected at any moment for the doors on the hovering bird to open, and for camo-clad mercenaries to begin firing down at them, or perhaps rappel from hanging ropes to surround them. If that happened, he would have only seconds to drive away, and even then, they would still be under the constant scrutiny of the hovering helicopter.

But then the helicopter banked and turned away. Will and Deke exchanged a look.

"Is that a good sign?"

Will shook his head, already assembling a mental picture of what had just happened. "That was a reconnaissance flight. They've probably been flying all over the place for a couple hours, trying to pick up our trail. To extend flight time, they would have been flying light. No passengers. But now that they know where we are, they'll head back to base, pick up Tadesse and his men. Figure half-an-hour round trip. That's how long we've got before they get back here."

"Enough time to be somewhere else."

"On these old trails, we'll be lucky to get ten miles. They'll come right back to this spot, and then fly a search pattern until they find us again."

Deke gave him a sidelong glance. "Not like you to just give up."

Will continued watching the helicopter recede into the distance, and as he did, his lips turned up in a confident smile. "Who said anything about giving up?"

TWENTY-THREE

TANEISHA STARED OUT the side window of the Project: RESCUE Land Cruiser, watching the now-familiar landscape pass by. Her gaze lingered on the rugged terrain, the mountains standing as silent sentinels to the passage of time and the ebb and flow of empires. The journey had been uneventful, the highway bringing them to the turnoff to the old mule path she had traveled the previous day.

During the long drive the conversation in the Land Cruiser had turned to Tadesse and the Volga Energy Corporation. Maisy's revelations concerning Tadesse and his involvement with the VEK had ignited a familiar fire within her.

"The new face of colonialism," Taneisha said, her voice carrying a hint of despair. "Did you know that Ethiopia is one of only two nations on the African continent that never fell under colonial rule?"

Maisy glanced at her through the rearview mirror. "I didn't know that," she admitted. "Didn't Italy control the country before World War II?"

"They invaded but never took full control. The Ethiopians fought back and eventually drove them out. Adwa Victory Day, celebrating the defeat of the Fascist forces in the Battle of Adwa is a national holiday, and a powerful reminder of what can be achieved against overwhelming odds." She shook her head. "But now I guess corporations are the new colonizers."

"It doesn't have to be that way," said Sanjeet.

"How can we stop it?"

"You can stop it. Tell the Tigrayan people what's really going on. If they realize that they're being manipulated, maybe they'll fight to preserve the peace, instead of letting VEK destroy it."

"I wish it were that easy." Taneisha leaned back, her thoughts returning to the outcome of her first visit to the village of Alem Tekle.

"Nothing worth doing is ever easy," said Maisy.

Taneisha laughed despite herself. "That sounds like something I might say."

Maisy shrugged. "Will says it all the time."

The conversation fell fallow as they began climbing up the narrow ribbon trail that snaked through the mountains, flanked by the occasional juniper tree and stretches of wild grass that swayed in the gentle breeze. Taneisha felt oddly protective of the wild, austere landscape—this was a place worth fighting for.

But as they rounded the last bend and caught sight of the settlement, the charred skeletons of three Range Rovers in the foreground gave a grim reminder that the odds were stacked against them. The vehicles had been gutted by fire, their metal frames twisted and blackened, the glass melted away.

Maisy brought the vehicle to a stop, and the silence that followed was heavy. Taneisha's heart clenched at the sight, the memories of that day rushing back in a torrent of sound and fear. She remembered the gunfire, the confusion, the desperate scramble for safety.

Sanjeet's calm voice broke through her despair. "Remember why you're here."

Nodding, Taneisha opened her door and stepped out of the Land Cruiser. The village of Alem Tekle lay before them, seemingly deserted, the silence punctuated only by the occasional whisper of wind through the juniper branches. The huts, made of stone and clay, pocked with scorch marks and bullet wounds, stood like empty shells, their doorways gaping open, abandoned.

She moved forward, her eyes scanning the settlement for any sign of life, any hint that the peace talks could still find fertile ground here. Maisy and Sanjeet followed, the latter carrying a backpack adorned with a red cross. Their presence a steady reassurance at her back.

Then, as if conjured by the very tension in the air, a figure emerged from the shadow of a hut—a young man, draped in a white robe that contrasted starkly with the dark rifle he held at the low ready. Taneisha's breath caught as she recognized him. "Ezana," she whispered, her voice barely audible.

Ezana Sengal, the grandson of Alem Tekle, stood before them, his youthful face hardened by the violence that had upended his world. His gaze met Taneisha's, a mixture of surprise and resignation in his eyes. "I did not think I would see you again," he said in Amharic, his voice steady but tinged with the weariness of one who has seen too much.

Taneisha stepped forward, her own resolve mirrored in her steady tone. "I was not sure if I would see you," she said. "Is your grandfather... is he well? Can I speak to him?"

Ezana's expression was unreadable. "Follow me," he said, turning on his heel.

Taneisha glanced at Maisy and Sanjeet, and after receiving encouraging nods from both, followed the young man. They passed through the middle of the settlement, past huts and small plots of cultivated land, the signs of daily life starkly absent, and emerged into a section of open ground on the outskirts of the village. The rows of crosses left little question as to the purpose for which this land had been set aside. Mounds of freshly turned earth marked the location of more than a dozen recent burials. A handful of village men and women worked solemnly, their spades turning the soil as they prepared for more. Others—older men and women, children, many of them sporting crude bandages—simply looked on, hollow eyed. Several shrouded bodies lay at the edge of the cemetery.

Ezana stopped before one of the graves, his back to Taneisha as he gestured toward the ground. "Here is my grandfather," he said, his voice devoid of emotion.

Taneisha's hand flew to her mouth, her eyes brimming with sorrow. "Oh, Ezana, I'm so sorry," she managed to say, her voice breaking.

Ezana remained unmoved, his eyes scanning the horizon as if searching for answers in the distance. He pointed to another set of graves, freshly filled. "Here are your fighting men. I'm sorry they could not protect you."

Taneisha thought about Rajesh Raj, whom she barely knew, and his Ugandan mercenaries, whom she did not even know by name.

All dead.

The gravity of their loss hit hard.

Sanjeet stepped forward. "You have injured," he said. "I'm a doctor. Let me help."

Taneisha was surprised to hear him speaking Tigrinya, then realized that the words had actually issued from his satellite phone.

A faint glimmer of hope and gratitude broke through Ezana's expression as he gazed at Sanjeet. "Yes, we have many who are hurt," he replied. "Your help... it would be welcomed."

Ezana's voice, weirdly speaking English, could be heard, after which Sanjeet unslung his medical pack and approached the villagers.

It was a small victory, a moment of connection in a place marred by loss and the looming shadow of conflict.

Ezana watched Sanjeet for a moment, then turned back to Taneisha. "When we have buried our dead," he said, his voice carrying the inevitability of a storm on the wind, "Those of us who can fight will leave to join the army of General Tadesse to prepare for the war that is coming,"

Taneisha stepped closer, her voice earnest. "Ezana, there's something you should know. General Tadesse is not the savior of Tigray." She gestured to the graves. "He did this. He's working with a Russian oil company. They're stoking the fires of war so they can pillage the natural resources of your country for their own gain. It's greed, pure and simple."

Ezana's eyes flickered with a mixture of anger and skepticism. "How do you know this?" he asked, his grip on the rifle tightening.

Taneisha gestured to Maisy. "She has proof. Tadesse wants this war, but he doesn't care about Tigray. He only wants riches."

Ezana stared at her for a long moment, then looked down at the graves, his expression unreadable. "My grandfather fought for Tigray all his life. In the end, he wanted peace, not more bloodshed."

"Then honor him by seeking the truth before rushing to battle," Taneisha urged, her gaze unwavering. "Don't let their greed destroy Tigray."

"Even if I do this, there are many who will follow Tadesse into war."

"Then you must tell the truth. Make them understand."

Ezana turned to her, his eyes burning with fierce intensity. "You tell them."

Taneisha was momentarily taken aback. "Why would they listen to me? I am an outsider."

"That is exactly why they will listen. You have proof of Tadesse's treachery."

Taneisha's mind raced to process Ezana's request. This was the very reason she had come to Ethiopia. "We'll tell them together. As many as we can."

Maisy, who had been silent during the exchange, now spoke up. "Taneisha, Will wants us to head on to Gondar. The longer we stay here, the more danger we're in. And not just us, but these people, too."

Taneisha turned to Maisy, her resolve strengthening. "I know the risks," she said. "But we have a chance to stop this war, prevent more bloodshed. If we leave now, we're turning our backs on the very people we came here to help."

Maisy was torn, the weight of responsibility evident in her furrowed brow. "My first obligation is to ensure your safety."

Sanjeet, who had evidently been listening to the exchange as he attended to the injured of the settlement, spoke up, his voice steady and sure. "We're Project: RESCUE, aren't we? Saving lives is what we do.

Maisy glanced at the villagers, their eyes filled with a mix of hope and despair, then back at Taneisha. "How long do you need?"

Taneisha looked to Ezana.

"I can send messengers to our neighbors. Gather their elders together to hear what you have to say. I will have them meet here at sunset."

Maisy stared back at Taneisha for a long moment, then looked to Sanjeet who just nodded. "All right," she said, and then shook her head resignedly. "Will's gonna kill me."

TWENTY-FOUR

Belém do Pará, Brazil

FORTY-FIVE MINUTES LATER, the helicopter returned. It emerged from behind the mountain crest, moving like an arrow toward the place where its crew had last observed the Land Cruiser, and then immediately began orbiting the spot in ever-widening circles, its crew and passengers methodically scanning the ground below.

The aircraft's presence was an intrusion, a noisy mechanical predator beating the figurative bushes in an attempt to flush out its prey. Its rotors beat a steady rhythm, a sound that grew louder and more insistent as it dropped lower, closer to the ground. The downdraft kicked up a storm of dust and debris. It was clear that those aboard were determined, willing to scour the landscape until they found what they were looking for.

The land below seemed to offer few places to hide from such a thorough search, yet there was no sign of movement, no indication that the targets of this intense scrutiny were anywhere to be found.

Will and Deke watched the aerial search from beneath the cover of a hastily built blind near the bank of the river, just two miles from the location where they'd first been spotted. They had chosen their hiding spot with care, selecting a natural depression near the riverbank that was surrounded by dense brush and overhanging rocks. It was a spot that was invisible from the air, especially to anyone looking for something as large as a Land Cruiser.

The two men had worked quickly after the helicopter's initial departure, driving the Cruiser into a shallow ravine where they had camouflaged it with branches rocks, and even a liberal application of dust to ensure it blended seamlessly with the natural environment. Then, understanding that the vehicle would be the first thing their pursuers would look for, they set out on foot, putting distance between themselves and the Cruiser. On foot, they would be smaller targets, harder to spot from the air, especially as the light began to fade.

The helicopter made several more passes, each one lower and more desperate than the last. But as the shadows grew longer and the light continued to wane, the search proved fruitless. Eventually, with the sun dipping below the horizon, the helicopter turned and headed back the way it had come, leaving the valley in peace once more.

Will and Deke waited until the sound of the rotors had faded into the distance before they dared to emerge from their hiding place.

"I was starting to think those guys would never leave," said Deke as he stretched the stiffness out of his limbs.

"I didn't think they would," admitted Will. "Not without putting some boots on the ground first."

"Lucky for us they didn't, or we'd be stuck here." Deke made a show of looking around. "So, what's the next part of your brilliant plan?"

Will surveyed the dimming landscape. "We keep moving."

"I figured that part. But are we driving or walking?"

"Walking. Our feet can take us places that wheels won't go. Plus, we're a lot less likely to be spotted from the air if we're on foot."

"It's going to be slow going in the dark," Deke pointed out.

"Can't be helped."

"And where exactly are our feet taking us?"

Will pointed toward the setting sun. "The main highway is only about ten or fifteen miles from here. We can cover that by morning, even if we take it easy."

Deke nodded. "And once we reach the road?"

"We try to hitch a ride. Worst case, we call and have Maisy and Sanjeet come pick us up. Whatever gets us out of Tigray the quickest. Speaking of which..." Will took out the sat phone and sent a call.

Maisy answered on the first ring, her voice was a mix of relief and urgency. "Will! Everything still okay?"

"That's up for debate." He quickly related the details of their journey, along with the decision to proceed the rest of the way on foot.

"Are you sure that's wise? Tadesse might send his people to watch border crossings."

"We'll burn that bridge when we come to it."

Maisy gave a nervous laugh, which was followed by a long pause on the line, and when she spoke again, her tone was hesitant. "Listen, we've had another slight change of plans on our end. We're staying here overnight. Taneisha is meeting with the local elders to try to convince them not to join Tadesse's rebellion."

Will wasn't the least bit surprised to hear it.

"She believes it's the right thing to do," Maisy went on, as if to rebut criticism he hadn't given. "Sanjeet and I do, too. And they've got wounded here. He's helping patch them up."

"It's okay, Maisy," Will said when she paused to take a breath. "I support whatever decision you make. Just be careful."

"We will." Will could hear the relief in her tone. "You, too."

"Let me guess," Deke said when Will ended the call. "Taneisha's making them stay."

"Just for the night."

Deke shook his head, a wry smile on his face. "That woman is relentless."

"Maybe that's what it takes to stop a war." Will put the phone in his pocket, and with a final look around, said, "We should get moving."

"How do you think Scott's going to react when you tell him we ditched the Land Cruiser?"

Will shrugged. "That's what insurance is for."

TWENTY-FIVE

THE AIR IN the village was thick with anticipation and the scent of burning frankincense. For hours, they had trickled in, small groups of three or four—the elders of neighboring settlements, draped in traditional white shawls, and their wives and sons and daughters—bearing food and gifts which they presented to Ezana, along with their condolences.

Despite the near total absence of technology, word of the attack and the death of Alem Tekle had spread quickly, and with it, a rising war furor. From what Maisy could tell, a narrative had already taken shape, in which the Ethiopian government was responsible for the massacre, a crime which would not go unpunished. Not if General Tadesse had anything to say about it. Taneisha, who stood alongside Ezana, introducing herself to each of the elders as they arrived, made no effort to correct the misunderstanding. That would happen later, when all the invited were present.

Sanjeet had spent the afternoon caring for the injured of the village. Most of the wounds were minor—the seriously wounded had not survived the first night—but infection was a problem, and his antibiotic stores were quickly depleted. "Elena will have a supply at her clinic," he concluded after reporting the shortage to Maisy. "We should travel there tomorrow."

Maisy groaned at the thought of making that trip. Every delay that kept them in Tigray just increased the likelihood that General Tadesse would come looking for them. But like Elena and Taneisha and Sanjeet, she found that the real and immediate need of the Tigrayans was something she couldn't ignore.

She had spent the afternoon researching the information Will had forwarded to her. Translating the Cyrillic text he'd sent had been the work of a few minutes. The first one contained powdered aluminum, commonly used in making metallic paints as well as fireworks. The second contained ferrous oxide. The two substances were often combined to make thermite, a powerful incendiary compound capable of producing intense heat, which had a variety of industrial applications, but could also be used for sabotage. That Will and Deke had discovered the compounds in close proximity to General Tadesse was more than a little concerning.

Determining the identity of the man in the video clip proved harder. Will hadn't been able to get a clear look at his face, which negated the possibility of using facial recognition software, but after making some inquiries, Maisy had hit upon a different solution. She began with the assumption that the man was an employee of Volga Energy, and then, with a little help from an old friend at Defense Intelligence Agency, was able to sift through the VEK personnel files and assemble a list of candidates who might be a good match. Since the man's muscular physique not only hinted at a military background, but also made it unlikely that he would be someone working in a research lab, she was able to further refine the search parameters. Narrowing the list down to half-a-dozen men, all of them former soldiers and all of them doing security work for VEK, which Maisy gathered involved a lot more than simply standing guard duty at their facilities. Of that group, the likeliest candidate was Mikhail Andreyevich Sokolov, a former GRU Spetsnaz operator with experience in several theatres, including the Horn of Africa, and who was now listed as "associate director of operations."

It was plain to Maisy that Sokolov was working with Tadesse to restart the Tigray War in order to advance VEK's interests in the region, but how that figured into Boris Petrov's global strategy was not immediately clear. She noted that the VEK VP was slated to take the stage at the COP 30 climate conference in just a few hours, and wondered if his address to the delegates would shed any light on his plans for Tigrayan oil shale.

What was obvious was that VEK and Tadesse had to be stopped, but whether Taneisha could accomplish that with diplomacy remained to be seen.

When she finished a summary report of her findings for Will, she went looking for Sanjeet. She found him examining a young boy who, aside from looking a little under-nourished, showed no obvious signs of injury.

"How's it going?" she asked.

Sanjeet's expression turned grave as he looked up at Maisy. "I fear my young patient here is showing symptoms of visceral leishmaniasis," he said, his voice barely above a whisper. "It's a parasitic infection transmitted through the bite of infected sand flies, and affects internal organs like the spleen, liver, and bone marrow, which can lead to severe anemia. Early symptoms are fever, weight loss, and an enlarged spleen and liver." He nodded to the boy, indicating that all of these warning signs were present.

"It can take months for symptoms to appear after the initial bite," he went on, "which means he may not be the only one here who's infected.

"Is it...?"

"Fatal? If untreated."

Maisy felt sick at the thought of the child's suffering. "But you can treat it?"

Sanjeet sighed heavily. "The standard treatment involves antimony-based drugs. Elena will have those in her clinic, but I fear with the current situation and the threat of still more war, the outlook is not good."

"Let's hope Taneisha can talk them out of it."

Sanjeet nodded, and after murmuring a few words of reassurance to the boy and sending him on his way, turned back to Maisy. "Let's go see how she's doing with that."

They found Taneisha, along with most of the village and the visitors, in a large central courtyard, while elsewhere the evening meal was being prepared. The air was redolent with the rich scents of cumin, coriander, and cardamom, and the smoky aroma of grilled meats. Taneisha was sitting with Ezana, but rose to greet Maisy and Sanjeet, and invited them to sit with her.

"How go the negotiations?" Maisy asked.

"The real conversation won't begin until after we have eaten," she said, gesturing toward the spread of food that awaited them. "But in my experience, sharing a meal is a great place to begin finding common ground."

As the sun settled behind the mountains, kerosene lamps were lit to illuminate the gathering, after which a train of village women began setting out platters of food, which Taneisha dutifully identified for Maisy and Sangeet. There was *tihlo*—balls of barley dough covered with meat and berbere-based sauce. A flatbread called *ambasha* was used in lieu of eating utensils, to scoop up a spicy stew called *beso*. The villagers had also prepared *gaa't*, a porridge made from barley. The repast was washed down with cups of *suwa*, a traditional honey wine, though Sanjeet, observing the dietary restrictions of his Sikh faith, stuck to tea.

Despite the simplicity of the ingredients, the flavors were rich and satisfying, each dish carrying the warmth and hospitality of the villagers, and as they all partook of the communal feast, Maisy couldn't help but feel a sense of rising hope.

The feeling was short-lived.

Even before the meal was cleared away, an air of tension began to circulate about the gathering. Many of the elders listened intently as Taneisha warned of General Tadesse's double-dealing and urged them to continue supporting the peace, but their expressions remained guarded. One woman with deep lines of wisdom on her face, spoke out. "We have heard your words," she said. "But we have also seen the General's generosity. He has provided for us when others have not."

Another elder, an ancient man with a weathered face, chimed in. "What proof do you have that he is not acting in our best interests?" he asked.

"We have proof," explained Taneisha. "A recording of Tadesse talking about the attack which was meant to kill me and the others who came to speak with Alem Tekle in hopes of sustaining the peace."

"A recording?" The elder seemed dubious. "And how will we know that it is really Tadesse speaking?"

Ezana jumped in. "I have heard it, and I believe it to be Tadesse. But even if it is not... Tadesse wants war. That is not in dispute. We have seen the destruction that war brings. We have already suffered enough. We cannot trust a man who has shown us such disregard for our well-being."

From there, the discussion devolved into a free-for-all with the elders voicing their doubts and concerns. Maisy tried to follow with the instant translation app on the phone, but there were too many voices, often speaking over each other, for her to get a clear picture of what was being said. Nevertheless, she could see that Taneisha and Ezana's words were falling on deaf ears. The villagers trusted Tadesse, and without concrete evidence of his treachery, they were unwilling to turn against him.

"I take it that's not going over very well?" she whispered to Taneisha.

"The other elders trust Tadesse to bring about the dream of a free Tigray," she explained in a low voice. "Ezana and I have tried to tell them that Tadesse isn't who they think he is... That he's responsible for the attack that killed Alem, but I don't think they want to believe it."

The elders continued to murmur animatedly among themselves. Maisy felt a heavy weight settle in her chest as she realized the gravity of the situation. They had come here in the hopes that Taneisha might be able to defuse the impending crisis. She had not anticipated the loyalty of the villagers to Tadesse, and that was a very real problem.

Tadesse's own words came back to her.

We have been given a second chance to finish what we started.

She looked around the room, noting that some of the younger men who had accompanied the elders supporting Tadesse were watching Taneisha very closely.

Maisy leaned in close to the diplomat, her voice barely above a whisper. "Tadesse wants you dead. If he has supporters here, then you're in real danger."

Taneisha looked back at her, eyes widening in comprehension, but then her resolve returned. "We can't just give up. We have to make them understand what's really going on."

"You're not going to. Talk isn't going to do it. You've got to show them proof of Tadesse's treachery. Something they can't argue with. But right now..." She shot another glance at the young men who were still openly staring at them. "Right now, we need to go."

Taneisha reluctantly paid her respects to Ezana and then followed Maisy and Sanjeet through the village toward the waiting Land Cruiser. Outside the courtyard, the darkness was nearly absolute, prompting Maisy to activate the flashlight in her sat-phone to illuminate the way. With the hum of conversation from the courtyard diminishing behind them, the night felt ominously quiet, which only deepened Maisy's sense of urgency. She dug into a cargo pocket for the key fob to the Land Cruiser and clicked the button to unlock the doors.

The soft click of the mechanism seemed unnaturally loud in the stillness. As if the noise was a signal, three young men stepped out from behind the vehicle. blocking their path. Maisy recognized them as the same men who had been watching Taneisha earlier.

Maisy's heart skipped a beat as she took in their stance—shoulders squared, arms crossed, and eyes narrowed in an open display of suspicion and hostility. One of them spoke, a short utterance in what Maisy guessed was Tigrinya. Belatedly, she thumbed the screen of her phone to activate the translation app.

Taneisha, assuming a defiant posture, answered. "We are leaving. Please step aside."

The man who had spoken first shook his head and spoke again. The app supplied a simultaneous translation. "It's not safe to travel at night. You must stay here."

"Something tells me traveling is a lot safer than staying here," Maisy murmured.

"We can see to our own safety." Taneisha's voice was firm, her eyes locked on the young men who stood defiantly before them. "Now, please let us pass."

But the young man only shook his head. "You are not leaving. General Tadesse must know of the lies that you have told about him."

With the mention of Tadesse, Maisy realized that the situation had escalated beyond the point where they would be able to simply talk their way around the young men.

"Ezana is the elder here," Taneisha replied, her tone unwavering. "You have no authority to detain us."

At the invocation of Ezana's name, the young men exchanged uncertain glances, but then one of them reached behind his back and drew out a machete-like chopping knife, brandishing it menacingly.

"You will stay here," he declared, his eyes fixed on Taneisha.

Maisy's mind raced to find a way out of this standoff. She knew they couldn't fight their way through; they needed a plan that would allow them to escape without violence.

"Put that away," Taneisha said firmly, her voice echoing through the night. "You dishonor Ezana and all who live here with your threats of bloodshed."

This time, the mention of their host's name had no effect. The young men's hostility was unquenchable, and their intentions were clear. They were determined to hold them captive for General Tadesse.

"What are you doing?" The challenging voice—Ezana's—came from behind them, and when Maisy turned to look, she saw that he was holding his AK-47. He was not aiming it at anyone, holding it loosely with the barrel pointing at the ground, but its mere presence was significant. He strode forward, passing around the three visitors, and facing the young men.

"Put that knife away," he said, his tone firm but not threatening. "You will not treat my guest with such disrespect."

Cowed by Ezana's presence, or more likely, the fact that his rifle trumped their blade, the young men immediately slunk away, their departure as silent as their arrival.

Taneisha's confident mask fell away, as she turned shakily to regard Ezana. "Thank you," she said, her voice quavering with relief.

Ezana nodded, his expression grave. "I am sorry that happened, but I think you are right to leave. I fear you may have stayed too long already. General Tadesse will soon hear of this."

Maisy stepped forward. "We will be careful," she assured Ezana. And then to Taneisha added. "Come on. We have to move."

She quickly circled around to the driver's side and climbed into the Land Cruiser, starting the engine. Its hearty rumble offered some comfort after the confrontation, but Maisy knew that they were a long way from safety. When Sanjeet and Taneisha were aboard, she put the vehicle in gear, and with a final wave to Ezana, circled around and headed back down the trail.

The headlights cut through the darkness, but the uneven terrain cast long shadows ahead of them. For several minutes, a tense silence came over them as Maisy focused on driving.

Finally, Taneisha broke the silence. "I really thought we had a chance," she said miserably.

"You did all you could," replied Sanjeet. "Believe me, I know what that feels like."

Taneisha accepted this with a nervous laugh. "So what do we do now?

Maisy fielded the question. "I don't think it's safe to try for Axum. Will wanted us to head south to Gondar, but that's a long trip, and I don't know if we dare try to make it at night. Especially if Tadesse is watching the border, which seems pretty likely now."

"We could go to Elena's clinic," suggested Sanjeet. "Adi Gebru isn't far, and it's on the way to Gondar. We could stop there, at least for the night. Rest and regroup and then decide what to do in the morning."

Taneisha nodded. "Sounds like a good plan to me."

Maisy, however, let out an involuntary snort of laughter at the suggestion.

"What?" asked Sanjeet.

Maisy shook her head. "Sorry. You're right. That's probably our best bet. It's just... We came here for the sole reason of escorting Elena out because it was too dangerous to stay, and now we're going to her for refuge."

Sanjeet chuckled softly. "Well, we *were* right about the danger."

TWENTY-SIX

Belém do Pará, Brazil

PETROV FELT ALMOST giddy as he stepped onto the stage and gazed out at the sea of faces, men and women from every corner of the globe, waiting in anticipation. In front of him, the teleprompter displayed the opening lines of his speech, words which he had meticulously assembled over the course of several months in anticipation of this moment. It was a declaration that would shake the world.

He knew how they would receive his words. They would revile him.

But later, when they had no other choice, they would accept that this was the only way to save their world.

Petrov cleared his throat and began to speak, his voice resonating through the hall. "Ladies and gentlemen," he started, his tone commanding yet measured, "Honored delegates. We are here today because the world is burning. Our forests are ablaze, our ice caps are melting, and our oceans are rising. The evidence is irrefutable, the science unequivocal, and the consequences undeniable."

Petrov paused, his gaze sweeping over the audience, and let the words sink in. It wasn't anything they hadn't heard a hundred times already, but coming from someone such as himself, it must have sounded like divine revelation.

"As a leading petroleum producer," he continued, "My company has been a part of the problem. I freely admit it. We have fought fiercely to preserve our own wealth, even going so far as to deny the reality of what is happening before our very eyes. And do you know why? It is because these hydrocarbons—petroleum and natural gas—they are buried treasure, and we have the map. And if we don't dig it up, somebody else will.

"That, you see, is the fundamental problem we face. It is the reason... The only reason, why nothing ever changes. I, Boris Ivanovich Petrov, in the name of all mankind, could foreswear all further extraction, close down Volga Energy for good... and yet, what difference would it make? I would die a pauper, and someone else would simply come along and take the treasure I have eschewed." He paused a beat, and then gesturing forcefully with a knife hand to emphasize every word, said, "This. Must. Change."

A murmur rippled through the crowd, a mix of surprise and skepticism.

He looked at the teleprompter, but his next words came from the heart. "Change is never easy, and the path ahead is fraught with challenges. Solving this problem will be costly, yet the cost of inaction is far greater. We must act, not tomorrow, not next year, but now.

"We face a moral crisis. Make no mistake, that is what it is. We all know what the *right* thing to do is, but we are opposed at every turn by entrenched economic interests. Eventually, we will have no choice but to change our ways, accept the reality of our situation and the urgency of our need, but history *will* judge us. Our children's children will ask our ghosts, 'What took you so long?' And what will we say?"

He shrugged. "It cost too much?"

He paused again and then raised a finger, a cue to begin projecting visual aids onto the screen behind him. When the first image appeared, an unpleasant murmur rippled through the audience.

The image was of a flyer, printed two centuries earlier, advertising the sale of African slaves.

Petrov allowed the discomfort to build for a few moments before resuming. "Consider the slave trade, an abhorrent chapter in human history. Many benefited, both directly and indirectly, from the forced labor of enslaved persons. Many more knew in their hearts that it was morally reprehensible. Yet nothing changed for centuries because the economic advantages of the status quo were a more powerful incentive than moral outrage."

On the screen behind him, the displayed image changed to a similar flyer, but this one carried an anti-slavery message. "Nevertheless, in time, the outcry to end this abominable practice eventually led the British Empire—the greatest world power at the time, and the largest slave trading power—to first outlaw the slave trade, and then to emancipate every enslaved person in the Empire. It was not easy. But it was the right thing to do." He paused a beat before adding, "No matter the cost.

"Much like the fossil fuel industry today, the slave trade was deeply integrated into the economy, and its abolition required not only moral conviction, but also significant economic restructuring."

He paused again, allowing his listeners to fully embrace his analogy. "Today, we are called upon to undertake a similar transformation. The abolition of slavery was not the end of progress—it was the beginning of a more just world. Likewise, transitioning away from fossil fuels is not the end of our prosperity; it is the beginning of a sustainable future."

Petrov's words hung in the air, a challenge to the assembly to rise to the occasion as the abolitionists did centuries before, to confront the moral and economic crisis of their time with courage and determination. The applause that followed was tentative, however. These people were used to hearing empty rhetoric and were waiting for Petrov to drop the other shoe.

He did not disappoint.

"When the British Empire abolished slavery, the greatest challenge was how to convince slave owners to release their slaves, the very source of their wealth. Simply enforcing the rule of law would not have worked. There would have been open revolt, just as would later happen in the United States. No, a different solution was needed. A hard, but necessary decision was made."

He let the unasked question linger before answering it himself. "Compensation. The government paid vast sums to slave owners as recompense for their 'losses'. It was a pragmatic solution to a moral crisis, one that recognized the economic realities of the time."

The delegates shifted in their seats, their discomfort palpable as they began to see where he was taking them. A low murmur arose as those listening began whispering expressions of incredulity.

Petrov pressed on. "Today, we face a similar situation with fossil fuels. The industry, and indeed, entire economies, are deeply invested in these resources. To ask those of us who produce petroleum to simply walk away from our buried treasure is unrealistic. But what if, like the slave owners of the past, the nations of the world were to offer us fair compensation in exchange for doing just that?"

The murmur grew increasingly louder, a swelling cacophony of anger and disbelief. Shouts of "Extortion!" and "Scam!" erupted from the audience like steam from fumaroles. Several delegates were on their feet, moving into the aisles. Many were simply making for the exit, but some of the younger attendees were heading for the stage with murder in their eyes.

Petrov drove on. "We stand at a crossroads, much like the British Empire did when it faced the moral imperative to end slavery." The image on the projection screen changed, displaying a graph of rising temperatures and sea levels, an undeniable visual representation of the crisis at hand. "They chose to pay compensation to slave owners, a decision that was—"

Suddenly the screen went dark, as did the stage lights, and Petrov realized that his microphone was no longer working. "A decision that was both costly and controversial," he went on, shouting to be heard.

Lena Andersdotter, flanked by a pair of beefy-looking security personnel, emerged from off-stage and stalked toward him, putting herself between him and the audience, arms folded defiantly. "Mr. Petrov," she said, her voice barely audible over the din. "I think you're finished."

Petrov wasn't sure if she was referring to his speech or something more. In truth, he had said everything he hoped to say, and despite the response, which was exactly as he had anticipated, he had accomplished his purpose.

He'd let the genie out of the bottle. There would be no putting it back.

Unbowed, Petrov stared back at her, "You say that we must battle climate change no matter the cost. *This* is the cost."

Andersdotter shook her head. "I should have known better than to trust you. You are like the scorpion in the fable, unable to overcome your nature." She let the rebuke sink in for a moment, then went on. "For your own safety, I am revoking your attendance privileges, permanently," she continued, her tone leaving no room for argument. "I think it would be best for all if you left Belém immediately."

"You can throw me out," he retorted. "But you know I'm right. This is a real solution."

"Will you leave on your own?" she asked, with a nod to the security guards. "Or do you need someone to walk you out?"

Laughing, Petrov turned away and headed for the wings, with the two guards trailing a few steps behind him.

As he neared the exit, the familiar drawl of Jack McAllister cut through the din. "You sure have got a pair," said the lobbyist, falling into step beside him. "I'll give you that."

"Revolutionary ideas are never popular," replied Petrov. "Real change is always difficult. But one day, I will be proved right. Perhaps sooner than you think."

"Now I get why you were buying up all those shale oil leases," McAllister went on. "If they paid even a fraction of the gross market value of those reserves, you'd stand to make a hell of a lot more leaving it in the ground than you would if you had to actually extract it. Plus, you get to act like you're the one who saved us all from climate change."

Petrov shrugged. "Capitalism, no?"

McAllister shook his head. "You had to know they were never going to go for it."

"Oh, I think they will." Petrov allowed himself a triumphant smile. "When the world gets hot enough, they will."

TWENTY-SEVEN

Tigray National State, Ethiopia

WITH THEIR PLAN set, Will and Deke shouldered their go bags—backpacks containing the bare minimum survival essentials that were just another application of Will's Law of Luck—and ventured out under the twilight sky. The shadows continued to deepen around them, but as their eyes grew accustomed to the low-light conditions, they were able to move with a degree of confidence.

They followed the river's course, its constant murmur joining the chorus of nocturnal creatures to accompany their silent march, but after a few miles, its course bent south, diverging from the route Deke had plotted on the GPS that would bring them back to the highway just north of Adi Gebru.

"Maybe we can stop in and say 'hi' to Elena" said Deke after showing Will the proposed route. "I'm sure she'd be thrilled to see you."

"Us, you mean," Will corrected. "And we've already got enough people who want us dead right now, thank you very much."

"Thou doth protest too much, methinks," replied Deke with a chuckle.

Will just ignored him.

THEY CONTINUED ONWARD, navigating the uneven terrain by starlight, only occasionally using the headlamps from their go-bags to illuminate their path. Not surprisingly, the terrain bore little resemblance to what was displayed on the GPS satellite map, with unexpected ravines and boulder fields necessitating detours, but for the most part, they stayed on course.

A few hours into the journey, they reached what looked on the GPS map like a shortcut—a narrow slot canyon that would, they hoped, take hours off their journey.

The canyon was quite a change from the open terrain they had traversed earlier. The walls to either side were sheer, looming above them and shutting out the starlight. The air was cool and still, carrying with it the scent of earth and stone.

As they ventured deeper into the canyon, the GPS signal began to falter, and the path ahead became less certain.

After about half an hour of travel, Will blundered into what seemed to be a dense thicket completely obstructing their route.

"That's weird," muttered Will.

"I'm afraid to ask." Deke's low voice rumbled out of the darkness. "What's weird?"

"Finding brush down in here. There's not enough sunlight for plants to grow."

After a few abortive attempts to push through it, Will flicked on his headlamp and inspected the barrier. He was surprised to see, not the leaves and branches of some hardy sedge, but instead a tangled mass of oxidized metal, formed into a lattice like the girders of a radio tower or some similar structure, but twisted into an almost unrecognizable mess. "Deke, check this out."

Deke approached, his headlamp flickering to life. "What the hell is that?" he asked, squinting at the wreckage. "Looks like something an angry kid might have made with an Erector Set."

Will gave him a sidelong glance. "Do they even make those anymore?"

Deke shrugged. "No idea."

Will rubbed a thumb across a section of the gray-white metal, noting the almost powdery feel of it. "I think this is aluminum. We could be looking at wreckage from an airplane."

"A plane crashed in here? What are the odds of that?"

"The pilot probably misjudged the width of the pass. Could have crashed higher up and then gravity did the rest and brought the wreck down here. Would have been easy for searchers to miss." He shone his light back and forth, looking for any gaps in the barrier, but found none. "We're probably the first people to come in here since it happened."

"Maybe a military flight? Shot down in the war?"

"Maybe. But not the last war. I'd say this has been here at least a few decades."

Will turned his light into the wreckage, looking for anything identifiable. Farther in he could see larger pieces of debris that might have been aluminum sheeting, but those and the twisted girders might have belonged to any sort of large airplane. Yet, somewhere in the skeletal remains of the craft, there would be more recognizable pieces of wreckage—engines and other parts with serial numbers and information that could be traced back not only to a particular design, but perhaps even to a specific missing plane.

But despite his curiosity, Will knew solving the mystery would have to wait. "We'll report it when we get back. Right now, we just need to get past it."

Deke grasped one of the girders and made a futile attempt to give it a shake. "Solid. We're not going to be able to push through this."

Will nodded. "As I see it, we've got three options. Find a way through, climb over, or backtrack and take the long way around."

"You might be able to squirm through that mess," said Deke. "No way in hell I'm gonna fit."

"We'll lose a couple hours if we turn back. How do you feel about option two?"

Deke grasped the exposed girder again, this time with both hands, and then shifted his full weight onto it. Once more, it refused to yield. "Seems pretty sturdy. And I'm current on my tetanus shot. I guess it's worth trying."

"All right, I'll find the route," Will said. He took a step back, analyzing the wreckage as he might examine a sheer rock wall in preparation for a free solo ascent. If the rest of the obstruction was as solid as the girder Deke had tested, the climb wouldn't be too much more challenging than climbing a ladder, albeit a ladder with irregularly spaced, oddly slanted rungs.

After mentally mapping out the first few steps, he reached up and took hold of an overhead girder, then stepped up onto another, and began to climb. His movements were slow and deliberate, each step calculated to avoid the jagged metal edges.

Despite the appearance of solidity, with each step up, the metal lattice creaked and groaned ominously.

"Careful now," Deke called out from below. "Don't get skewered."

Will didn't reply, but kept his focus unbroken as he made his way up ten, twenty, thirty feet, until the spacing of the girders opened up enough to allow him to make a transverse passage through the wreckage. He paused there, sweeping his light back and forth, checking for the safest path through the forest of girders.

He was surprised at the apparent depth of the wreck. The tangle of girders extended down the length of the canyon well beyond the reach of his headlamp, causing him to reconsider his theory that they had found the remains of a crashed aircraft. That was when he caught a glimpse of something seemingly suspended in the midst of the tangle, like a cocooned insect in a spider's web. It was difficult to determine the size or even the shape of the object, but it appeared quite large, almost completely spanning the width of the canyon. The most logical explanation was that it was a boulder, fallen from above to become wedged in between the sheer walls, but something about its placement, in the midst of the wreckage rather than atop it, further aroused his curiosity.

"Come on up," he called without looking down. "There's something up here I want to check out."

"Climbing," Deke shouted up to him.

Deke's ascent was accompanied by the same foreboding creak of metal fatigue. Will listened for a moment or two, then started forward, carefully picking his way through the girders. He had only gone a few steps, however, when a loud snap, like a gunshot, echoed through the canyon, simultaneous with a shout of dismay. "Damn it!"

Will froze, a surge of adrenaline rushing through his veins as an ominous vibration shook the girders he was holding onto. For an agonizingly long moment, he thought the whole chaotic assemblage would collapse under him. When the moment passed, he called out, "Deke! Are you okay?"

There was another long moment of silence before Deke's voice came back. "I'm fine. Just a little rattled."

"What happened?"

"I guess this old wreck isn't as solid as it looks. Broke under me when I tried to step up. I caught myself, but it wasn't pretty."

"Want to turn back?"

"I don't know. I'm not loving the idea of having this mess come crashing down underneath me. What do you think?"

Will stared at the strange shape suspended in the girders and weighed the decision.

If this had been a mountaineering expedition, he would not have hesitated to employ the precautionary principle. Climbing was about managing risk, doing everything possible to mitigate the inherent dangers, choosing the safest route when there was a choice, and rigidly observing safety margins with ropes and equipment. That Will would have already turned back.

But he really wanted to get a closer look at whatever that big shape was.

"I think we'll be okay," he said. "Just take it slow."

"Slow and steady," replied Deke. "That's me."

He resumed climbing, once more accompanied by the creaks and pops of the aluminum framework shifting under his weight. Despite his curiosity, Will stayed put until Deke reached his position, where the latter paused to catch his breath.

"Okay," he said after a moment. "What are we looking at?"

Will turned and shone his headlamp forward at the bulky shape. "I'm not sure what it is," he admitted. "But I'm starting to think this isn't an airplane wreck."

"Then what is it?"

"I don't know, but I think the answer might be in there."

Deke gazed at the shape with a skeptical eye but then nodded in resignation. "I guess I'm not gonna talk you out of having a look, am I? Lead on."

Will nodded and then immediately began traversing the forest of girders, moving between them with the alacrity of a child on playground monkey bars. As he drew nearer, it became apparent that the object was definitely not a fallen boulder, but something manmade—a long, almost tubular structure that, despite being battered out of shape, looked almost aerodynamic.

"Kind of looks like the fuselage of an airplane," he said.

"I thought this whole thing was an airplane," Deke countered, moving cautiously up to join him.

"I'm not really sure what all this is," admitted Will. He moved in close enough to lay his hands on it and saw, to his surprise, that it was not made of metal but lacquered wood, and upon closer inspection, looked more like a trolley car or a ski lift gondola than a modern aircraft.

It also appeared to be upside down.

He squatted down and peered through an opening that had once been the front windshield. His headlamp piercing the gloom, revealing a strange tableau of corroded metal, crumbling wood panels, and debris covered in a layer of dust. He desperately wanted to go inside, but hesitated out of a very real concern that the wooden structure would collapse under his weight. Instead, he drew back and looked under the structure to determine if it was supported by the framework of girders. To his surprise, he found that not only was it supported by the girders, it was attached to them.

Realization dawned. "Deke! I think this is an airship."

"Airship? You mean like the Goodyear blimp?"

Will furrowed his brow, searching his memory for any bits of trivia relating to airship design. He'd studied the history of aviation during his astronaut training, but only a small portion of it had dealt with lighter-than-air flight. He did recall that there was a distinction between non-rigid blimps, which were essentially balloons filled with lifting gas that relied on air pressure to maintain their shape, and rigid or semi-rigid dirigibles which had an internal frame and would not collapse if deflated. This wreck appeared to be an example of the latter, and judging by the sheer size of the debris field, it would have been quite large.

"I think this is a zeppelin."

"Zeppelin. Like the Hindenburg? They made others?"

"Quite a few, actually."

"Did any of them crash in Africa?"

"This one did. The Hindenburg was one of the last ever built, so this one is probably an earlier model."

"So it's... what, eighty years old?"

"Probably closer to a hundred." Will peered into the gloomy interior. "I'm going to go inside and have a look around."

Deke sighed. "Of course you are."

Will grinned and then carefully lowered himself headfirst through the window opening, testing the dust-covered inverted ceiling to make sure that it would support his weight before proceeding.

As he moved farther into the cabin, he could make out the outlines of seats bolted to the floor that were hanging down like stalactites, and a large central console. The control panels were complex, with dials and levers encrusted in verdigris, frozen forever in time.

When he was a few yards inside, his hand brushed a piece of debris that rolled away amida small cloud of fine dust that swirled in the beam of his headlamp. Through the dancing motes, he saw that the disturbed object was actually a peaked cap, as might have been worn by a military officer or pilot. The insignia on the cap—a crown device—was unfamiliar to him, but it was the sight of the skull beneath it that brought a sudden stillness to his heart. The realization that this airship was also a tomb, containing the remains of its crew, was a sobering thought.

He remained there for a moment, headlamp casting an eerie glow on the lifeless form, feeling a mix of emotions. Respect for the lives lost and curiosity concerning the mystery of their fate battled within him. After a moment of reflection, he knew he had to continue his search. There were answers here, secrets waiting to be uncovered.

His light illuminated a brass plaque above the helm wheel. He rubbed away the crust of verdigris and was just able to make out the upside-down letters engraved upon it.

Placca di Dedica dell'aeronave "Esperia"

"*Esperia*," he murmured.

"What's that?" asked Deke.

"*Esperia*. It's the name of this zeppelin."

"Doesn't sound like a very German name."

"It's not." Will continued rubbing the plaque, revealing more of the engraving. It wasn't in a language he understood, but three words stood out.

Regia Marina Italiana.

"It's Italian."

"I thought Germany made the zeppelins."

"They did. I mean, they made *the* zeppelins. But the name applies to a style of rigid airships—airships with a frame, as opposed to blimps which are just big gas bags. Anyway, this one belonged to the Royal Italian Navy."

"That tracks," said Deke. "The Italians invaded Ethiopia back before World War II." He paused a beat. "Okay, mystery solved. Time to go."

"I wonder what they were doing here," said Will, ignoring his friend's exhortation. He tried to imagine *Esperia*'s final moments. There was no evidence that the airship had suffered the same fiery fate of the Hindenburg. Rather, it seemed more likely that it had simply crashed, perhaps blown into the mountains above the canyon.

He noticed an open passageway at the back of the cabin. "Be right back."

Deke gave a heavy sigh but offered no further protest. He knew his friend well enough to recognize that, until Will had satisfied his curiosity, they weren't going anywhere.

Just beyond the passageway was a companionway that would have given the crew access to the interior of the rigid lifting envelope where the gas cells were housed. Now, the steps merely disappeared into the tangled girders below. Will squeezed past the steps and continued through another passage into a large, empty cargo bay.

Correction, he thought as his light fell upon the broken pieces of a single, large wooden crate resting on the inverted ceiling. *Mostly empty.*

He crawled closer until the light penetrated the interior of the crate and was reflected back with a glint of gold.

Will gasped, utterly stunned. "Uh, Deke. I think you should come take a look at this."

"Really?" complained Deke. "Can't you just take a pic and send it to me?"

"Just get back here."

Grumbling, Deke crawled into the cabin and made his way back to the cargo hold. As he came up alongside will, however, his eyes widened in disbelief. "Holy..."

"Yep."

"Is that what I think it is?"

Will nodded solemnly. "I think it is."

Inside the broken crate, nestled in dry straw packing material, lay another box, or more accurately, a reliquary. It was about four-and-a-half feet long, two feet wide, and two feet high, made entire-ly—or so it appeared—of gleaming gold that seemed to radiate an otherworldly aura.

Remarkably, although the crate had obviously been tossed about the interior of the cargo hold during *Esperia's* final moments, it had come to rest in an upright position, a fact easy to ascertain by the orientation of the lid of the reliquary, which was adorned with two very distinctive winged figures.

"The Ark of the Covenant," murmured Deke. "God help us."

TWENTY-EIGHT

NEGOTIATING THE OLD trail had been bad enough by daylight. At night, it was a trial of patience and endurance. Fortunately, gravity was on their side. Descending the rugged terrain was easier than climbing. In some places, all Maisy had to do was feather the brakes as they slid down slopes covered in loose scree. And the farther down they went, the easier the going got. The last mile and a half to the highway was on a dirt road across nearly flat ground.

When they reached the asphalted surface of the B30, Maisy had to fight the urge to floor it. Nighttime was no time to speed down an unfamiliar highway. Fortunately, Adi Gebru, the town where Elena had set up shop, was only about ten more miles down the road.

Like many Ethiopian towns, Adi Gebru was easy to miss, especially in the dark. There was no explicit business district. There were businesses—grocers, coffee shops, a gas station—and a school, but there was little in the way of signage to differentiate them. Rather, there was simply a marked increase in the density of houses and other buildings along the roadside, which was even harder to detect at night when all the lights were out. Since electricity was available only on an intermittent basis, especially since the war, the locals adhered to the traditional practice of rising and setting with the sun.

All of which meant that, without the GPS to guide them, they would easily have overshot their destination.

The clinic was not actually in the town proper, but rather a mile or so to the west, up yet another dirt road, not far from one of Tigray's historic churches. There was little to differentiate the small, flat-roofed, rectangular edifice, built from stone, wood, and mud in the traditional fashion. The only indication of its function was a large red cross with equidistant arms—the universal symbol of medical care.

The night air was cool as they approached the clinic's front door, their breaths visible in the night air. Maisy raised her hand to knock, but before her knuckles made contact, the door creaked open to reveal Dr. Elena Ramirez, illuminated by the battery-powered lantern she was holding. She was wearing sweatpants with STANFORD printed down the left leg and a plain T-shirt. Her tousled hair suggested that she'd been roused from slumber by their approach; her facial expression—a mix of bleariness, surprise, and irritation—confirmed it.

When she realized who her visitors were, Elena's frown deepened. "You're wasting your time," she snapped. "I'm not going back."

Sanjeet spoke up. "That's not actually why we're here, Dr. Ramirez. The truth is, we need your help."

Elena's eyes narrowed, as she gave them all an appraising look. "Unless this is a medical emergency," she said, "you can come back during office hours. I open at sunrise."

Taneisha stepped forward into the light of the lantern. "Dr. Ramirez," she began, her voice firm yet respectful, "We haven't met. I'm Taneisha Hayes. I'm with the Africa in the 21st Century Initiative. We're trying to create a roadmap to long-term peace in Tigray."

Elena's expression softened slightly at the mention of the organization. "I've heard about A21I. You do good work."

"Thank you. I've heard good things about you as well."

This brought a smirk to Elena's face and her gaze flitted to Maisy and Sanjeet. "Is that right?" She brought her attention back to Taneisha. "You're the one Will ran off to save yesterday."

Maisy thought she heard just a hint of jealousy in Elena's assertion.

"Will and Deke *did* save my life, and the lives of my colleagues," replied Taneisha. "For which I'm very grateful. We were attacked by a group of insurgents fighting for General Tadesse. It seems not everyone in Tigray wants peace. Our security team was wiped out, and we would have been next if Will and Deke hadn't shown up when they did."

"So, did they—" She thrust her chin toward Maisy. "—bring you here to convince me that it's dangerous to stay?"

"Not at all. As Sanjeet said, we need your help."

All right, I'm listening." Elena crossed her arms over her chest. "Why are you here?"

"Like you," Taneisha began, "I'm not a fan of leaving before the job is done, so I convinced Maisy and Sanjeet to take me back up to the village I was visiting yesterday. Unfortunately, too many of the locals are loyal to Tadesse and we were threatened again."

"So, you're throwing in the towel?"

Taneisha grimaced. "I'm not giving up on Tigray. But I also recognize that the direct approach isn't going to get the job done. I'll be able to do more from the outside. Bring international attention to what's going on here."

"We're heading south to Gondar," supplied Sanjeet. "But it's dangerous to travel at night. We were hoping we could stay here until morning."

Elena scrutinized him with her stare, then turned to Maisy. "That's all? You're not going to try to convince me to leave with you?"

Maisy shrugged. "Technically, we're still under contract to Doctors Without Borders to bring you home, so..." She gave a half-grin. "We might *try*."

Elena stabbed a warning finger at her. "Do you want to stay here or not?"

Maisy raised both hands in a show of surrender.

"All right," said Elena. "Don't just stand out there in the cold. Come inside."

The interior was as rustic and utilitarian as the outside. There were no decorative touches or bookshelves, only tables and cabinets filled with medical supplies. A couple of beds and some old exam tables were the only furnishings.

"Find a place to get comfortable," Elena said. 'Sorry, there's not much here in the way of creature comforts. We do get some walk-ins, but most of our work was outreach."

"What sort of medical issues are you dealing with here?" asked Sanjeet, showing professional interest.

"Some injuries. The usual farm accidents. Parasitic infections are a big problem."

Sanjeet nodded. "A boy in the village was showing early symptoms of visceral leishmaniasis."

Elena nodded gravely. "The leishmaniasis epidemic here is a direct consequence of the war. Over four-million people were displaced, and a lot of them ended up in refugee camps in the lowlands in areas infested with sand flies, living in close quarters without proper sanitation. The fighting was especially intense along the highway, so a lot of these people were among the displaced. When they returned, they brought the flies with them, not to mention the parasite. The risk of transmission is higher than ever."

Sanjeet's brow furrowed with concern. "What about treatment? Are you able to provide it to everyone who needs it?"

Elena sighed, her gaze falling on the medical supplies around them. "We do our best, but resources are stretched thin. The internal displacement has created a perfect storm for diseases like leishmaniasis to thrive. People are stressed, malnourished, and their immune systems are compromised."

"It's a dire situation," Sanjeet said softly.

"It is," Elena agreed. "But we're not giving up. We'll continue to fight this epidemic, one patient at a time." She cocked her head to the side as if gazing into the distance. "It's just one of the reasons why I can't leave. There's just too much to do."

"If General Tadesse succeeds in stoking the fires of war," intoned Taneisha. "Then history is going to repeat itself."

"I've heard about Tadesse," said Elena. "What does he want, anyway?"

"You mean aside from causing chaos? He's selling the dream of a free Tigray, but what he really wants is to exploit the region's natural resources."

Elena raised an eyebrow. "What natural resources?"

"Oil shale." Taneisha nodded toward Maisy. "She discovered that he's working for a Russian oil corporation."

"Oil." Elena spat the word out like it was a bad taste. "You wouldn't believe some of the things I've seen... The absolute devastation left behind by these oil companies. They come in, with absolutely no environmental regulations. Drill and spill.

"I worked in the Niger Delta with the Ogoni." Elena's eyes darkened with the memory, her voice tinged with a mix of anger and sorrow. "Thirty years of oil spills contaminated water sources, killing fish and poisoning the land. The environmental impact was catastrophic. The forests are dead, just barren wastelands. And the air is so thick with fumes, it actually rains crude oil."

She paused, taking a deep breath before continuing. "The people there have chronic respiratory problems from the polluted air. Skin diseases from contact with contaminated water. Birth defects. Cancer." Her hands clenched into fists as she spoke. "And the worst part? The oil companies just walked away. They paid the government a pittance to—" She made air quotes with her fingers. "'Clean up the mess'. Not a cent of it actually went into cleaning things up." She fell silent for a moment, then looked at Maisy. "You think it's going to happen here now?"

Maisy chose her answer carefully. "There are considerable oil shale fields in Tigray, and VEK, a Russian petroleum outfit, seems to be in the process of setting up an operation. They hired Tadesse and some of his former soldiers for security, and it appears that the attack on Taneisha's team was carried out by them. We can only assume that it has something to do with exploiting the oil."

Elena shook her head. "Nothing ever changes."

The direction of the conversation reminded Maisy to check her newsfeed for the latest on Boris Petrov's speech at COP 30 which, given the time difference, would have been given sometime in the last hour or two. As expected, there was an alert with a link to another *Huffington Post* article headlined: **OIL EXEC SHOCKS COP-30**.

Maisy clicked on it and began reading silently.

Belém—In a bold move, Boris Petrov, a senior vice president at one of Russia's leading petroleum extraction companies, delivered a speech today at the COP 30 climate meeting in Belém, that left attendees stunned. His acknowledgement of his industry's role in creating the climate crisis was shocking enough, but it was his proposed solution that nearly caused a riot.

Petrov drew parallels to the British Empire's abolition of slavery, specifically to the payment of compensation, not to the enslaved people, but rather to the enslavers for financial losses. He then went on to propose that a similar economic incentive, in the form of compensation to petroleum producers for not extracting what he called "their buried treasure" would be an effective, if controversial solution to the climate crisis.

His speech sparked intense debate among attendees, with many expressing outrage at what one delegate characterized as the "naked cynicism" of the proposal. Spokes-

men for other leading oil producers signaled interest in exploring the possibility of a compensation scheme but were quick to reject Petrov's characterization of the fossil fuel industry as morally equivalent to the practice of slavery.

Maisy stopped reading and looked up, shaking her head in astonishment.

Taneisha took note. "What?"

Maisy took a moment to think about where to begin. "After we learned about the connection to VEK, I set up my news filter to flag any references in the news. This may not be related to what's going on here but..." She took a breath. "One of their senior executives just gave a speech at the climate conference in Brazil, in which he suggested that oil producers should be paid to leave the oil in the ground."

Elena laughed. "If that's what it takes, I say fine."

"Well, who exactly would write that check?" wondered Taneisha.

"I don't get the impression that he's being taken seriously," said Maisy. "What I can't figure is why VEK would be staking claim to oil shale deposits if their plan is to take a payoff to leave the oil in the ground?"

"I'd say it's typical behavior for these companies," said Elena. "Say one thing, do another. Either way, the foreigners get rich exploiting the natural resources, and the locals are left with nothing."

"I suppose," said Maisy. "But still, why even put an idea like that out there?"

It was a rhetorical question, to which none of her companions would venture an answer. Sanjeet finally broke the awkward silence. "It's late. We should get some sleep while we can."

Maisy nodded in agreement.

But long after Elena passed out blankets and switched off her lantern, Maisy kept turning over the paradox. If Petrov was even a little bit serious about his compensation scheme, why secure leases and exploratory permits for oil shale—one of the least profitable sources of petroleum—in places like Tigray, and why throw the region into a state of war.

Her poker playing instincts told her that Petrov had an ace up his sleeve, and that, with his speech in Belém, he'd just gone all in. But what would happen when he finally showed his hand?

Unable to conceive of what the Russian might have planned for Tigray, she tapped out a quick text message to Will, updating him on their decision to relocate to Adi Gebru, and then rolled over and somehow managed to fall asleep.

TWENTY-NINE

DEKE POINTED AT the golden relic, still unable to accept what he was seeing. "Is that really...?"

"Really *the* Ark of the Covenant?" Will chuckled. "I want to say it looks like it, but then nobody really knows *what* it looked like."

In fact, the reliquary, at least what little of it was visible, bore only a passing resemblance to the prop created for the Indiana Jones movie. The craftsmanship was much more primitive, as one would expect from the Bronze Age nomadic culture in which it was supposedly created. But even that was no guarantee of its authenticity.

"Is it gonna melt our faces off?"

Will shrugged. "Depends. Are you going to try to use its powers for evil?"

"Hell, no."

"Then I think we're good."

"How'd it wind up here?"

"According to local legend, the Ark was brought to Axum during the time of Menelik, the son of King Solomon and the Queen of Sheba. The Ethiopian Orthodox Tewahedo Church claims that it's been here ever since, kept in a chapel at the Church of Saint Mary of Zion. There's a lot of debate about whether the story is true, since nobody's allowed to see it. I'm not sure even if they could that there would be a way to prove that their ark was the real one. If there even *is* a real one.

"I know the story," said Deke, shaking his head. "I meant, how did it wind up here?" He gestured to the crate.

"When the Italian army captured Axum, they must have confiscated it from the church and tried to sneak it out on this airship. Obviously, they didn't get far."

"And nobody noticed it was missing?"

"I'm sure the priests did, but they probably didn't want anyone to know that their most sacred relic had been taken."

"Ah." Deke chuckled. "They covered it up to avoid looking bad."

"It's a tale as old as time."

"What do we do about it?" asked Deke.

"We can't take it with us." Will took out his sat-phone, activated the camera, and snapped a picture of the relic. "Once we're somewhere safe, we'll let someone know where to find it."

"Someone *who*?" pressed Deke. "Who do we trust with this? The Ethiopian government? The Tigrayans? Seems like either side might try to turn it into a political symbol. You know, like 'God is on our side.'"

"You're not wrong," admitted Will. "Fortunately, we don't have to come up with an answer right now. C'mon. Let's get going."

THEY MADE THEIR way cautiously through the cabin and back out onto the wreckage. Satisfied that there were no more mysteries to be uncovered, Will refrained from further exploration and charted the shortest path through the debris field. They soon found their way back to the canyon floor, and half an hour later, emerged from the pass. Once out in the open, Will's phone buzzed, notifying him of the receipt of a text message from Maisy. The message had been sent almost two hours earlier, but the canyon walls had blocked the incoming signal.

The message read simply: *Overnighting with Elena in Adi Gebru. Meet us in a.m.?*

Seeing Elena's name on the screen brought an unexpected smile to his face, which quickly turned into a frown as he thought about the conversation that would follow their arrival. Now more than ever, it was imperative that all of them—Elena included—get out of Tigray.

He decided against telling Deke about the text.

There was also an email from Maisy, sent earlier in the evening, which supplied a translation of the Russian writing on the labels on the material they'd found in the equipment shed in the oil shale field, and a tentative identification of the man Will had recorded in Tadesse's camp.

Will only had time to glance at Maisy's report, but quickly came to the same conclusion she had: the Russian working for VEK— Sokolov—was stockpiling the ingredients to make thermite. The answer to the question of why, however, eluded him. The in-situ oil shale extraction process required raising the temperature of the rock to about 450 degrees Fahrenheit. Thermite produced temperatures in excess of 2,500 degrees, and even as high as 4,500 degrees.

He could think of one possible explanation, but it had nothing to do with oil shale. When used in conjunction with the ammonium nitrate explosives, thermite could be used to create a thermobaric explosive device.

Thermobaric bombs worked on the principle of creating and then igniting an aerosolized fuel cloud—in this case, the powdered aluminum—to produce a flash of intense heat and a massive vacuum pressure wave that not only collapsed buildings but could literally suck a person's lungs out. Military-grade thermobaric bombs were the most destructive non-nuclear devices available, and their effects so terrible that many countries had called for their use to be banned entirely.

Will shuddered to think what a man like General Tadesse might do with a single thermobaric bomb. They would have to share this information with the Ethiopian authorities, of course. Unfortunately, the mere fact that Tadesse possessed the capacity to build such a device almost ensured renewed fighting in Tigray.

Like the possible Ark find, that would have to be a conversation he had with authorities later.

Their route quickly brought them to a dirt road which, if Deke's plotted course was correct, was part of a branching network that would eventually bring them to Adi Gebru. The going got easier after that, but they remained vigilant, aware that each step forward was not necessarily taking them away from danger.

The first hints of dawn were just beginning to lighten the eastern sky when they reached their goal. There was no traffic on the highway. But if not for the GPS, they might have stumbled across the empty asphalt without even realizing it.

Will glanced at the display screen of his phone, noting the time, and saw the text he'd received earlier. "Maisy and Sanjeet are here. They spent the night at Elena's clinic."

Deke raised a knowing eyebrow, which Will pretended not to see. "We should wait until sun-up," he went on. "No sense in waking everyone up early."

Deke nodded, looking up and down the highway for any sign of activity. "Makes sense. Plus, we can see who's around before we make a move."

They found a sheltered thicket and settled in to rest until dawn. Will plugged the sat-phone into the portable battery pack he kept in his go-bag, set the alarm for ninety minutes, and then stretched out on the bare ground and tried to get comfortable. Exhausted after hours of cross-country travel, he quickly fell fast asleep.

An hour and a half later, the two men rose, stretched out the kinks in sore, tired muscles, and then prepared for the short walk through town to the clinic. Will sent a text to Maisy, letting her know that they were about fifteen minutes out, and then he and Deke started walking.

Their passage through the town did not go unnoticed by locals—mostly women and children—who were also up with the sun. Curious stares followed them as they walked, the silence of the town punctuated by the soft sounds of their footsteps.

"Think Tadesse has spies here?" Deke asked in a low voice.

Will kept his gaze fixed ahead. "It only takes one. Let's make sure we're gone before he gets word."

They left the staring townsfolk behind and made their way up the dirt road to the clinic. The sight of the second Project: RESCUE vehicle parked out front raised Will's spirits. While their ultimate destination, Gondar, was still hundreds of miles away, the border between Tigray and Amhara, was only thirty miles away. Once across it, Tadesse's ability to menace them would be greatly reduced.

As they approached the door to the clinic, Maisy emerged, her face a mix of relief and concern, and rushed out to greet them.

"You made it," she cried, and threw her arms around Will first, then Deke.

"Can't get rid of us that easy," said Deke.

Will gestured to the clinic. "Since you wound up here, I take it Taneisha's talk with the village elders didn't go well?"

Maisy shook her head. "They still worship Tadesse and refuse to accept that he wants war for selfish reasons."

Will nodded slowly. "Well, she tried. I'm not sure what else we could have done. Is she finally willing to admit that it's time to go?"

"I think so." Maisy hesitated for a moment before adding. "Elena's a different story. She won't leave, no matter what. And I get the distinct impression that if you even mention it, she might throw something at you."

Will returned a grim smile. "I'll be sure to duck."

As if on cue, Elena called out from the doorway. "Did she tell you I'm not leaving?"

Will turned to face her. "You know the war is about to heat up again."

"All the more reason why I have to stay." Elena crossed her arms, defiant. "I appreciate your concern, Will, but I'm staying. There's just too much to do here."

"I'm worried about your safety, Elena, but I'm not going to drag you out of here kicking and screaming."

"Unless you're into that sort of thing," quipped Deke, earning a scathing look from Will.

"I get how important this is for you," Will went on. "And that's why, even though the thought of leaving you here kills me, that's what I'm going to do."

This raw admission moved Elena visibly. She swallowed, and then managed a smile. "Thank you."

Will turned to Maisy. "Are Sanjeet and Taneisha ready to go?"

"I'll get them."

Elena stepped out of the way as Maisy went inside, but kept her gaze fixed on Will. "Can't you stay for breakfast?"

Will shook his head. "I don't think that's a good idea."

She narrowed her eyes at him, as if trying to find subtext in his statement.

"The longer we stay here, the more danger we're in," he clarified. "All of us."

A moment later, Maisy came out, followed by Sanjeet and Taneisha. The latter paused for a moment, as if sensing the tension between Will and Elena, but then followed the others to the waiting Land Cruiser.

Will turned back to Elena. "Take care," he told her, his tone softening. "Maybe we'll meet again, someday."

He started to turn away, but Elena called out. "Will?"

He turned back but didn't speak.

"Are things here really that bad?"

"I hope not."

She nodded. "You be careful, too."

Knowing that any further exchange would only make leaving harder, Will turned away without another word and strode toward the Land Cruiser.

As he climbed into the driver's seat and started the engine, he was peripherally aware of Elena, standing there outside her clinic watching them, but he refused to let himself look in her direction.

"You okay?" asked Deke from the front passenger seat.

Will put the Cruiser in gear, and simply said, "I'm good."

THIRTY

THE BRIDGE ACROSS the Tekezé River was less than ten miles from Adi Gebru, but despite the fact that a significant portion of the route involved negotiating a series of hairpin switchbacks through the foothills of the Simien Mountains, the GPS indicated that they would reach the bridge in about fifteen minutes time.

After the awkwardness of their departure from the clinic, Will felt a change of subject was called for, so as they left the switchbacks behind, he caught Maisy's eye in the rearview mirror. "I didn't get a chance to thank you for getting me the information I asked for."

Maisy nodded. "That's the easy part of the job."

"I can't figure why they're stockpiling the ingredients to make thermite. It's not used in the in-situ extraction process. Or for anything else I can think of."

"It can be used to make a bomb," said Maisy. "Maybe the oil shale operation is just cover for a bomb-making operation. The man you recorded... Sokolov. He's former Spetsnaz. His unit specialized in training insurgent forces."

Will nodded. "I was thinking along similar lines. But I still can't quite figure out what VEK is really after. It's not like oil shale extraction is that profitable under the best of circumstances."

Maisy gave a thoughtful hum. "There is something... Maybe it doesn't have anything to do with what's going on here... But one of the senior execs at VEK gave a speech at the COP 30 climate conference in Belém."

"An oil exec talking to the tree huggers?" remarked Deke. "I bet he was a big hit."

"It was unusual, to say the least," said Maisy. "And it went over about as well as you'd expect it to."

"What did he have to say?" asked Will.

"Well, among other things, he compared climate change to slavery."

This comment elicited raised eyebrows from both Deke and Taneisha. "I think you left that part out when you told us about it last night," said Taneisha.

Maisy offered a guilty shrug. "Specifically, he said that both slavery and climate change are moral crises. Everybody knows that what they are doing is wrong, but they aren't willing to disrupt the status quo."

"I'm sorry," said Deke. "I thought you said this guy was an oil exec."

She nodded. "I did."

"Hypocrisy much?"

"It gets better. He continued with the slavery parallel by referencing how the British Empire paid compensation to slave owners to get them to give up their slaves."

Deke stiffened in his seat, all humor gone from his demeanor. "Are you kidding? They paid the slave *owners* reparations?"

Taneisha provided the answer. "It's true. The Empire spent something like forty percent of the entire treasury to do it. In today's money, it would be close to twenty-billion dollars."

"To the *owners*? What did the freed slaves get?"

Taneisha just shook her head.

Maisy went on. "Petrov tried to make the point that, even though it was expensive, it was the only way to get everyone to do the right thing."

"We didn't do that in America," countered Deke.

"No," agreed Taneisha. "We just fought a war over it instead."

"I think I see where this is going," intoned Will. "This Petrov thinks the only way to solve the climate crisis is to pay the oil producers to stop producing oil."

"That's extortion," said Taneisha, shaking her head. "I can't believe anyone would even consider it."

"That was pretty much the general reaction of the conference attendees," said Maisy. "Sounds like he almost started a riot."

Will steered into another sweeping right turn that brought them parallel to the course of the river. According to the route map, the road continued alongside the river for a ways, then turned left onto the bridge. "I can't imagine that he would have expected any other reaction," he said when the road straightened out again. "So why do it? Why go on the national stage to propose something so ludicrous?"

"It's like Elena said last night," offered Taneisha. "Corporate double-speak. Say one thing, do another. And then claim that people don't really want to do what it takes to solve the problem."

"Or maybe he just thinks we're desperate enough to actually go for it and was taking a gamble," said Deke.

Will stiffened as if an electric shock had just gone through his body. "Say that again."

Deke looked at him sidelong. "I said, maybe he thinks we're desperate enough." He paused a beat. "Okay, I know that look. You're thinking something, aren't you?"

Will's mind was racing, turning the pieces of the puzzle this way and that to see if they would fit the picture that was already coming together in his head. But before he could articulate an answer, the paved highway on which they had been traveling abruptly ended, giving way to a badly maintained dirt road. The new road immediately veered left toward the water, passing through the shattered ruins of a small community that had once occupied the approach to the bridge.

The riddle of Petrov's speech and the Tigray oil shale scheme went to the back burner of Will's mind as he gazed at the bombed-out structures lining the road. Their route research had indicated that the bridge that had been destroyed by Tigrayan fighters during the war had subsequently been repaired by the Ethiopian government after the ceasefire, to facilitate not only the movement of goods in and out of Tigray, but also ENDF troops to keep the peace. The landscape through which they were now passing, however, was enough to make him question the accuracy of that report. If the bridge was still out, they were sunk.

But the bridge *was* intact. Though only a single-lane wide, the new span stretched out above the hundred-yard-wide course of the Tekezé to meet the far shore.

That was the good news.

The bad news was that the road leading up to the bridge was blocked. A military checkpoint had been set up, limiting access to the crossing. The barrier, which consisted of little more than razor wire stretched between wooden stakes that had been tied to the bridge guardrails, was not exactly a formidable obstacle, but the half-dozen armed men in camouflage fatigues milling about in front of it—and one more standing behind a heavy machine gun mounted in the back of a dun-colored Toyota Hilux pickup—were another matter.

As Will slowed and brought the Cruiser to a full stop about twenty yards short of the roadblock, the posture of the soldiers became visibly more alert, their carbines coming to the low ready position. Two of them detached from the group and began approaching the Cruiser.

"This could be a problem," murmured Deke.

"Will, those aren't ENDF soldiers," Maisy said, her voice barely above a whisper. "The uniforms are wrong."

Will's heart sank. "Yeah, I was afraid of that."

"You think they're Tadesse's men?" asked Zeke.

"I don't think we can afford to take the chance that they aren't," replied Will, his hand hovering above the gearshift lever.

As the two gunmen closed in on the Cruiser, they brought their weapons up, taking aim at Will through the windshield. One of them took his hand away from his carbine just long enough to make a gesture, the meaning of which was easy enough to interpret.

Get out.

All the glass in the vehicle was laminated with a bullet-resistant layer which could stand up to limited small arms fire, so Will wasn't too worried what would happen if the men decided to pop off a few shots with their AKS-74 carbines. The heavy gun on the Hilux was another matter. The torrent of high-caliber rounds it could unleash against them would quickly tear through the safety coating and fracture the glass underneath. The Kevlar mats lining the SUV's body panels wouldn't fare much better.

"What's our play?" asked Deke, his voice betraying just a little of the urgency they were all feeling. "Want me to try talking our way past?"

Will's mind raced to determine the choices available to them, and the possible outcomes of each. Under any other circumstances, he might be willing to attempt negotiating with the men. Checkpoints were a favorite ploy of bandits in the world's dangerous places, but often all it took to get past was a generous bribe. But if these men *were* working for Tadesse, buying them off wasn't likely to work.

Ramming the roadblock was a possibility. The wire wouldn't stop the Land Cruiser, and once past it, all they would have to do is put the pedal to the metal and make a run for the border.

But that machine gun...

The bridge would be a free-fire zone, where they would be fully exposed to the heavy gun as well as the combined fire of the individual gunmen. And if the wire from the barrier got wrapped around the wheels, they could find themselves hobbled at the very moment when speed was what they needed most.

That left just one option.

The gunman, now increasingly agitated, repeated his gesture for them to exit the vehicle, adding a shouted command that, while not audible to the occupants of the Land Cruiser, was nevertheless easily understood.

"Will," warned Maisy. "Don't get out."

"Wasn't planning to," he replied. "Everyone, down!"

With that shout of warning, Will slammed the Cruiser into reverse and jammed down on the go pedal. The engine roared as they shot backward, tires flinging out gravel and grit showering the two gunmen even as they tried to bring their weapons to bear. A moment later, a hail of bullets began striking the windshield glass, the impacts staggeringly loud in the close confines of the SUV.

Will ignored the incoming fusillade, focusing instead on keeping the Cruiser running a true straight-line course back through the ruins of the settlement. It took only a few seconds for them to reach the turn that would take them back onto the pavement, but it was more than enough for the rest of the gunmen to join the assault, intensifying the storm of lead. When he reached the turn, he slammed on the brakes, letting the Cruiser skid to the edge of the unmaintained road, then threw the gearshift into 'drive' and stomped the gas again, cranking the wheel hard to the left and pulling back onto the asphalt. A final volley peppered the passenger side and then the gunmen were behind them. The windshield was now glazed with dozens of spiderweb fractures, but not a single bullet had gotten through.

Whether they could survive another head-on assault was another matter.

Pushing the Cruiser harder than before, Will raced back toward the foothills. As he rounded the first big turn and started climbing, Deke rose from where he'd been huddled and took a look around.

"Are we safe?" he asked.

Will checked the mirror but the terrain limited his view. "Not sure," he admitted.

Deke also took a long look in the rearview, then turned back to Will. "Would this be a good time to talk about what we're going to do next?"

Will gave a slight shake of the head. "We'll figure it out, Deke. Right now, our priority is just getting away from those guys."

"But what then?" asked Taneisha from the back. "Do we try going back to Axum?"

"Something tells me there will be a surprise party waiting for us there," opined Deke.

"Or somewhere along the way," added Maisy.

Will shook his head again. "We can't risk going back there. But there are other places we can go. If we stick to the back roads, we can bypass Axum, keep going east to Adwa or somewhere else... Anywhere Scott can send a plane to get us. As long as those guys don't come after us, we'll figure something out."

Deke glanced in the mirror again. "Uh, sorry to break it to you, but they're coming after us."

THIRTY-ONE

AS HE LACED up his running shoes, Sokolov noticed that the soles were already wearing through. The rough shale was murder on footwear designed for tarmacadam. He shook his head in disgust. He needed a new pair, but the odds of getting a delivery now, out in this benighted place, were next to zero.

He stepped out of his tent, and was greeted by the cold, biting air of early morning. The camp was eerily silent, the only sounds the occasional rustle of the wind beating the sides of the tents. Tadesse and his men probably wouldn't be up for another hour or so.

After a few quick stretches, he set off at a steady pace, his breath visible in the chill as he set off down the poorly maintained dirt track. The oil shale field stretched out ahead of him, a vast, barren expanse. He kept his stride even, focusing on the rhythm of his breathing and the pounding of his feet against the ground. He ran to stay in fighting shape, as well as to find a reprieve, if only fleetingly, from the relentless tedium and frustration that had come to define his stay in this desolate place.

His mind wandered as he ran. He thought about all the things he would do when he got back to civilization. Contemplated the luxury of a hot shower, the simplicity of a decent meal, the comfort of a bed with sheets and pillows, and the women he would find to share it with him. These musings only heightened his frustration. He needed this operation to be done. Unfortunately, Tadesse's recent string of failures was complicating matters. Petrov's plan was contingent on raising the chaos level in Tigray, but Tadesse kept falling short, first with his failure to kill the diplomats, and then letting the two Americans escape.

Maybe it's time to put a boot in his ass, Sokolov thought.

His frustration mounting with each step, he glanced at his watch, noting the time, and then turned back. The morning run had done little to alleviate his restlessness. If anything, it had aggravated it.

He wasn't yet within sight of the camp when he felt his phone buzz in his pocket. He pulled it out and saw Petrov's name displayed. Sokolov's heart rate, which had not exceeded eighty beats per minute during the run, quickened with a rush of anxiety. He wasn't looking forward to telling Petrov of Tadesse's failures.

"Boris Ivanovich," he said, trying to keep his voice steady.

"Mikhail, how are things progressing?" Petrov sounded unusually upbeat.

Sokolov paused, taking a moment to gather his thoughts before responding. "We've hit a few complications," he admitted, choosing his words carefully. "Tadesse's men failed to eliminate the diplomats as planned. And now, those two Americans... they've slipped through our fingers."

There was a brief silence on the other end of the line, during which Sokolov could almost feel Petrov's patience waning. When Petrov finally spoke, his voice remained composed but tinged with unmistakable disappointment. "Mikhail, the chaos in Tigray must escalate according to plan. Earlier today, I delivered my ultimatum. It is time to proceed to the next stage of the plan, but in order to do that, Tadesse and his movement must pose a clear threat to the region."

Despite feeling Petrov's quiet wrath, Sokolov also experienced a slight thrill of exhilaration at Petrov's readiness to proceed with the next stage. Because once that happened, his long exile to Tigray would be at an end.

"I understand, Boris Ivanovich," Sokolov replied. "I will ensure that Tadesse becomes the bogeyman we need him to be."

"How soon can you make this happen?" Petrov asked, his impatience barely concealed.

Sokolov hesitated for a moment, calculating the risks and necessary preparations. "Give me eight hours," he finally responded confidently. "I will orchestrate a disruption that will escalate tensions and break the ceasefire convincingly."

"Make it four," Petrov said. "This needs to happen quickly. I'm on my way back to Moscow, and I have a feeling Minister Ivanov is already sharpening the knives."

"Four hours, then," Sokolov assured him, though he was far from certain that Tadesse could accomplish his part of the plan so quickly.

Still, the idea that, in four hours' time he would be on his way out of Ethiopia filled him with purpose. It might take a day or two to get back to Moscow, but at least he would be done with Tigray.

But first, he would have to put the squeeze on Tadesse.

After the call, he felt like running again, and reached the camp in under four minutes. As the tents came into view, he was pleased to see some of Tadesse's men already up and preparing the morning meal. Porridge, again, no doubt. Nevertheless, the thought that this might be his last breakfast in Tigray brought a smile to Sokolov's face.

The smile fell a little when he saw Tadesse hurrying toward him, clutching a satellite phone. *Probably going to tell me how his men screwed up again,* thought Sokolov.

But when the Tigrayan reached him, instead of offering more excuses, Tadesse broke into a grin and waved the phone triumphantly. "I just heard from the men I sent to watch the highway crossing at the Tekezé River. The Americans just tried to cross. We have them!"

THIRTY-TWO

GRIPPING THE WHEEL with white-knuckled intensity, Will tore through the winding roads of the foothills. Behind them, the gunmen in the Hilux struggled to close the gap, getting close enough to fire off a few shots from the machine gun—none of which found their mark—but their sense of self-preservation must have been stronger than their motivation to catch the quarry because once Will entered the switchbacks, they lost sight of the pursuit.

With engine roaring and tires squealing, Will negotiated the switchbacks, tapping the brakes only as a last resort. As he accelerated out of the last hairpin turn, he called out, "Everyone still with me?"

"Where else we gonna go?" replied Deke with a shrug.

Maisy and Sanjeet were more subdued in registering their affirmative. Taneisha seemed positively shell-shocked at first, but then, in a trembling voice, managed to say, "It feels like déjà vu all over again."

Despite the tension, Will chuckled. "No landslide this time."

They were just descending into Adi Gebru when the pickup once more appeared in the rearview mirror.

"I don't think these guys are gonna give up," warned Deke.

Will didn't answer.

As the Cruiser roared through Adi Gebru, he laid on the horn, warning residents to get themselves and their livestock out of the way. At the north end of town, he braked and then, with a squeal of rubber on pavement, made a sharp right turn, heading onto the very same road he and Deke had followed out earlier that morning. In the full light of day, he saw a mixture of bare dirt and cultivated fields stretching out before them, and beyond them, the rising hills of the highlands.

Will didn't answer. He scanned the horizon, now visible in the daylight. The landscape transitioned from semi-agricultural fields, where neat rows of crops bordered the road, to more rugged hilly terrain.

"Speaking of déjà vu," remarked Deke, trying and mostly succeeding in maintaining an outward show of bravado. "Were we here earlier? This all looks kind of familiar."

"Couldn't say," Will replied. "It was dark."

His eyes darted from the road ahead—barely visible through the spiderweb fractures in the windshield—to the rearview mirror. There was little to see there; the combination of dirt road and speed was throwing up a plume of dust that could have been seen from space. If the Hilux was back there, and Will didn't doubt that it was, the gunmen would have little difficulty following them.

"So, you've got a plan B, right?" Deke continued, his tone half-joking but with an edge of seriousness. "Just asking."

Will glanced at him, the hint of a smile playing on his lips. "Always."

"Care to... You know... Share?"

Ahead, a fork in the trail appeared, and Will veered to the right without hesitation, the vehicle jolting slightly over the rocky path. Dust billowed in their wake, obscuring the view of their pursuers momentarily.

As they continued negotiating the roads and primitive trails, the landscape closed in around them, offering both refuge and uncertainty. The rocky terrain grew steeper and more difficult to navigate.

Will was focused on trying to backtrack the route they had taken the previous night, a hike through a landscape that had largely gone unseen. There were few memorable landmarks, and any that might have been visible in starlight, silhouetted against the night sky, were all facing the wrong way. Nevertheless, between what he remembered of the terrain and his internal compass, he was confident that they were moving in the right direction. Pushing the Land Cruiser—and himself—to the limit, what had taken him and Deke hours to hike during the night, they would traverse in a matter of minutes.

Suddenly, Deke looked sidelong at him. "Will, are you thinking what I think you're thinking?"

Will's eyes did not leave the trail. "I think so."

"Are you sure you don't want to... Maybe... Think again?"

"If you've got a better idea, I'm listening."

Deke sighed. "No, not really. But it's a hell of a gamble."

"We're not going to outrun these guys," Will replied, his grip on the wheel tightening as the trail narrowed further. "We need a game changer. This is our best shot."

Deke fell silent, trusting Will's judgment as he navigated the treacherous terrain. The path grew increasingly challenging, undulating over channels cut deep by seasonal rains, and littered with an obstacle course of boulders and jagged rocks. The Land Cruiser's suspension groaned under the strain, but it held steady, pushing forward with unwavering determination.

At length he spied the terrain feature he'd been looking for, a narrow, almost invisible cleft between two mountain peaks. "Everyone, hang on," Will called out needlessly as he maneuvered the Land Cruiser off the track they'd been following and began climbing the hill, toward the entrance to the canyon. The vehicle bounced and jolted over the uneven ground, the tumult of rocks thumping against the undercarriage almost deafening.

Will got to within a hundred yards of the cut before the terrain became impassable. When he had no choice but to slam on the brakes, the dust cloud that had trailed them almost since leaving Adi Gebru engulfed the Cruiser, plunging them all into deep gloom.

"Everybody out," he shouted. "But stay with the truck until I tell you it's safe to move."

Maisy was the only one to give voice to her trepidation. "Will, you know I trust you—"

"Then trust me," he said, cutting her off. "Out."

He didn't wait for any further discussion, but threw open the door. He'd stopped on an incline, with the front-end pointing upslope at an angle. As a result, the door wanted to fall shut on him, and he had to pull himself out of the seat and squirm past the door, only to then fall back against the side of the Cruiser. With the dense dust cloud swirling around them, visibility was measured in inches, so he kept one hand on the SUV as he moved down to the rear passenger door, which was giving Sanjeet problems.

"I got it," shouted Will, holding the door open so his friend could exit. Once Sanjeet was clear, Will gripped his hand. "Don't let go."

Sanjeet gave a reassuring squeeze. "I won't. Lead on."

They climbed upslope and around the front end of the vehicle where Will was relieved to see Deke waiting with Maisy and Taneisha, all holding hands in a line. Will pointed up the slope. "This way. Watch your step but move as quickly as you can. We need to be in that canyon before the dust settles."

The narrow canyon entrance loomed ahead, a shadowy cleft in the otherwise featureless landscape. The dust cloud had settled somewhat, but the air was still thick with particles, making it difficult to see more than a few yards in any direction. Nevertheless, as they passed into the cut, the canyon walls rose steeply on either side, creating an oppressive, claustrophobic atmosphere that felt more like the maw of a cavern.

Will hurried onward, leading the group deeper into the canyon. After the noisy drive, the near total silence was surreal. The air grew cooler by degrees as they moved deeper into the shadowy passage. It would still be many hours before the midday sunlight reached the depths of the canyon.

"What is this place?" gasped Taneisha.

"A shortcut," answered Deke, and then added, "Hopefully."

"Keep moving," Will urged, his voice steady but urgent. "We're almost there."

"Almost where?" asked Maisy, peering into the darkness ahead. "It looks like we're about to hit a dead end."

"Not a dead end," promised Will.

Still, as they closed the remaining distance to the massive obstacle that seemed to fill the canyon from wall to wall, Will could understand Maisy's concern. In the dark, able to see only what their headlamps could illuminate, Will hadn't really gotten a sense of just how massive the debris field was. A tangle of oxidized aluminum girders bent at impossible angles loomed over them like a Lovecraftian nightmare intent on devouring them.

"What the hell is that?" breathed Maisy, gazing up at the wreckage.

"A stairway to heaven," replied Will, reaching out for the girders. "And it's time to climb."

THIRTY-THREE

THE ROTOR BLADES of the helicopter thundered overhead as General Tadesse stared out the open side door. While utilitarian—the Russian made Mi-17 was a workhorse for the extraction industry, ferrying workers and equipment to VEK's far-flung operations—the aircraft represented a measure of wealth and power that he could only dream of.

Perhaps one day, when all of Tigray was his to rule, he would have a helicopter of his own.

The landscape below was a blur of dust and rugged terrain. Tadesse's grip tightened on the edge of the door, as he scanned the ground for any sign of the Americans. They had only been in the air for a few minutes, and yet already they were closing in on Adi Gebru, where a contingent of Tadesse's ground troops had last reported contact with the American spies. Such was the power of the helicopter. They could leap over mountains, traveling in mere minutes what might take hours of driving on circuitous routes to reach.

His men, many of whom did not share his fascination with the helicopter, sat farther from the door, their faces reflecting varying degrees of tension, apprehension, and in some cases, nausea.

"General," called out one of his men seated on the opposite side of the aircraft. "Look."

Tadesse carefully made his way to the other side of the cabin and peered down at the landscape. He squinted against the wind, his gaze fixing on two distinct dust clouds below. The larger one—closer and moving, or so it seemed, toward the helicopter—was in the lead, while the smaller trailed some distance behind.

"That's them," Tadesse said, pointing out the dust clouds. "The Americans are in the lead vehicle. Captain Negasi pursues them."

The intervening distance blunted his enthusiasm somewhat. Negasi's truck was at least a mile behind the American's vehicle, and to all appearances, the gap separating them was growing. He took out his sat-phone and dialed the number for Negasi, the commander of the troops in the Hilux and the man who had called him with the news that the Americans had been located. He held the phone firmly against his ear, straining to hear over the helicopter's din.

The call connected, but it took a moment for Negasi to speak. "Yes, General?"

"I'm above you in the helicopter," said Tadesse. "Why haven't you caught up to the Americans?"

He expected the captain to offer excuses, but Negasi's reply surprised him. "We stopped in Adi Gebru to ask where they might be going."

Tadesse was impressed by the young officer's forethought.

"We were only delayed a few minutes," he went on. "The roads in the hills are a maze with no way out. We are following their dust trail, but the terrain is very rough. If they keep driving the way they are, they will surely have a breakdown, and then we will have them."

"You are very clever, Captain," said Tadesse. "But I don't want to take the chance of them escaping again. Keep pressing them. We'll drive them toward you, and you can cut them off."

There was a brief pause on the other end of the line, then Negasi spoke again, his tone hesitant. "General, the villagers I spoke with mentioned another American. A woman doctor operating a medical clinic. It's northwest of town, near the church. The vehicle we are pursuing was seen leaving there earlier. I wonder if perhaps they are trying to draw our attention away from the others who might be hiding at the clinic."

Tadesse's mind began racing as he weighed the new information. Was the young captain correct? Were the Americans in the Land Cruiser trying to create a diversion, sacrificing themselves in order for the others in their group to escape?

"Very well, Captain. Continue with your pursuit. I will pay a visit to this clinic."

"Understood, General," said Negasi.

Tadesse ended the call and then got on the internal intercom. "Change course," he told the pilot. "Take us to Adi Gebru."

The pilot nodded and adjusted their heading, the helicopter banking sharply as it changed direction and shot forward. Tadesse watched the dust plumes a few moments longer, then returned his attention to the view ahead, where the highway town of Adi Gebru was already visible. He relayed Negasi's description of the clinic's location to the pilot who promptly overflew the town and followed a dirt road to the northwest. The tall steeple and cross of an ancient church atop a low hill came into view. Below it was a small cluster of stone houses.

A smile touched Tadesse's lips as he thought about the Americans who might be hiding in one of those buildings, imagining that they were safe. He would show them that no place in Tigray was safe for outsiders.

Tadesse's heart pounded with anticipation as the helicopter descended toward a flat patch of ground. He caught a glimpse of a red cross adorning the wall of one of the buildings before a storm of dust, stirred up by the helicopter's downwash, obscured his view.

"I will take the lead," Tadesse told his men. "We'll search every inch of that clinic if we have to. We can't let them slip through our fingers again."

He received a chorus of affirmatives.

A moment later, the helicopter touched down with a jolt. Tadesse jumped out, his men following close behind, careful to keep their heads down as they passed under the still spinning rotor blades. Once clear, they moved toward the clinic in a line, weapons at the ready. Tadesse kept his aimed at the clinic door.

Then the door opened.

Tadesse almost pulled the trigger, but stopped himself when he saw that the woman standing in the doorway was not one of the diplomats he'd been sent to hunt. She was white, but with a deeply tanned, olive-complexion that wouldn't have been unusual in North Africa, young and fit, with jet black hair tied in a single, long braid. He recalled that Negasi had mentioned a woman doctor, and realized that had to be who he was seeing.

Better to let her live, he thought, *at least until she can tell me where to find the others.*

Keeping his AKS-74 trained on her, he advanced until he was close enough to be heard over the roar of the helicopter. "I am General Tadesse," he called out. "I know that you are hiding the Americans in your clinic. Send them out, and there will be no further trouble."

The woman regarded him with a slightly perplexed look, then, speaking slowly, said, "Pardon me. I am still learning Amharic. What do you want?"

Tadesse muttered a curse. "Americans," he repeated, this time speaking Amharic. "Send them out."

The woman stared back at him, then shook her head. "There is nobody else here. This is a medical clinic."

Tadesse turned to the closest of his men. "Search everywhere. Find them."

The man nodded and then hastened forward, pushing past the woman doctor, and entered the building.

"Really," the woman insisted. Glancing over her shoulder as the soldier began moving through the clinic, overturning furniture as he went. "There is nobody here."

"We were told that the Americans left here earlier. Do you deny that they were here?"

"I am not political. I help anyone who comes to me."

Tadesse decided the woman spoke better Amharic than she was letting on. "Where were they going?"

"Gondar. That's what they told me. They left almost an hour ago."

"They are not going to Gondar. My men turned them back at the river. Where else would they go?"

The doctor shook her head. "I honestly have no idea."

The man who had gone in to execute the search now reappeared in the doorway behind her. "There is nobody inside, General."

Tadesse narrowed his eyes at the doctor. She was telling the truth, or at least, was not explicitly lying. But did she know something more that she wasn't saying?

He stared at her for a long moment, then realized what he needed to do. He gestured toward her, then addressed his soldiers. "Bring her."

THIRTY-FOUR

TANEISHA STARED AT the metal monstrosity before her and felt panic rising. *I'm supposed to climb that?*

She was already out of breath from the jog through the canyon. Her body was still adjusting to the altitude of Tigray, and even moderate physical exertion left her panting. The fact that none of the others seemed to be the least bit winded only made her feel out of shape and inadequate.

"It's the wreckage of an old Italian zeppelin," explained Deke. "It crashed here, probably back when Italy invaded in the thirties. We found it when we came through here earlier."

Maisy let out a low whistle and gestured to the chaotic tangle. "This has been sitting here for ninety years? And you want us to climb up it?"

"Up and over," explained Will. "It's the only way to reach the other end of the canyon. Once past it... Well, we'll have a bit of a hike, but after that..."

Deke gave a knowing nod. "The other Cruiser."

"They were looking for us with a helicopter," explained Will. "We had to ditch it and continue on foot. It should be right where we left it."

"But they're right behind us," said Taneisha. "Won't they just follow us?"

"Getting over this isn't as easy as it looks," explained Will, then quickly added. "Unless you know what you're doing, and I do. Just follow my lead. Step where I step, and we'll get through it. Just like climbing a ladder."

"I hate climbing ladders," muttered Taneisha. It was true. She didn't even like standing on stepstools to change light bulbs.

Maisy looked up at the towering wreckage, her expression a mix of fear and resolve. "We don't have much choice, do we?"

"No," Will admitted. "But we can do this. Everyone stick together and move carefully. We can't afford any mistakes."

With that, he began to climb, using the girders as makeshift rungs. The metal groaned under his weight but held its shape. When he was a good fifteen feet above their heads, Deke nodded to Sanjeet. "You're next, Doc. Can you remember the route?"

Sanjeet, ever the stoic, nodded and immediately began climbing with the sure-footedness of a gecko. When he reached the same spot where Will had been, Deke signaled Maisy to begin. Meanwhile, overhead, Will had moved past the edge, disappearing from view.

Taneisha glanced nervously at Deke. "Who's next?"

"You're up," he said with a confident smile. "Don't worry. You've got this."

Taneisha stared at the twisted lattice of girders, her heart pounding like a jackhammer in her chest. Deke's confident smile did little to calm her nerves. She took a deep breath and stepped forward, her hands trembling as she reached for the first metal bar. The oxidized metal felt powdery, almost porous in her grasp.

This isn't going to hold me, she thought.

She knew that was just her fear talking. The others had climbed up with no problem, there was no reason to believe it wouldn't support her.

"You've got this," Deke repeated, his voice steady and encouraging. "Just take it one step at a time."

Her hands were slick with sweat, making her grip feel precarious. She took another deep breath, trying to calm her racing heart. "Okay, here goes," she muttered to herself. She lifted her foot, trying to find a stable place to step. The girder felt cold and unforgiving beneath her boot.

She pulled herself up, her arms straining as she ascended slowly. Each movement felt awkward and uncertain, and she couldn't shake the feeling that she was going to slip and fall at any moment.

"Just keep moving," Deke called from below. "You're doing great."

Taneisha wasn't sure she believed him, but she kept climbing, her muscles protesting with each step. Halfway up, her foot slipped, and she let out a gasp, clutching desperately at the metal bars. The girder groaned with the shock of her sudden movement, and for a fleeting instant, she was sure the whole thing would collapse beneath her, the metal struts slicing her apart like enormous garden shears or impaling her like skewers. She froze there, her breath coming in ragged gasps. She could feel the metal edge biting into the skin of her palm and fingers.

"You're okay!" Deke's voice was firm and reassuring. "Just find your footing and keep going. You're almost there."

With trembling hands, she found a more secure grip and steadied herself. She couldn't afford to let fear paralyze her now. She forced herself to keep moving, inch by inch, until she was halfway up. Her arms and legs burned with the effort, but she refused to give up.

Above, she could see Maisy, who had already reached a stable spot and was looking down at her. "You're doing it, Taneisha! Just a little bit more!"

Maisy's encouragement gave her a boost of confidence. She focused on the next hold, then the next, each one bringing her closer to the top.

Finally, she reached the point where Maisy was waiting. Maisy extended a hand, and Taneisha grabbed it gratefully. With a final heave, she transitioned from vertical to horizontal movement, and saw the irregular lattice of struts and girders stretched out before her. Farther ahead, Sanjeet and Will were making their way across with surprising alacrity, finding a path through the metal maze.

"There's more?" she gasped.

"The hardest part is behind you," assured Maisy. "Just step where I step."

And with that, the elfin woman started moving, taking long steps across yawning gaps, grasping vertical protrusions for stability as she went. Taneisha waited until Maisy was a good twenty feet ahead of her, and then, summoning up her newly discovered confidence, she began the traverse. Her breath was coming in short, sharp bursts, but she kept moving, Maisy's example giving her the courage she needed. Behind her, Deke had finished his climb and was observing her.

"All right," he said approvingly. "I told you, you got this."

Maisy echoed the sentiment. "You're almost there. Just a little bit more."

Before she knew it, she was nearing the far end of the debris field, where Will was waiting, assisting the others with the transition to the descent. As she got closer to him she noticed the silhouette of a large, enclosed structure—it almost looked like the body of an airplane—partially hidden among the girders. It was completely out of place amid the twisted wreckage.

"What's that?" she asked, her voice still shaky.

Will followed her gaze, and with just a hint of a smile, answered. "That is the zeppelin's cabin."

His reaction further piqued her interest. "Anything interesting in there?"

"You wouldn't believe me if I told you."

Taneisha frowned, her curiosity growing. "Try me."

"Let's just say it's got the answer to a very big question." He cocked his head to the side as if struck by inspiration. "And maybe a solution to a more immediate problem."

"You don't have to be so damn cryptic about it," she scolded.

He laughed, "It's quite a story. I promise I'll tell you all about it once we're somewhere safe."

Just then, Deke arrived, breathing more heavily than Maisy would have expected, and with a strained look on his face. "Company's coming," he gasped. "Time's up."

THIRTY-FIVE

SOKOLOV'S FACE WAS a mask of indifference as he watched the helicopter bear Tadesse and his men away. It was only when the aircraft disappeared over the horizon that he allowed himself a smile of satisfaction. With Tadesse on the trail of the Americans, the primary obstacle to the success of Petrov's plan had finally been overcome. Now only one thing remained.

He returned to his tent and retrieved the hard plastic tough box. It was heavy, filled with wire and electronic components—everything he would need to turn the chemical constituents in the trench at the bottom of the equipment shed into a bomb that would, as Petrov joked, shake the world—but he carried easily under one arm over to Tadesse's pickup truck.

The sturdy vehicle was canted at a slight angle due to the fact that the tire used to replace the one vandalized by the Americans was the wrong size. Sokolov set the container down in the bed, securing it tightly with bungee cords, then climbed into the cab and started the engine.

The truck roared to life, a cloud of dust rising in its wake as he drove the short distance to the nearby equipment shed. He had to take it slow, both because of the mismatched tires and the uneven terrain. The drive was short but bumpy, each jolt reminding Sokolov of how much he was ready to be done with Tigray.

He carried the tough box into the shed, his way lit by a headlamp, and went directly to the trench. It had taken ten long days to excavate the trench, scooping out rock and dirt by the bucketful, an essential, if tedious, labor. In order for Petrov's plan to work, it was necessary to get below the bedrock layer, where the oil shale lay, it's organic matter fused into the rock by the weight of millions of years of sedimentary accumulations. He'd done the work himself—it wasn't the sort of thing he could trust to Tadesse and his ilk.

Once at the bottom of the trench, he opened the tough box and began laying out its contents. His fingers moved deftly, almost reverently, as he began assembling the device. Twelve years in the elite GRU-Spetsnaz had taught him everything he needed to know about building bombs.

The device came together quickly, his practiced hands working with precision, inserting the pencil detonators into the bags of ammonium nitrate, connected them with long strands of insulated wire, securing them in place with anti-tamper devices that would instantly trigger the device if someone attempted to remove them. He didn't think anyone would. Tadesse and his men were under orders to stay out of the equipment shed, and there wasn't anyone else around who might wander in, but Sokolov didn't like to leave even the little things to chance.

He chuckled at the thought of how easy it had been to manipulate Tadesse. The general's fierce nationalism, not to mention his insatiable greed, had made him the perfect pawn. He did not doubt that the Tadesse was secretly planning to double-cross VEK and keep the oil for himself once he came to power.

If the fool only knew.

When all of the detonators were in place, he connected them to the master control switch, which would synchronize the detonators such that the small charges in the aluminum powder would go off a fraction of a second ahead of the charges in the ammonium nitrate, creating a cloud of fine metal particles that would tremendously amplify the explosive power of the ammonium nitrate. Lastly, after checking his watch, he set the timer for three hours and fifteen minutes, and then armed the backup remote failsafe detonator which would allow him to instantly detonate the device with a phone call, should the need arise.

Satisfied with his work, he climbed out of the trench and got back in the truck. He did not return to the camp, however, but instead drove several miles away, seeking higher ground.

He found a suitable spot overlooking the camp, a natural vantage point that offered a clear view of the surrounding area. Far enough away to escape the blast, but close enough to observe and, if necessary, trigger the device.

As he settled into his makeshift surveillance post, Sokolov checked his watch again—just a little less than three hours to go— and smiled. At long last, all the pieces were in place, and all that remained was to wait.

THIRTY-SIX

ALMOST BEFORE DEKE'S warning was given, the sound of gunfire began reverberating between the canyon walls. The tangled wreckage rang with the sound of bullets striking and ricocheting amid the girders.

Will ducked reflexively, even though there was little chance of a slug finding its way through the impenetrable screen. Still, little chance was not the same as zero chance, and there was the added possibility that the random bullet strikes might critically destabilize the wreckage, bringing it down under them like a house of cards.

He faced Taneisha. Her eyes were wide with fear, her body already unconsciously hunching into a semi-fetal protective curl. He gripped her shoulder.

"Taneisha, listen to me." He had to shout to be heard over the din, but strove to keep his tone steady and confident. "We have to move. Now."

She managed to nod.

"Downclimbing is a little trickier because you can't always see where to put your feet. Just feel for solid holds with your feet and trust your hands. Keep your body close to the structure and take it slow."

Taneisha nodded again and tried to steady her breathing. "Okay, I'll try."

"You've got this, Taneisha," said Deke. "You're almost there. Just take it one step at a time. We're right behind you."

Will watched as she started her descent. "That's it. Good. Keep going, just like that."

As Taneisha cautiously made her way down, the tumult abruptly ceased.

Will and Deke exchanged a glance. It made sense that Tadesse's men would figure out that they were just wasting bullets. But what would they do next?

In the sudden silence, the sound of the girders groaning and creaking with new stress answered the question.

Tadesse's men were attempting the climb.

Will berated himself for having underestimated their resolve. "I thought we'd have more time," he muttered, then facing Deke, added, "Your turn."

Deke glanced down at Taneisha, and after judging that she was far enough along, commenced his downclimb.

Will could feel the wreckage shuddering with the increased load of so many bodies moving about. It had never been designed to support so much weight—hell, it hadn't been designed at all. It had been created by a random event, its equilibrium determined by the force of gravity and its own compromised structural integrity. Now, with addition of new mass and the energy of the climbers stepping up, pulling on the girders, lifting themselves, the equation was no longer balanced.

"Deke," he murmured. "I've got a bad feeling about this."

"I feel you," agreed Deke, his voice tight with effort and urgency. "We need to get the hell off this thing."

Movement at the opposite end of the debris field caught Will's eye. He looked back down the way they'd come just as the head and shoulders of one of Tadesse's men rose into view. Across the distance, their eyes met, and then the man was unslinging his weapon.

There was no time to waste.

Will swung his body out over the edge even as the rifle's report thundered in the air around him. The haphazard structure lurched several inches as the rifle's recoil, comparatively slight though it was, added its energy to the wrong side of the equation. The groan of stressed metal echoing through the canyon like the screams of the damned, and from somewhere deep inside the tangle of metal, the sound of girders snapping apart was almost as loud at the preceding gunshots.

Taneisha let out a cry as her grasp failed and she fell back. Fortunately, she was only a few feet above the canyon floor, and Maisy and Sanjeet were waiting to catch her.

Will clung to his hold for a moment, hoping desperately that the swaying would abate. Twenty feet below him, Deke was similarly stranded. The sway of the wreckage made it impossible to move, much less find good handholds.

"Get clear!" Deke shouted down to the others. His voice barely audible over the tumult. "This whole thing's about to go!"

Maisy and Sanjeet, still holding Taneisha, both looked up, eyes wide with terror as they saw Deke's dire prophecy already coming to pass.

Then, heeding his own admonition, Deke leapt backward. He was a good ten feet from the canyon floor, a fall that could easily result in serious injury, but if his years playing football had taught Deke anything, it was how to land. As soon as his feet made contact with the ground, he went limp, absorbing the energy of the sudden stop by crumpling, and in the same motion, threw himself sideways into a roll. A moment later, he was on his feet, gazing up at Will.

"Hurry!" Deke shouted again. "It's going!"

Will stretched out his feet, groping blindly for footholds, but found it nearly impossible with everything shifting around him. The wreckage writhed and bucked, the slumbering metal monstrosity come to life at last, intent on devouring them all.

"There's no time," shouted Deke. "You need to jump!"

The urgency in his friend's voice compelled Will to desperate action. With no time to think, he let go of his tenuous hold and leapt into the air. As he did, the wreckage underwent a violent shift. Girders snapped apart, shards of metal flung out like a volley of arrows, whizzing past, some of them barely missing him.

Will did his best to emulate Deke's landing technique, but he had a lot farther to fall. The impact jarred every bone in his body, and when he attempted to throw himself into a roll, it was like being hit by a bus. The wind was knocked out of him, and the world seemed to spin. But then Deke was there, grabbing him and dragging him away from the collapsing structure.

The sound was deafening, a constant roar of metal tearing and clanging in a cacophony of destruction, that seemed to vibrate in his bones. Will thought it sounded like the end of the world. A massive cloud of dust and debris engulfed them, choking the air and turning the world a hazy, suffocating brown.

"We need to move!" Deke yelled, his voice barely cutting through the din. He pulled Will to his feet, half carrying, half dragging him away from the debris field.

Will struggled to breathe, his lungs burning with the effort. Sharp stabs of pain radiated through his feet, up his ankles, all the way to his knees, but his legs bore his weight. His vision swam as he tried to peer through the haze. He stumbled, but Deke's grip was strong, keeping him upright as they fled down the canyon. Behind them, the wreckage continued to settle with bone-chilling groans and snaps.

Gradually, however, the tumult subsided. When they reached a point where the air was clear, and Will could breathe without choking on dust, he looked back.

The wreckage had not fallen completely flat; there was simply too much of it for that to happen. Rather, it seemed to have been compressed under its own weight. Many of the near-ancient girders had snapped apart, triggering a cascade of failures that had ultimately resulted in a new equilibrium. The canyon was still blocked, but now the wreckage did not rise quite so high.

And somewhere in the embrace of that twisted mass of metal, the zeppelin's cabin waited, protecting its sacred prize.

Will wondered if any of Tadesse's men had been caught in the collapse, or if they had managed to get clear. He hoped the latter was the case. Being crushed under tons of metal wreckage was a fate he wouldn't wish on his worst enemy.

Hopefully, they would think twice before making another attempt to cross the debris field.

Will looked away, still leaning heavily on his friend.

"So was that how you planned it?" asked Deke.

"Not quite," admitted Will.

Deke chuckled. "Let's not do that again."

"Amen to that," replied Will. "Come on. We need to keep moving."

Maisy, Sanjeet and Taneisha were waiting just a little farther up the canyon. Will checked in to see if anyone had been injured. He was relieved that aside from some scrapes and bruises, everyone had come out unscathed. The initial pain Will had felt after his hard landing had faded enough to let him move with only mild discomfort. He'd probably stressed some tendons and maybe sustained a stress fracture or two, but nothing that would leave him debilitated. Which was a good thing considering what they would have to do next.

"Okay, listen up," Will said, his voice still hoarse from the dust and exertion. "We've still got a ways to go, but at least there won't be anything as dangerous as what we just survived."

Taneisha gave a shaky nod. "Thank God for that."

They started toward the canyon exit, moving cautiously but with purpose. With the dust settling and the sun rising in the sky, the gloomy atmosphere had receded like the tide, revealing a landscape that, while rugged, seemed almost benign compared to the chaos they had just endured. Will allowed himself to nurture an ember of hope.

Maybe, just maybe, they were going to make it out of this alive.

Then, with the exit to the canyon just fifty yards away, a new sound began to echo down the earthen walls, a low, rhythmic thump that quickly grew louder.

A helicopter.

Will's heart sank, but he pushed back against the wave of dread that threatened to engulf him.

"Everybody, wait here," he ordered. "Take cover if you can. They could just be looking for us. I'm going to check it out."

Without waiting for a response, he broke from the group and, sidling along the shadowy east wall, approached the end of the canyon. Although his attention was forward, he detected movement from the corner of his eye and turned to find Deke right behind him.

Will frowned. "I thought I said to wait."

Deke gave him a mischievous grin. "Oh, I didn't think you meant me." Then, he sobered. "But seriously, brother, we're in this together. All the way."

Will felt a rush of gratitude for his friend's unwavering support. He nodded. "All right, let's go."

They advanced, edging forward slowly, staying in shadow. As they neared the exit, the helicopter's rotors became deafening, sending gusts of wind that kicked up dust and small stones. Will and Deke pressed on, finally reaching a vantage point where they could see beyond the canyon's mouth.

What they saw caused Will's heart to plummet.

The helicopter was on the ground, a hundred yards beyond the entrance to the canyon, its rotors still turning.

Closer in, Tadesse and half a dozen of his men were standing in a tight group, staring intently into the cleft as if waiting for someone to emerge.

And there was one other person with them.

"Damn it," breathed Deke. "They've got Elena."

THIRTY-SEVEN

THE HELICOPTER'S ROTORS continued to churn the air, creating a constant thrum that added to the tension. Tadesse's men stood in a semi-circle, weapons at the ready, flanking their leader who stood behind a defiant Elena. Tadesse gripped her biceps and held a pistol against her ear.

"I've got to go out there," Will said, his voice low but urgent.

Deke shook his head. "You've gotta have a better plan than that."

"Tadesse took Elena hostage. That means he might be willing to negotiate.

"But what are we bringing to the table?" Deke countered. "We've got nothing to bargain with."

Will's eyes narrowed, a hint of a smile playing at the corners of his mouth. "As Maisy might say, we've got an ace up our sleeve."

"Maisy wouldn't say that because Maisy doesn't need to cheat." Deke narrowed his eyes at Will. "What ace?"

Before Will could elaborate, a shout echoed through the canyon. Tadesse's voice, loud and commanding. Although the words were incomprehensible, the threatening tone sent a chill down Will's spine. He quickly activated the translation app on his phone, just in time to hear the demand repeated.

"—last warning. Surrender or this woman dies."

Will's mind raced. He knew what he had to do. He looked at Deke. "Wait here. I mean it this time."

Deke shook his head, his expression determined. "He knows we'll be together. But maybe we can make him think it's just the two of us."

Will hated that he couldn't refute Deke's logic. "Okay, then. Let's go."

With a deep breath, Will raised his hands and stepped into the open, Deke right beside him.

As Will and Deke emerged, Tadesse's eyes locked onto them. He shook Elena roughly, his expression a mixture of anger and determination. His men immediately trained their weapons on the approaching pair.

Tadesse barked another command, and his electronically reproduced voice blared from the phone's speaker. "I know there are more of you. All of you come out, or she dies."

He gave Elena another shake for emphasis.

Will caught Elena's eyes and gave her what he hoped was a reassuring nod as he mouthed the words, "It's going to be okay."

Then, he brought his gaze back to Tadesse and continued advancing, ignoring Tadesse's repeated warnings to halt. He had to get close enough to be heard over the helicopter's noise. Deke stayed right beside him.

"I said stop!" bawled Tadesse.

But Will pressed on until he was within earshot. "General Tadesse," he called out, his voice firm and unyielding. "Let's talk about what you really want."

Tadesse looked taken aback, uncertain how to respond. Will seized the moment by looking past the general, into the cabin of the idling helicopter. "Where's Sokolov? Is he with you? Or did he send you off to do his dirty work?"

Tadesse sneered, but there was a flicker of doubt in his eyes. "That is none of your concern. Tell your comrades to come out. Now."

"I want to talk to Sokolov," pressed Will. "Not his underlings."

A slight tilt of Tadesse's head told Will that his barb had stuck. "What do you know of Sokolov?"

"I know that he's calling the shots on behalf of VEK. Let me talk to him. I'm sure he'll listen to what I have to say."

Tadesse gave him a narrow stare. "Why do you think he would listen? He's the one who ordered me to kill you and the others."

Will managed a cynical chuckle. "Like I said. You're just doing his dirty work. I'll bet he didn't even let you in on the real plan."

Tadesse's look of suspicion deepened, confirming the truth of the statement. Will raised an eyebrow, affecting a look of surprise. "Oh, he didn't tell you. I guess I'm not surprised. What did he promise you? A share of the oil wealth?"

Despite himself, the general answered, "When Tigray is a free country, yes. The oil will make us all rich."

"There isn't going to be any oil wealth. VEK isn't interested in developing the oil shale field."

Tadesse's eyes narrowed further. "You are lying. You would say anything to save your skin."

"I told you before. I want to help the people of Tigray. We actually want the same thing. Which is more than I can say for VEK."

Will glanced at Deke, who nodded slightly, signaling his support. Then he turned back to Tadesse. "Let me see if I'm reading this right. Sokolov, representing VEK, told you that if you start up the civil war again, destabilize the region, he'll fund your revolution and help you establish a sovereign Tigray, after which you'll get a share of the profit from the sale of the shale oil produced by the Naeder Adet field." He didn't need the Tigrayan to verbalize an answer; the general's face said it all.

"There isn't going to be any oil revenue," Will went on, "Because VEK isn't going to develop the field." He paused a beat, then played his ace. "They're going to destroy it."

As the words were translated into Tigrinya, Tadesse just stared back at him, dumbfounded. Then, he gave a harsh laugh. "That's funny."

The reaction confused Will, but only until he realized that the word Tadesse had used had been mistranslated. What Tadesse had been trying to say was that he found the idea preposterous.

"Have you seen what's in that storage shed near your camp?" Will went on. "Explosives. Oxidizing agents. Powdered metal. The ingredients to make a thermobaric weapon. Do you know what that is?"

Will could see by the look on Tadesse's face that the app wasn't painting the picture he wanted, so he clarified. "It's a fire bomb. He's going to set the oil shale on fire."

Tadesse shook his head. "Why would he do that? Then his masters wouldn't have any oil to sell."

"VEK doesn't care about the oil. They're going to create an environmental disaster right here in Tigray. A fire in the shale that will be impossible to put out. It will just burn and burn and release carbon—" He stopped himself, remembering to simplify the concept. "Poison gas into the atmosphere. Poison gas that will change the weather for the entire world."

A gleam of something like humor appeared in Tadesse's eyes. "Poison gas that changes the weather. And will this be done with witchcraft?"

Will suddenly saw a flaw in his plan. He was certain that he'd solved the puzzle of Petrov's scheme. With a thermobaric device, Sokolov could set the Naeder Adet shale ablaze—a fire so hot that it would cause a chain reaction, vaporizing the oil from the rock to sustain the fire indefinitely, releasing nearly half-a-billion tons of carbon dioxide into the atmosphere. Half-a-billion tons wasn't much compared to the global annual output of thirty-seven-billion tons, and wouldn't move the needle very much, adding less than a quarter of a part-per-million—a mere drop in the bucket—but with worldwide emissions still on the rise, it might be the drop that caused the overflow.

Or the final straw.

A disaster in a remote corner of the world that nobody even cared about might be just the thing to convince industrial nations of the world to reconsider Petrov's extortion scheme. And since it would appear that General Tadesse, a known Tigrayan revolutionary, was behind the bombing, no one would suspect that it was all Petrov's doing.

Will could just imagine how the Russian would spin it. *What a terrible disaster. And this could happen anywhere. Pay us to leave the oil in the ground, and the problem goes away.*

But how was he going to convince Tadesse of that when the man had probably never even heard of climate change?

Then Elena said something. Whatever language she was using, it wasn't Tigrinya because the phone didn't translate it, but her words had an effect on Tadesse. She turned her eyes to Will. "I told him it's not witchcraft. It's science." She paused a beat. "Are you sure about this, Will?"

He nodded. "The explosives are there, right in the middle of the oil shale field. The Russian is going to blow it up and let the world blame Tadesse for it. All so his oil company can blackmail the world into paying them to leave the rest of their oil reserves in the ground. Can you explain that to him?"

Elena began speaking haltingly to Tadesse, but he waved her off. "I understand what he is saying," he said in Tigrinya. "But you expect me to believe that the Russian oil company doesn't want our oil?"

"You don't have to take my word for it," said Will. "Ask Sokolov. Ask him why he has a supply of those materials. They aren't used in the extraction process. The only reason to have them is to create a bomb that burns so hot, it will set the rocks on fire."

Tadesse studied Will, weighing his words. Finally, he gave a slight nod. "Very well. I will accept your proposition, but the rest of your group must surrender. My men will stay here to watch over them while you and I fly back to the camp to see what Sokolov has to say."

Will almost balked at this demand, but then realized that there was really no alternative. Maisy, Sanjeet and Taneisha were trapped in the canyon, and if Tadesse wanted to, he could just send his men in with guns blazing.

Deke spoke up. "I'm coming, too."

Tadesse's eyes narrowed. "And why should I permit that?"

"It's a show of good faith," said Deke. "A sign that we trust each other. Besides, I'm the smart one. I'll be able to tell if Sokolov is lying to you."

Will didn't think Tadesse would buy the argument, but after a moment, the general nodded. "Very well. But I will also bring her." He gave Elena another shake. "If you try anything, she will be the first to suffer the consequences."

Will's heart tightened, but he kept his face impassive. "Let me go tell the others."

He turned and headed for the canyon entrance. Tadesse barked orders to his men, and four of them followed, their guns trained on him.

As they approached the cleft, Maisy, Sanjeet, and Taneisha emerged, their hands raised in a show of submission.

"We heard," said Sanjeet.

"Are you sure about this?" added Maisy.

"Am I sure that Sokolov is planning to set Tigray on fire? Absolutely. Do I trust Tadesse?" He waggled his hand. "But I don't see that we have much choice."

"Whatever else he is," said Taneisha. "Tadesse is a patriot. He believes in Tigray. That's the one thing you can count on."

"That helps," Will said. Then, with a reassuring nod, he added. "Stay strong. We'll be back soon."

He turned and went back to Tadesse. Without another word, the general gestured with his pistol for them to board the helicopter. Escorted by two of Tadesse's men, Will and Deke made their way toward the waiting aircraft, followed by Tadesse and Elena.

The rotor wash whipped at his clothes and the dust stung his eyes, but Will barely noticed. He was hyper-focused on what lay ahead. They had a chance, a slim one, but a chance nonetheless, to stop Sokolov and just maybe, save Tigray from war.

THIRTY-EIGHT

THE HELICOPTER'S ROTORS filled the cabin with a dull roar that was, while not exactly deafening, certainly not conducive to quiet conversation. Will was a little surprised then when Elena, who had taken the seat next to him, leaned close, so close that he could feel her breath on his neck, and half-shouted, "I'm sorry."

Her closeness sent a tingle through him, and he cursed the timing. He put his mouth close to her ear. "For what?"

"I should have listened to you. I should have left when you told me to."

Will managed a smile. "You couldn't have known."

"If I'd listened, we wouldn't be here. I put everyone in danger." She laid a hand on his arm, her touch conveying both regret and a need for reassurance.

And something more?

He shook his head. "Deke and I would still be here. This doesn't have anything to do with you. You just got caught up in it. If anything, I'm the one who should apologize."

She raised an eyebrow, as if questioning the logic of his argument.

"Maybe this is for the best. If we can stop Sokolov from setting the shale on fire and prevent Tadesse from restarting the war, then it's a good thing that we're here."

Elena smiled, then leaned in even closer, their foreheads almost touching. "You always find a way to see the silver lining, don't you?"

Before Will could reply, Tadesse spoke, pulling them back to reality. Will's phone supplied the translation. "We're approaching my camp."

Will drew back from Elena, noticing Deke's smirk as he did, and gazed out the open door. He was surprised at how quickly the helicopter had covered the distance. It had taken him and Deke hours to drive from the camp to the river, and then half the night to walk from there to the canyon. By air, it had taken less than fifteen minutes.

Through the open door, Will could see the dull metal cube of the equipment shed off to the left, and the row of canvas tents directly ahead. Aside from the wind rustling the fabric of the tents, there was absolutely no activity in the camp.

"The truck is gone," Tadesse shouted, his face betraying confusion. "Sokolov must have taken it. He isn't here."

Sokolov's absence complicated things. Without his admission, or for that matter, his insincere denial, it would be difficult to convince Tadesse that he'd been played by the Russians. But Will realized that there might be another way to achieve the same outcome. "Land by the equipment shed. The proof of what he's doing is in there."

Tadesse considered this for a moment, then nodded and relayed the instructions to the pilot. The helicopter banked gently, angling away from the tents, and instead descended toward the enormous metal structure.

When it touched down, Tadesse exited first, apparently no longer seeing a compelling need to keep his gun on Elena. Will took that as a positive sign. He disembarked next, followed by Deke and Elena, with the two gunmen stepping out last. As soon as they were clear, the helicopter's turbines roared louder, and it rose once more into the sky.

"Hey," cried Deke. "That's our ride."

"He must go to Adwa to refuel," explained Tadesse. "I will call him back when we are ready to be picked up."

Will was a little distressed by the fact that they were now no longer just a hop and a skip away from their friends, but there was nothing they could do about it. Hopefully, they would be able to quickly convince Tadesse of Sokolov's duplicity, and have the helicopter return for them in short order.

"Inside there," Will said, gesturing to the shed, "You'll see what Sokolov is up to."

Tadesse gestured for one of his men to open the door. The guard complied, swinging it open to reveal the gloomy interior. Will stepped inside, followed closely by Tadesse and Deke, with Elena bringing up the rear. At a command from Tadesse, the guards remained outside, keeping watch. This might have signaled a further easing of tension between the general and his captives, if not for the fact that Tadesse kept his pistol in hand and walked at the rear of the line.

With only the light from Will's phone to show the way, they moved to the trench and started down. As they descended, Tadesse gazed at the cut stone wall with a look of wonder. "Why did he dig this?"

Will glanced back. "He didn't talk about it?"

"We were—" He paused, searching for the right word. "*Encouraged* to keep away from here."

"Oil shale is found below the bedrock layer. In order for his bomb to set it on fire, it has to actually reach the shale."

Deke nodded in understanding. "So that's why he was storing all that stuff down here."

Will nodded, and shone the light ahead, illuminating the pallets and their lethal contents. Even from a distance, it was obvious that something was different about them.

"Those wires are new," remarked Deke, with just a hint of concern.

The sight of the completed device sent a chill down Will's spine. He had been expecting to find the materials to make a bomb, not the actual bomb itself.

His every instinct told him to turn around and walk... no, run away, as fast as his feet would carry him.

He wasn't the only one. Tadesse let out a yelp of dismay and started to turn away. "It is a bomb. You were telling the truth. We have to go."

"Wait!" cautioned Will. "Don't move. We don't know what the trigger is."

The wisdom of the admonition broke through the general's primal fear and kept him rooted in place.

Will played the light around the immediate area, looking for trip wires or pressure plates. Finding none, he took a cautious step closer.

"Will," Elena said, whispering as if fearful that her voice might trigger the device. "Are you sure that's good idea?"

"We need to see what we're dealing with."

"And you're a bomb expert now?"

Will smiled despite himself. "Not an expert," he admitted.

In truth, his science background and NASA training had given him, at best, a theoretical understanding of how chemical reactions could produce explosive results. Maisy, with her military and intelligence background, would probably have understood the device better, but she was miles away, so it was up to him.

He eased forward another step.

The beam of his flashlight revealed a tangled web of wires snaking out from a large plastic tough box set atop one of the pallets of ammonium nitrate, connecting to blasting caps inserted in several of the bags of the chemical. Affixed to the each of the connections was a little plastic rectangle that looked sort of like a keychain-sized carpenter's level. Nestled inside the tough box was a smaller black device about the size of a shoe box, displaying a countdown timer.

"Sokolov's finished it," he said, his voice tight. "This isn't just materials. This is the bomb. And it's armed. The good news is, we've got some time."

"How much time?" asked Deke.

"Two hours, twenty-eight minutes, and change."

"I don't suppose there's an 'off' button?"

Will shook his head. "If there is, I don't know what it looks like. But there are tilt-indicators on the connections. Probably some sort of anti-tamper switch. If we try to pull the blasting caps or move them in any way, it will go off."

"I saw the movie," muttered Deke. "So why would he finish it now? What's changed? Is it because we showed up?"

"I think this was always the plan. Petrov's speech was the signal to implement the final phase." He glanced at the general. "He sent you after Taneisha's team as the first act in the new Tigray War. That way, you'd take the blame for the bombing."

"Creating a disaster they could exploit," finished Elena.

Tadesse's face tightened with anger and confusion. "So, he was using me all along?"

Will didn't know what to say, but then he recalled what Taneisha had told him just before he'd left with the general. "Using you. Using your love for Tigray."

Tadesse dropped his gaze. "I would have killed you," he murmured. His eyes found the pistol, still in his hand. With a brusque motion, he shoved it into its holster on his hip.

"Hoo-ray," said Deke with uncharacteristic sarcasm. "We're all friends again." He gestured to the bomb. "Now, what in the hell are we going to do about that?"

The question hung in the air. Will looked around at the faces of his friends and allies. Elena, who had risked everything to get here; Deke, his steadfast companion; even Tadesse, a man who had been manipulated just as they had.

"We have to find a way to disarm it," Will said finally.

"You said we have two hours," said Elena. "Can't we call someone?"

"Call who?" replied Will. "The kind of expertise we need is at least twenty-four hours away, not two." He shook his head. "It's us, or nobody." Then he narrowed his eyes at her. "Or maybe just one of us. There's no reason all of us need to be here."

Deke made a face. "Well, somebody needs to hold the light for you."

"I'm staying," Elena said firmly. "You may have noticed, I have a thing about leaving unfinished business."

Will turned to Tadesse. "You should go. Someone has to tell the world the truth about all this. Especially if—"

"I am also staying." The general's expression was a mix of determination and regret. "I need to see this through. For Tigray."

Will felt a twinge of frustration and a tidal surge of gratitude for the loyalty of his friends. "Okay," he said. "We do this together. Let's save the world."

THIRTY-NINE

SOKOLOV FELT A tingle of apprehension when he heard the distant sound of the helicopter. He searched the skyline until he spotted the Mi-17, cruising around one of the peaks and making for the general vicinity of the camp.

He tried to tell himself that this was a positive thing. That Tadesse had finished off the Americans and was simply returning to his camp, but some primal instinct rejected that explanation.

Tadesse wasn't that clever. The Americans, on the other hand, were.

He grabbed his binoculars off the passenger seat and trained them on the aircraft, following its descent toward the camp, and was dismayed when, seemingly at the last minute, it veered away from the customary landing site, and drifted toward the equipment shed where it touched down. The rotors whipped up a cloud of dust, momentarily obscuring the figures disembarking, but as they moved out from under the spinning disc, he saw three unfamiliar faces accompanying the general.

Tadesse hadn't killed the Americans; he'd brought them back as captives.

Sokolov cursed loudly, then swore again when he saw the group moving toward the door of the shed.

A cold sweat broke out on his forehead.

Tadesse knew better than to go in the building. The only explanation for this act of insubordination was that the Americans spies had somehow convinced him to do so. And when they found the bomb....

Then he remembered that there was a simple solution to the problem.

He set the binoculars aside and picked up his phone. He'd entered the number for the remote detonator in his speed dial, so the solution was literally at his fingertips. Petrov would be disappointed at the premature detonation, but on the plus side, not only would the bomb set the oil shale on fire, but Tadesse and the Americans would be eliminated in the process.

He brought the number up, hit the send button, and waited for the fireworks.

Nothing happened.

He glanced down at the phone and saw the message "call failed" displayed on the screen. He hit the "retry" button and this time watched the phone. Even as the "calling" notification pulsed gently, he realized why the signal hadn't gone through. The receiving unit was more than fifty feet underground and covered by a metal roof.

He cursed his shortsightedness.

When he had armed the remote detonator, it had been almost an afterthought. A backup to the backup. The timer was the primary trigger, and if anyone attempted to disarm or move the bomb, the anti-tamper measures would serve as a secondary trigger.

And that was still true. One way or another, the bomb would detonate. The oil shale would catch fire.

But what would Tadesse do when he discovered that Sokolov had betrayed him? Would he tell the world of the Russian's treachery? Point the finger at VEK for sabotaging their own operation?

Petrov's plan would come apart at the seams.

He swore again.

He knew what he had to do.

Muttering one more curse for good measure, he tossed the phone down on the passenger seat, and started the pickup's engine.

FORTY

FOR SEVERAL MINUTES no one spoke, but all eyes were on Will as he studied the intricate web of wires, the tilt switches and the thousands of pounds of ammonium nitrate, aluminum powder and ferrous oxide to which they were all attached.

It wasn't just a bomb; it was an environmental holocaust hanging over the world by a thread.

Finally, Will broke the silence. "Okay, I think I know how we're going to beat this thing. Sokolov has rigged it up so that there is a bag of ammonium nitrate and a detonator on each of the pallets with the aluminum powder and the oxidizer. Those charges will blow first, scattering the aluminum powder and the oxidizer into the air to form a fuel cloud, and then the rest of it will go up a fraction of a second later.

"We can't stop it from blowing. I'm not sure anyone could. But what we can do is reduce the bomb's destructive power by removing the aluminum powder and ferrous oxide from the equation. To do that, we'll have to *very carefully—*" He paused to emphasize the words. "Move the wired bags of nitrate off those pallets and stack them off with the rest. There are tilt switches on the detonators that will trigger the bomb if tilted or moved too abruptly, so we'll have to work together, slow and smooth. Once we've done that, we'll need to move the aluminum and the oxidizer as far from the bomb as we can. Or at least the oxidizer. That's what will make the fire burn hot enough to start a cascade reaction in the shale. The aluminum is really only dangerous if it's aerosolized. The bomb will still blow, but it won't be hot enough to set the shale on fire, and we'll be miles away when it finally goes.

"Move it?" asked Deke. "What, are we gonna carry it out on our backs?"

"We'll use the excavator. Bring it down here, load up the bucket, and then drive it out.

"That's the plan," he finished.

"Have you got a Plan B?" murmured Deke.

Will shook his head, ruefully. "Not this time.

"How do the tilt-switches work?" asked Elena.

"They're designed to switch a motor or pump off if it isn't kept perfectly level. There's a small drop of mercury sitting in a little detent atop a disc. At the outer edge of the disc, there are two concentric copper rings about a sixteenth of an inch across, connected to the power source. Movement in any direction will cause the mercury to slide down, bridging the gap and completing the circuit which sets off the alarm. Or in this case, triggers the device."

Elena took a deep breath. "But you think we can move those bags without disturbing the mercury. How are we going to do that?"

Will returned a cryptic smile. "With magic."

Deke raised an eyebrow. "Magic?"

"We're going to use a variation of the levitation trick. Just like the slumber party game we all used to play as kids—light as a feather, stiff as a board."

"I never played that game," said Deke.

"Neither did I," added Elena.

Tadesse, listening to the translation, shook his head. "I have no idea what you're talking about, but I will not be a party to witchcraft."

Will's smile slipped. "It's not witchcraft," he assured the general. "It works by distributing the weight of an object between several people, and then perfectly synchronizing our movements. These bags weigh about thirty pounds each. That's not much, but if any of us, even Deke, tried to pick one up, there would be enough movement to shake the tilt switch. But working together, using just our fingertips, the bag will seem to float."

When none of the others showed the slightest bit of confidence in the scheme, Will offered a compromise. "We'll practice on some of the bags that aren't wired. You'll see."

He directed them to the closest pallet, which contained sacks full of aluminum powder, stacked around a single sack of AN from which trailed a detonator wire. Will selected a bag of aluminum that was well clear of the AN and directed the others to position themselves around it. "Now, slide your fingertips under it just a little... Good. Now, together, we're going to chant, 'light as a feather, stiff as a board.'"

"You're kidding, right?" said Elena.

Deke jumped to Will's defense. "No, he's right. Chanting will synchronize our movements. We'll be working together on a subconscious level."

Will nodded. "All right. Let's begin."

He led the chant, keeping a slow, steady rhythm. Deke joined in immediately, but it took Elena and Tadesse a couple cycles. Tadesse chanted the words in Tigrinya but matched their rhythm. When he felt sure that they were all in sync, Will inserted the word: "Float!"

The sack seemed to rise like a cloud, floating on their fingertips.

Keeping up the chant, they followed Will's lead, walking their shared burden a few steps away from the pallet where they set it down with ease.

"Good," Will said, breaking the rhythm. "I think we can do this."

His confidence was not as contagious as he might have hoped, but none of the others dissented outright. After clearing away the rest of the sacks of aluminum covering the wired bag of AN, he directed them all to take their places.

Despite the earlier success, and despite his sincere belief that they *could* do this, Will's heart pounded in his chest as they all slid their fingertips underneath the bag. The slightest deviation would end them all in the blink of an eye.

He took up the chant. "Light as a feather..."

He did not rush, allowing several repetitions of the shared chant to ensure that they were perfectly in sync before adding the command, "And float."

The bag rose slowly, their shared movements careful and deliberate. When the detonator wire bobbed a little, Will felt his heart stop cold, but then it settled. The bead of mercury, visible in the center of the tilt-switch, vibrated ever so faintly but did not move.

Sweat beaded on Will's forehead, streaming down his face like tears as he gave the next directive, "And move."

As one, they stepped away from the pallet. Every crunch of gravel underfoot was as ominous as a death knell, but their chant did not fail. Their movement was not as perfectly synchronized as he might have hoped for, but the chant and the unconscious body-communication they shared, kept the bag perfectly steady on their fingertips. Together, they walked the sack a distance of about fifteen feet and then gently set it down atop one of the pallets of AN.

"Perfect," he said, exhaling a breath he hadn't realized he was holding. "Now, we just have to do that three more times."

FORTY-ONE

MINUTES FELT LIKE hours as they methodically moved the remaining wired bags of AN. Each successful transfer was a small victory, but the tension never eased. They were constantly aware of the ever-present danger of a single misstep. When the last wired bag was successfully moved, they all collapsed against the wall of the trench, as exhausted as if they had just completed a marathon.

The break, of necessity, was short. Will rose and, after a check of the time remaining—a little less than an hour and a half—started up the slope to retrieve the excavator.

"Hang on," called Deke. "I'm coming with you."

Will considered pointing out that driving the excavator was a one-man job but was grateful for the company.

The machine—a sturdy, diesel-powered Caterpillar 320 GC—loomed large at the top of the trench. Its extended hydraulic arm and bucket looked like the neck and head of a sleeping dragon.

As Will climbed up onto the tracks and entered the control cab, Deke called out, "You know how to run that thing?"

"Heck of a time to ask," said Will, laughing. "I've worked with some similar machines. They were smaller, but it shouldn't be too different. Just give me a few minutes to get familiar with the controls."

He settled into the seat and took a moment to orient himself. The dashboard was filled with gauges, switches, and levers, each serving a specific function. He'd spent a couple seasons fighting wildland fires and had learned how to operate a bulldozer. The excavator performed a slightly different function, digging rather than pushing, but the operation of the twin tracks on which it rolled was almost identical.

"Okay," he muttered, flipping the ignition switch. The engine roared to life, a deep rumble reverberating through the cab. Thick plumes of exhaust belched from its exhaust pipes.

Deke leaned in through the open cab door. "This thing is loud as hell," he shouted. "I'm going to open the shed door for some ventilation before we get gassed out. Don't know if it will help."

"You should probably tell Tadesse's guard what we're doing," Will replied, adjusting the seat and familiarizing himself with the foot pedals. "I'm sure they'll be wondering."

"Good point." Deke leaped down from the platform and jogged over to the large shed door, heaving it open. Will saw him talking to the two Tigrayan guards who listened, their expressions a mix of skepticism and reluctant acceptance, then brought his attention back to the matter at hand.

After a deep breath, he found the lever to activate the hydraulic arm and raised the scoop off the ground. The machine shook as the added load changed its center of gravity. He retracted the arm, bringing the bucket in closer, then gripped the joysticks that operated the treads. The Cat was a powerful machine, its every movement accompanied by the growl of the engine. The mechanical clanking of the tracks on stone vibrated through the cab with tooth-loosening ferocity, but Will maintained a deft touch on the controls, maneuvering the yellow beast to the edge of the trench, easing it down the incline with painstaking care.

Deke ran up alongside him, gesturing to get his attention, so he eased back on the joysticks. "What's up?"

"You're shaking the ground," shouted Deke.

"So?"

"So, what's it going to do to those mercury switches?"

Will hadn't considered that. If the vibration from the excavator moving overground was as bad as Deke said it was, then it might be enough to trigger the delicate tilt switches. The simple act of moving the heavy machine in close proximity to the device might set off the bomb they were trying to defeat.

He blew out his breath. "I'll just have to be careful," he called back.

Knuckles white on the joysticks, he resumed the downward journey, moving the machine at a crawl to minimize the vibrations. The roar and exhaust fumes transformed the narrow slot into a veritable hell pit. The heat in the cab was stifling. Will's eyes watered, and he had to blink rapidly to clear his vision. He couldn't afford any mistakes now.

At long last the machine reached the flat bottom of the trench. The Cat's headlights lit up the cut with an intensity that their phone flashlights could not begin to match. In its beam, he saw Elena and Tadesse staring back nervously at the mechanical behemoth. He eased it forward until it was about twenty yards from the nearest pallet, and then cautiously extended the arm, positioning the scoop bucket so that its opening was facing up, and shut off the Cat.

Will climbed out of the cab, wiping the sweat from his brow. The roar of the engine faded, leaving a ringing silence in its wake. Deke joined him there, and together they approached Elena and Tadesse, who were still staring at the excavator with a mix of awe and apprehension.

"Okay," Will announced. "We need to get those bags of ferrous oxide into the bucket. I think it will hold both pallets' worth. I hope so anyway, because we're not going to have time to make a second trip. Unfortunately, we'll have to load them into the scoop by hand."

"Light as a feather?" asked Elena with an almost playful gleam in her eye.

"Not this time. We'll do it like a bucket brigade. Pass each bag from person to person."

Following Will's direction, they formed a line, with Will at the pallet, passing the bags to Elena, who handed them off to Tadesse, who then gave them to Deke to place in the excavator's bucket. The bags weren't that heavy, but the repetitive action took its toll, especially on Will who had to reach down lower to lift each sack as the pallet was unloaded. Nevertheless, working as a team, they emptied the first pallet and were down to just a couple layers on the second when Deke announced that the bucket was full.

Will stretched and twisted his torso to work out the knots in his muscles. "All right, I'm going to drive this thing back up, get that stuff as far away as I can. Once I'm clear, you guys come up and put some distance between yourselves and this place. You don't want to be anywhere near here when it goes off."

"How far away do we need to be?" asked Elena.

"The farther the better. The blast radius might only be a couple hundred yards wide, but it could throw rocks and debris a couple miles."

"Terrific," groaned Deke, stretching. "More hiking."

Will laughed, then headed for the cab of the excavator.

But just as he was climbing up onto the tracks, a dull but distinctive popping noise echoed through the trench, followed quickly by another. The four exchanged a glance, and then Tadesse drew his pistol, recognizing the sound—as they all had—as gunfire.

FORTY-TWO

AS HE APPROACHED the equipment shed, Sokolov saw two of Tadesse's men moving toward him. There was no sign of the general or his American prisoners—they were all likely still in the shed.

The revolutionary soldiers moved with an almost indifferent air, their rifles, not held in a ready position but slung across their backs. They clearly did not perceive Sokolov as a threat.

He slowed the pickup, coming to a full stop a few yards from the men and got out. The closest, a tall soldier whom Sokolov knew by the name Sergeant Yohanas, addressed him in Tigrinya, "General Tadesse was looking for you. He is with the Americans inside."

Sokolov nodded, forcing a smile. "Thank you," he replied in accented Tigrinya. "I need to speak with him."

Then, with practiced ease, Sokolov drew his pistol and fired it into Sergeant Yohanas's face. Before his companion could even begin to comprehend what was happening, Sokolov shot him as well. Both men crumpled to the ground, dead.

Stepping over their bodies, Sokolov continued to the open entrance to the shed, the pistol held out before him. He cleared the entrance by edging around the door frame, then went inside. The gloomy interior of the shed was thick with exhaust fumes and dust, but through the haze, the Russian immediately noticed that the excavator was gone. His heart rate quickened as he realized what had happened to it. The Americans had somehow contrived a way to neutralize the bomb and were going to try to move it... Or perhaps bury it... With the excavator.

He approached the edge of the trench cautiously, peering down into the darkness. They were down there, he was certain of it, but had wisely extinguished their lights to avoid drawing fire.

Shooting down at them was tempting, but the risk was too great. An errant bullet could trigger the bomb and doom them all. Instead, he decided on a different approach. Affecting a companionable tone, he called down into the trench. "General Tadesse! Are you down there?"

Tadesse's voice echoed up from the depths. "Betrayer! You would use me to destroy Tigray for your own twisted aims."

Sokolov stifled an impulse to laugh. *Took you long enough to figure it out,* he thought. "It was never about you, General. It was always about the bigger picture."

Another voice, speaking English, rose up. "Sokolov?" There was a pause, and then, the same voice went on. "We haven't actually met, though our paths almost crossed yesterday. I'm Will. Will Irons."

Sokolov peered into the darkness, trying to isolate the location of the voice. "Ah, yes," he said. "The American CIA agent."

"American, yes, but not CIA. Though, I do imagine they'd be interested in hearing what you and your boss Petrov have been up to here." There was a pause and then the man—Will—went on. "Listen, it's over and you've lost. We've found a way to defeat your bomb. My advice to you is to get out of Tigray while you still can."

Sokolov laughed. "You're bluffing. If you had truly deactivated it, you wouldn't still be down there."

"It's true," intoned a new voice, a deep baritone that could only belong to the black American. "We've removed the components of your bomb to keep it from setting the shale on fire."

Sokolov's eyes narrowed as he scanned the darkness below. If the man was speaking truthfully, then the Americans *had* found a weakness to exploit. But surely it was only a theoretical problem. To remove the fuel or oxidizer from the device, they would have to overcome the anti-tamper devices.

No, the bomb was still armed. It had to be.

"And yet, you are still down there," he replied. "No, I think this was your plan, but you haven't been able to actually make it happen. I advise against it. All you will do is set the bomb off. I have a better idea. Why don't you come up so we talk face to face?"

"We're fine where we are," replied the black man. "How 'bout you come down here, instead?"

Sokolov laughed to hide his anxiety. This standoff did not work in his favor. He couldn't remain here indefinitely. He didn't believe for a second that the Americans had actually carried out their stated plan of altering the bomb, but that didn't mean they wouldn't attempt it. When they did, no matter how careful they were, they would surely trigger one of the anti-tamper switches and detonate it. If he was still here, he would die along with them.

"Be reasonable," he called out. "Even if you have done what you say, the device is still active. And in—" He checked his watch. "Oh, my. Twenty-eight minutes, it will detonate. But you don't have to die. Come up. Surrender and I will let you walk away. You have my word."

Tadesse shouted his answer in Tigrinya. "Betrayer. How can we trust your word?"

"The general's right," said the black man. "We come up there, and you'll just shoot us."

Sokolov muttered a curse under his breath. If only the remote detonator had done its job. He was trying to come up with a more persuasive argument when the first American—Will—spoke up. "Actually, Deke. I think he's right. We don't want to be down here when the bomb goes off. I think we *should* go up there."

The reversal apparently surprised Deke as much as it did Sokolov, because after a moment of stunned silence, the big American's voice carried up from the depths—not a shout, but louder than a whisper. "You sure about this?"

Will's reply was equally distinct. "What's rule number one?"

"Always have a plan."

Then Will called out again. "Sokolov. Get ready. Here we come."

The assuredness in the American's voice made Sokolov wary. They were up to something, attempting some sort of desperate gambit to save their skins. *Well, let them try,* he thought, aiming his pistol down into the shadows.

All of a sudden, the lightless depths came alive with sound and fury, the unmistakable roar of the excavator's engine coming to life.

FORTY-THREE

WILL SAT IN the cab of the excavator, his hands steady on the joysticks as the machine roared to life, its powerful engine sending vibrations through the seat and up his spine. As soon as its systems were powered up, he raised the bucket, and then engaged the cab's rotation mechanism.

The powerful hydraulic system responded smoothly, and the cab began to swivel on its axis, the arm and bucket following in a graceful arc. He kept his eyes on the surroundings, ensuring he didn't accidentally slam into the trench wall. Once the cab had completed a 180-degree turn, he gently centered the joystick, locking the cab into its new position, with the arm and bucket now facing the opposite direction. Then, he worked the joystick controlling the treads, and the excavator began rolling back toward the sloping ramp.

Moments before, recognizing that a standoff would only end disastrously for them, Will had quickly outlined his plan for their escape.

"We don't have many options here. Sokolov's not going to let us walk out of here alive. And we can't stay where we are. We have to head up."

"Anything is better than staying in this hole," said Elena, her voice betraying an eagerness to seize the initiative.

"What's the plan?" asked Deke.

"We use the excavator to get back to the top. I'll drive, you guys stay behind me. The excavator will give you cover, though I don't think Sokolov will start shooting at us right away." He turned to Tadesse, speaking softly into the phone. "General, you're the only one of us who is armed. You'll need to be the one to take on Sokolov."

Tadesse's jaw had tightened, his eyes hard. "I look forward to it."

"And Plan B?" asked Deke. "If the general here doesn't have the shot."

"Then one of us will have to get the job done."

While it was a core tenet of the FAST Team to pursue non-violent solutions, that did not mean aggressive action was off the table. Their guiding principle, that violence should be used only as a last resort, recognized the possibility that a situation might arise where no other options were viable. They did not carry weapons, but the four of them had undergone intensive training for combat situations—the use of weapons, but also techniques for moving under fire.

One thing was certain. While he lived, Sokolov would do everything in his power to kill them and ensure that his bomb set Tigray ablaze.

He had to be stopped.

Deke had clapped Will on the shoulder. "Let's do this."

Now, with the excavator creeping up the incline, its headlights showing the way, Will focused on the task at hand. Burdened with more than a ton of ferrous oxide powder in its bucket, the machine was a lumbering giant, its movements slow and deliberate. The metal tracks clanked against the rocky ground, the cab vibrating with each turn of the treads.

The roar of the engine filled the trench, drowning out all other sounds. The cab was filling up with the smell of diesel fumes mixed with the acrid scent of sweat and fear, but Will's hands were confident on the controls.

Up ahead, the end of the sloping ramp was in view. They were almost there. Twenty yards. Ten.

Will took a deep breath, steeling himself for what was to come.

Sokolov was up there, armed, waiting to shoot, but Will also knew that they had a secret weapon. The excavator was not just a machine; it was both a shield and a battering ram which they would use to smash Sokolov's plans.

Behind the machine, Deke, Elena and Tadesse moved in unison, crouching low, the latter with pistol in hand, occasionally peering around the rolling treads for a look up at the rim of the trench where Sokolov surely waited, ready to strike.

Each second felt like an eternity. Will knew that once they reached the top, everything would hinge on Tadesse. The general's shot had to be true, or they'd all be dead within moments.

"Get ready!" he shouted. "We're almost there!"

The excavator strained with the transition onto flat ground, the treads slipping as the angle of the ascent reduced their contact. Will gritted his teeth, working the controls to extend the arm forward, using the loaded bucket as a counterweight. This had the desired effect of tilting the machine forward, over the lip and onto flat ground, where it promptly surged forward.

It also left him exposed to Sokolov.

He glimpsed the Russian, standing just ten yards away at a slightly oblique angle to the trench, at almost the same instant that the man fired his weapon. The bullet punched into the cab's window, the polycarbonate pane cracking but holding together.

A miss, but a close one.

"Tadesse, now!" Will shouted, pushing the machine ahead as if intent on running Sokolov down.

Tadesse, stepped out from behind the excavator, took aim, and fired his pistol. The muzzle flash illuminated his face, and the shots echoed through the shed. Sokolov ducked away, returning fire. The tumult of the reports drowned out even the throaty roar of the Cat's diesel engine. Bullets whizzed past the cab, a few ricocheting off the treads.

Will pivoted the cab, causing the excavator's arm to swing in a wide arc. The headlights cast eerie shadows about the interior of the shed, adding to the chaotic tableau. Will had hoped to hit Sokolov, or at the very least, keep him occupied so that Tadesse could shoot him, but Sokolov, sensing the attack, rolled out of the way at the last second. Bags of ferrous oxide fell out of the bucket, smashing to the ground, breaking open on impact. Will did not relent. He spun the machine around, the tracks grinding against the earth, and advanced after Sokolov.

Sokolov darted out from his hiding spot, firing another shot at the cab. Will ducked instinctively, feeling the rush of air as the bullet punched through the window glass, shattering it, and narrowly missed his head. He swung the excavator's arm again, this time coming dangerously close to the Russian. Sokolov rolled to the side, narrowly avoiding the scoop, and fired back, forcing Will to duck in his seat. Thankfully, Tadesse chose that moment to fire off another volley that drew the Russian's attention away from Will.

The exchange of gunfire continued, the general and the Russian locked in a deadly game of cat and mouse, a dance of bullets and movement. Will kept the excavator moving, trying to use its bulk to shield Tadesse and just maybe catch Sokolov off guard.

But then, without warning or apparent cause, the guns fell silent. Will looked around frantically, wondering where Tadesse was. In the same instant, Sokolov changed tactics. The Russian moved with a sudden burst of speed, running headlong toward the Cat. Will tried to swing the arm to intercept, but Sokolov was too quick, slipping past the arm, and scrambling up onto the platform. In a heart-stopping instant, the Russian was standing at the door to the cab, eyes cold and determined, pistol aimed directly at Will's heart.

"End of the line, American," he growled, and pulled the trigger.

FORTY-FOUR

ONE MOMENT SOKOLOV was there, standing right in front of Will, finger tightening on the trigger.

The next, he was gone, swept away as if struck by lightning.

The lightning had a name.

Deacon James.

While Sokolov had been occupied with the dual threat of Tadesse and the excavator, Deke had gone wide, sweeping around in a flanking maneuver, looking for a position from which to strike should the need arise. His football days of spur-of-the-moment maneuvers with seconds left on the clock would hopefully save Will's life.

He was Will's Plan B.

When Sokolov managed to reach the excavator, Deke had launched into motion, covering the distance in a split-second to hurl himself onto the excavator where he crashed into Sokolov as if smashing through an opposing team's entire offensive line. The unsuspecting Sokolov was swept off his feet and both men went flying. The impact knocked the Russian's pistol from his grasp, even as he broke the trigger, loosing a wild shot that nearly parted Will's hair.

Sokolov was no pushover, however. A hardened combat veteran and trained killer, he reacted almost as quickly as Deke had struck, twisting in mid-fall, pushing away from Deke to land cat-like on his feet.

Deke was not so lucky. He landed badly, and went sprawling on the rough ground, but if his years on the gridiron had taught him anything, it was how to take a hit and get back up. He bounded to his feet in an instant.

Just in time for Sokolov's counterattack.

The Russian delivered a flurry of punches, his fists moving in a tornado of violence, striking Deke's face and torso dozens of times in rapid succession. He was employing *udar kulakom,* a Spetsnaz fighting technique, meant to overwhelm an opponent in a blur of controlled violence.

Deke staggered under the assault, his large frame absorbing the blows even as he flailed his arms in a futile effort to ward them off. Blood flew from his mouth and nose, and trickled from a cut above his eye, but he didn't go down. Instead, after enduring several seconds of the assault, he lashed out with a punch of his own, a roundhouse that, while failing to land, forced Sokolov to back-pedal. He followed up with several jabs which, while not as rapid as Sokolov's rapid fire attack, were filled with raw power. One or two struck home, driving the Russian back, forcing him to dodge and weave, but Sokolov, unlike Deke, showed no sign of tiring. He danced back a few steps, then landed a brutal kick to Deke's midsection, doubling him over, followed by an elbow to the back of his neck that drove Deke to his knees.

Desperate, Deke swung out with one arm, knocking Sokolov's legs out from under him, and as the Russian fell back, Deke seized him with both hands and hurled him bodily against the excavator. The metal rang with the impact, but Sokolov rebounded quickly, his fists a blur once more.

The fight was brutal, ugly. More a brawl than a choreographed ballet of violence. Sokolov's training showed in every precise strike and calculated movement, while Deke relied on sheer toughness and brute force. Sokolov aimed a series of quick, sharp punches at Deke's ribs, trying to find a weak spot, but Deke absorbed the punishment and retaliated with a powerful right hook that connected with Sokolov's jaw, sending him sprawling.

Sokolov rolled to his feet, blood dripping from his lip. He feinted left, then lunged right, tackling Deke and driving him to the ground. The two men grappled, their breaths coming in ragged gasps. Then, before Deke knew what was happening, Sokolov managed to get around behind him. He wrapped an arm around Deke's neck and began to squeeze.

In that instant, Deke knew he was done for. He gripped the arm, digging his fingers in, trying to wrench it loose, but Sokolov was strong. Deke's vision started to blur, the blood supply to his brain cut off. Unconsciousness was moments away, a black tunnel closing in on him. With a last, desperate surge of strength, he bucked his hips and twisted, loosening Sokolov's hold just enough for him to slip a hand between the Russian's arm and his own neck. The easing of the pressure brought immediate relief, and Deke capitalized on it by twisting out of Sokolov's grasp. He brought his knee up, catching Sokolov in the ribs and knocking the wind out of him.

The two men rolled away from each other, gasping for breath, but then, impossibly, Sokolov was back on his feet first, launching another series of rapid punches. Deke blocked as best he could, but a few strikes got through, dazing him. Just as Sokolov prepared to deliver a finishing blow, Deke surged forward, using his weight to tackle Sokolov to the ground.

Pinned beneath Deke's massive frame, Sokolov struggled, but Deke's sheer mass kept him down. Deke pressed his unexpected advantage by slamming his fist into Sokolov's face. The impact bounced the Russian's head against the hard ground. The blow should have been enough to put him down for the count, and for a moment, it looked as if it had. Sokolov seemed to go limp beneath Deke. But the Russian was far from done. With a sudden twist, he rammed his knee into Deke's side, creating just enough space to roll free.

Both men staggered to their feet, battered and bruised, but determined to fight on. Unlike the Russian, however, Deke was no fighter. The relentless pounding had taken its toll on him. He was out of breath, slowing down. Sokolov, on the other hand, still moved with the lethal grace of a predator, and immediately launched another barrage of punches, each one a potential knockout blow.

Deke, worn down by the punishing assault, could barely keep up. Sokolov's fist connected with his jaw, snapping his head back. Another punch landed on his ribs, and Deke felt something crack. He fell to one knee, gasping for breath, his vision swimming.

Sokolov seized the opportunity, stepping in close. He grasped Deke's hair with his left hand, and raised his right for a blow that would almost certainly finish Deke off.

"This is the end for you," the Russian hissed through bloody, gritted teeth.

With nothing left to give, Deke braced himself for the inevitable.

Sokolov's fist began its descent, but before it could connect, a loud mechanical roar sounded. Sokolov raised his head, eyes going wide with terror, as the bucket of the excavator swung into him. The impact lifted him off his feet and sent him flying through the air. His scream of surprise and pain, barely audible over the roar of the diesel engine, was abruptly silenced as his body vanished into the depths of the trench.

FORTY-FIVE

WILL SHUT OFF the excavator's engine and leapt from the cab, rushing to Deke's side. What he saw nearly took his breath away.

In their years of working together, they'd mostly avoided physical altercations, but there had been a few times where the situation had escalated to the point where they'd gotten their noses bloodied, literally. Those occasions paled in comparison to the beating Deke had just taken.

He looked like a tenderized piece of meat. His face was streaked with blood from cuts and gashes too numerous to count, one of his eyes was swollen shut, and his arms were wrapped around his abdomen as if he was trying to hold himself together.

"You okay?" Will asked, resting a hand on his friend's shoulder. He was afraid to try to move him.

Deke's good eye found him, and he nodded weakly, wincing with the effort. "I'll live," he managed, his voice hoarse. "Thanks to you."

"I should have done something sooner," Will lamented, though in truth, he'd seized the first opportunity that had come along. The fight had been so fast and brutal, there simply hadn't been any other chance to come to Deke's aid. "Can you walk?"

"I'd prefer not to, but I guess I'm gonna have to, aren't I?" Deke extended a hand. "Help me up."

After assisting Deke to his feet, Will looked around the shed for the others. "Elena?"

Elena's voice reached out to him. "Over here."

He turned, orienting on the sound, and spotted her, kneeling over Tadesse, her hands covered in blood, pressing down on the bullet wound in his chest.

"Oh no," groaned Will, and hurried over to them.

Tadesse was conscious, but it was obvious at a glance that the injury was severe. His breath was a shallow rattle, his eyes glassy with pain. This, Will now realized, was why the shooting had stopped.

"How bad is it?" Will asked, though he already knew the answer from the look on her face.

"Bad," said Elena, her tone grim but professional. "The bullet punctured his lung. I need a pressure dressing and a chest seal. Damn it. I need my bag." She glanced up at Will. "Give me your shirt."

Will stripped off his shirt without a second thought, balling it up and then, without being prompted, knelt beside Elena and pressed the shirt down on top of the wound. The fabric quickly darkened, saturated with blood.

Elena pulled her hands away, then began looking around for anything else that might serve as a field expedient dressing.

Deke hobbled up to them a moment later. "What can I do?" he asked.

Elena started to answer, then did a double take when she saw the extent of his injuries. "What the hell—"

"It's okay. You should see the other guy."

She just nodded. "I need a piece of soft plastic or rubber. Something that can form an air-tight seal."

Deke glanced around for just a moment, then walked over to one of the broken sacks of ferrous oxide. He picked up the paper and turned it over. It was lined with a thin membrane of plastic. "Will this do the trick?"

Elena nodded, took it and knelt down over her patient.

"Okay, move the bandage away," she told Will.

When he did, Elena grasped the front of Tadesse's uniform and tore it open, revealing the wound, which alternately pulsed blood and then made a strange, wet sucking sound when the general tried to draw a breath. Elena placed the plastic membrane against the wound, holding it lightly in place. When Tadesse breathed in, the plastic was sucked down over the wound to prevent air from entering his chest cavity, and when he breathed out, some of that air blew out.

Suddenly, Tadesse's eyes opened wide, his hand gripping Will's with surprising strength. His lips moved and then he said something, the words bursting forth in a spray of blood.

"I don't understand," whispered Will, squeezing the general's hand. "Just hang on."

But then Tadesse's grip loosened, and his eyes lost focus.

"General," Will said.

Elena pressed a hand to Tadesse's throat. "No pulse. We've got to start compressions—"

She faltered, staring down at Tadesse's body helplessly. As a healer, it went against her every instinct to admit defeat, to stop treatment when there remained even a sliver of hope that a patient could be saved. But Tadesse didn't have even a sliver. In a hospital emergency room, or even in her primitive clinic, with the right equipment, she might have been able to pull him back from the brink, but here....

Will took his hands away from the makeshift dressing and faced Elena. "He's gone."

She nodded, her eyes glistening with emotion.

"He said something," Will went on. "I didn't understand."

"'Save Tigray,'" she whispered. "That's what he said."

Will gazed down at the unmoving form. "I will if I can, General. I promise."

He turned to the others. "Come on. We've got to get the oxidizer away from here."

Elena blinked away the tears, and after a last look at Tadesse, met Will's gaze. "How long do we have?"

Will shook his head. "Fifteen minutes. Maybe more. Climb up into the cab. We'll all ride out together."

Elena took a long, last look at Tadesse's unmoving form, then followed Will and Deke up onto the platform above the excavator's treads. The cab wasn't designed to accommodate passengers, so Elena and Will had to hang outside it, clinging to the door frame. As he fired up the engine, the machine roared to life, and they began their journey away from what would soon become ground zero for the blast.

Will had to extend the load to lower the arm so that they could ease through the door, but once outside, he brought the scoop in close and pushed the joysticks ahead for maximum speed, which was slightly faster than a walking pace. The machine lumbered across the uneven terrain, its powerful engine growling as it crushed loose rock and vegetation under its treads. The excavator moved steadily, but its speed was limited both by the uneven terrain and the heavy load it carried. Every bump and jolt reminded Will of the precariousness of their situation. They had no way of knowing how much time they had left or how far away was far enough. Even though it was physically separated from the device, the chemical payload in the bucket was still part of a ticking time bomb. If the blast caught them and the ferrous oxide ignited, then everything they had fought and sacrificed for would be in vain. Tigray would catch fire.

FORTY-SIX

SOKOLOV LAY IN the darkness at the bottom of the trench, his body shattered and twisted from the fall. He could feel the warm, sticky pool of blood spreading beneath him. Every breath sent waves of agony through his broken ribs, but he clung to consciousness, refusing to accept the release of oblivion.

He was dying and he knew it.

But he wasn't beaten.

He couldn't feel his legs, and when he tried to move his broken right arm, the flare of pain nearly rendered him unconscious. But his left arm worked, and he used it to drag himself across the rocky ground. His fingers scraped against the cold earth, nails breaking as he pulled himself forward inch by agonizing inch. Every movement was a fresh torment.

He couldn't see where he was going, but figured that eventually he would run into a wall and from there, be able to orient himself. Sure enough, after what seemed like an eternity trapped in the hell of his broken body, his fingers encountered the vertical wall of the trench.

Now which way?

One way would take him to the ramp and back to the surface. They other would take him to the bomb.

He chose to go right, using the wall to guide him, and resumed dragging himself along, inch by bloody inch until his outstretched fingertips encountered the softer texture of a wooden shipping pallet.

His hand trembled as he groped blindly, feeling the smooth surface of the bags, exploring them, searching. Then his fingers brushed against the thin, insulated detonator wire. He curled his hand around it like he was gripping a lifeline.

But it wasn't a lifeline. Just the opposite, it was the thread under which was suspended the sword of vengeance.

It was getting harder to breathe, as if his body, having reached the instrument of his retribution, was shutting down.

He closed his eyes for a moment, summoning the last reserves of his strength, feeling the wire in his fingertips. Such a little thing, and yet it contained so much power. A surge of grim satisfaction coursed through him. He would die, most assuredly, but he would take his enemies with him.

His grip tightened, and with a final, desperate effort, pulled.

FORTY-SEVEN

FROM ONE INSTANT to the next, everything changed.

The excavator was crawling across the rugged landscape, the vibrations and roar of its engine were the only sounds Will could hear. He kept his eyes on the horizon, never looking back. They were several hundred yards away already, far enough, or so he reckoned, to not be instantly vaporized when the blast came, but was that enough distance to escape the shock wave or the heat the explosion would generate?

He decided he would just keep driving until the question was definitively answered. And then, it was.

He saw the flash, like lightning in the sky, and just had time to shout, "Cover up," before the world turned upside down.

The deafening roar of the explosion drowned out everything, slamming into them like a giant's fist. The ground under the treads heaved with a tremendous force. Will's grip on the controls slipped, and the excavator lurched violently. Will was thrown against the cab walls as the machine toppled over. His body was tossed like a rag doll. He lost sight of Elena and Deke as a wave of dust and debris crashed over him. The noise was unbearable, a cacophony of destruction that seemed to go on forever.

Then, as abruptly as it began, it was over.

The world was eerily silent, save for the faint ringing in his ears. He lay still for a moment, dazed and disoriented, trying to make sense of what had just happened.

"Deke! Elena!" he shouted, his voice sounding distant and muffled in his own ears.

His head throbbed, and his vision swam, but he forced himself to move. He had to find Elena and Deke. He had to make sure they were okay.

As the dust settled and the gloom receded, he was able to determine that he was still in the cab, lying atop one of the polycarbonate windows, which was now flat against the ground. The excavator lay on its side, half-buried in the churned-up earth. Thankfully, it had not gone over onto the side with the entrance; if it had, he would have been trapped inside, or worse, thrown outside and crushed beneath the machine's bulk.

He got his feet under him, and after ascertaining that he was merely battered but not broken, crawled out onto the exterior of the cab.

"Deke!" he croaked. "Elena!"

A groan from nearby caught his attention. He lowered himself to the ground and moved toward the sound, until he found Deke, half-buried under a heap of dirt and loose rock.

"Deke, you okay?"

Upon seeing Will, a relieved look came over Deke's dust-caked face. "Yeah, I'm good." He broke off, coughing, then added. "Just a bit banged up. Well, a lot banged up now since I was already banged up before the blast."

Will gripped his friend's shoulder. "I'm going to find Elena."

"Go," urged Deke through another coughing fit. "I'll help you as soon as I catch my breath."

Then a weak voice reached out to them. "I'm here!"

Will oriented on her voice and found her seated, leaning against the upturned tracks of the excavator. Will rushed over to her, relief flooding through him.

"You're okay?" he asked.

She nodded, tears leaving tracks like roads and rivers on the map of her face, but her smile did not diminish. "I'll live. Help me up."

He pulled her to her feet and held her steady. She, in turn, wrapped an arm around his waist and held on tight, as if fearful of collapsing. They moved together to join Deke, who was just getting his feet under him, and then, almost as one, they turned their eyes toward the massive cloud of dust rising skyward above the spot where the storage shed had once stood, and where now there was only a vast crater gouged out of the earth.

Will found himself holding his breath as he scanned the crater, looking for smoke or flames... Any indication that the explosion had ignited the organic material sealed up between layers of shale.

There wasn't any.

The shale wasn't burning.

He let out the breath, a weight lifting off his shoulders. "We did it."

Elena's arm tightened around his waist. "*You* did it. You saved Tigray. You kept your promise."

Will didn't challenge the statement, but in his heart he knew that, while they had prevented an ecological disaster, Tigray's fate was far from resolved.

They stood there for a long time, watching as the dust settled and the air began to clear.

Deke finally broke the silence. "I suppose the plan is to walk out of here?"

"Looks that way."

"No Plan B?"

Will flashed a rueful grin. "Not this time."

FORTY-EIGHT

Moscow, Russia

PETROV SAT IN the back of his black sedan, the leather seats sticking to the sweat-dampened fabric of his suit. His mind racing, he wiped his brow with a handkerchief, and then splashed a measure of his prized Russo-Baltique vodka into a glass.

"Bulletproof," he muttered after downing the shot. "I am bulletproof."

But the warm glow of the liquor could not melt the icy grip of fear that bound his heart.

Things had not gone as planned in Tigray. There had been no word from Sokolov and no news of the fire. Now, he had been summoned to a late-night meeting in the office of Energy Minister Ivanov.

Outside the entrance to 42 Shchepkina Street, Petrov stepped out of his car and straightened his tie with shaking hands. The office building was a typical Brutalist Soviet-era structure that always looked to Petrov like a giant had taken a step pyramid, turned it upside down, and driven it into the ground so that only the base and a few of the step layers were protruding. It was far too ugly a building for a government ministry with so much influence, but then that was the point. Just like oil and the power it created, the Ministry concealed itself behind a façade of ordinariness. After dark, and all but abandoned, the building seemed even more like an ancient crypt. As he entered the foyer, the cold, austere ambience did nothing to soothe his nerves.

Minister Ivanov's office was as imposing as the man himself. The energy minister sat behind a massive desk, his eyes cold and calculating as he regarded Petrov.

"Sit," he commanded.

Petrov complied, sinking into the chair opposite the minister, feeling more like a schoolboy awaiting punishment than a senior vice president of one of his nation's leading companies.

Ivanov wasted no time. "I've learned of VEK's involvement in a plot to destroy an oil shale field in Ethiopia," he said, his voice icy. "Do you realize the position you've put us in? The Ethiopian government blames *us*... Mother Russia, for trying to sabotage their oil shale fields. They've not only revoked your exploratory permit, but are demanding a renegotiation of terms for our oil exports to the region."

Petrov swallowed hard. "Minister, I can explain—"

"Explain?" Ivanov interrupted, his voice rising slightly. "That is hardly the worst of it. Your speech to that climate conference has made a laughingstock of is all. You actually said that oil extraction is the moral equivalent of the slave trade? What were you thinking? You have given these environmental activists the rope they will use to hang us all."

Bulletproof. I am bulletproof, Petrov repeated the mantra in his mind, trying to muster the courage to answer the accusation. "Minister, the speech was necessary in order to fix the importance of the climate crisis in the minds of those scientists. Even though my plan to accelerate global warming by setting the oil shale field on fire did not materialize, the overall goal is not only sound, it is inevitable. One day, the industrialized nations of the world will realize it, and on that day, they will give us whatever we ask to leave fossil fuels in the ground."

Ivanov stared at him for a long moment. "Maybe one day, that will be true," he said. "But you will not see that day."

Petrov blanched, feeling the blood drain from his face. "I understand. What should I do?"

"Go home. Have a drink. Find a window..." Ivanov's voice trailed off ominously, leaving no doubt about what he meant.

Petrov stood shakily, nodding. "Of course, Minister," he said quietly, then turned and left the office.

As he exited the building and returned to his car, the world seemed to blur around him. He downed the last of the Russo-Baltique, drinking directly from the bottle.

Drained of its contents, the beautiful, gold-sheathed bottle was just an empty vessel, its bulletproof glass shielding nothing at all.

It didn't matter. Nothing mattered anymore.

The ride home was a blur, and when he finally stepped into his penthouse, the silence was deafening.

He walked out onto his balcony, feeling the bite of the icy wind on his face, feeling nothing at all, and gazed out at the city lights below. He went to the rail, took a deep breath, the weight of his failure pressing down on him like a physical force. The city yawned invitingly below.

He closed his eyes.

FORTY-NINE

Axum, Tigray National State – Three days later

WILL STEPPED OUT on the balcony of the upper story room at the Yeha Hotel, and leaned against the rail, gazing out across the ancient ruins outside old Axum. Below him, the obelisks of Axum stood as silent witnesses to the unfolding drama. The November air was cool, a refreshing change from the stifling environs of the room where Taneisha was leading the negotiations to determine the future of Tigray.

After preventing Sokolov from setting the oil shale field on fire, a lot of things had happened very quickly, starting with the egress from the wilderness.

Will, Deke, and Elena didn't have to walk far after all. Ten minutes after the bomb's detonation, the helicopter returned, following Tadesse's earlier instructions. The pilot, an employee of VEK, had been unaware of Sokolov's plot, and, upon seeing the explosion from a distance, had flown over, looking for survivors. He had then flown them all back to the canyon where they reunited with the friends who had been left behind. Deke managed to convince Tadesse's men that their general had joined forces with them against Sokolov, only to be killed by the Russian, dying a hero's death. With that crisis resolved, they flew back to Axum where Taneisha began organizing the peace talks.

Deke, still significantly bruised and battered from his brutal fight with Sokolov, had flown out on a charter flight arranged by Scott Devlon, accompanied by Sanjeet and all the members of the Doctors Without Borders medical team, including Elena, who had agreed to leave only on two conditions: first, that as soon as the peace talks bore fruit, she would be able to return and finish the work her team had begun, and second, that Will would take her out to dinner. Though he had no authority to accede to the first condition, Will happily accepted the second.

He and Maisy stayed behind to continue supporting Taneisha's efforts to maintain the fragile peace in the region. Unfortunately, judging by the lack of results in the first round of the discussion, that outcome seemed unlikely.

Will turned as the door opened and Taneisha stepped out to join him. Her expression remained resolute, but there was a weariness in her eyes that told him all he needed to know about the status of the talks.

"It's not going well, is it?" Will asked, leaning on the railing.

Taneisha shook her head. "General Yared won't budge on his demand for independence, and Mulatu is just as firm in refusing to grant it."

Yared was Yared Mulugeta, General Tadesse's successor to the leadership of the military arm of the Tigrayan National Front.

Taneisha had won a promise of safe passage for Yared from Colonel Tesfaye after threatening to reveal the latter's collusion with Tadesse. Once he heard the recording of his conversation with Tadesse, the self-serving colonel, recognizing that his hopes of secretly cashing in on a share of the oil shale riches had been dashed, quickly agreed that peace in Tigray was in everyone's best interests.

A fiery young man who had quickly risen through the ranks of the revolutionary army, Yared was determined to honor Tadesse's legacy by fighting for a free Tigray, and he was not about to compromise. He had agreed, only with great reluctance and at no small risk to his life or freedom, to attend the talks in hopes of accomplishing through diplomacy what his predecessor had been unable to accomplish with bloodshed.

Across the table from him, representing the Ethiopian government, was Mulatu Bekele, a seasoned diplomat in his late fifties with graying hair and a calm demeanor. He had spent decades in service to the Ethiopian government and had been instrumental in negotiating the original ceasefire to end the first Tigray War, but even he seemed to be struggling to find common ground with Yared.

The sticking point was the oil shale. Although its existence was no secret to the political leadership in Addis Ababa, most Tigrayans had been largely kept ignorant to the buried treasure in their territory, and now that they were aware of its potential, the stakes of Tigray's bid for sovereignty had escalated. The Ethiopian government saw it as a resource they could not afford to lose. They had revoked Volga Energy's exploratory permit and were looking for new foreign investors to develop the field.

"This isn't just about independence anymore," Taneisha went on, "It's about control over resources and power. The stakes are too high for either side to back down easily."

She gazed out at the view and sighed. "Solomon would know what to do."

"What's that?" asked Will.

She gave a guilty chuckle and thrust her chin toward a large pond to the northwest which, despite being filled with muddy water, glistened with the reflection of the afternoon sun. "That place is called 'Sheba's Bath', for the Queen of Sheba. Local legend has it that her palace was built here, and that was her bath. That got me thinking about King Solomon. According to the Bible, King Solomon's wisdom was of such renown that the Queen of Sheba journeyed from her kingdom to learn from him. There's no consensus among scholars as to whether the Queen of Sheba in the Bible was even from this region, but in Ethiopia, they put a lot of stock in the story. I was just thinking that we could use a Solomon here."

Will nodded. "So, what would Solomon do?"

She shook her head uncertainly. "Above all else, Solomon was a pragmatist. There's a famous story in the Bible about how he settled an argument between two women who came before him, each claiming to be the mother of the same infant. Solomon proposed to cut the baby in half, giving each woman a part. One woman agreed, but the other, overcome with horror, cried out to give the baby to the other woman, preferring to lose her child rather than see him harmed. Solomon then knew who the true mother was—the one willing to sacrifice her own happiness for the child's life."

Will, who was familiar with the story, returned a wan smile. "I'm not sure cutting the oil shale in half is a solution."

"It wasn't about finding a compromise that would satisfy both women," replied Taneisha. "It was about making them understand that there was more at stake than just the fact of possession. We need to make everyone here understand what's truly at risk. Not just the land or the resources, but the lives of the people who call this place home."

"I thought the story of Tadesse's sacrifice might sway them."

"Unfortunately, since we have only your report of what happened, there's some question regarding Tadesse's motives." She shook her head. "We have to find a way to make them see reason."

"Give up Tigray to save Tigray?"

"If that's what it takes." She sighed again. "Well, I guess I should get back in there."

Will nodded. "I'll join you."

Inside, the discussions continued, voices rising and falling in a cycle of argument and counterargument. Will followed along, the instantaneous translation playing through a Bluetooth earbud connected to his phone.

As he listened, he gazed about the room. In addition to Yared and Mulatu, several elders from nearby communities were in attendance, including young Ezana. Taneisha's colleagues from A21I were there as well, but had little to contribute while the discussion focused on whether or not there could even be a meaningful conversation between the participants.

The most noteworthy participant was the elderly Abune Tomas, Patriarch of the Tewahedo Orthodox Church. Attired in robes of purple and gold, adorned with intricate embroidery, he carried a golden crozier—the symbol of his office. Taneisha had invited him to the talks in the hope that his presence would add a layer of moral authority to the negotiations. Unfortunately, he had yet to signify his position on the matter, preferring instead to listen—Solomon-like—as the two sides of the debate made their positions clear.

"We will not surrender our fight for freedom," declared Yared forcefully, his voice ringing in the air. "Our claim to this land is ancient."

Mulatu Bekele responded with measured calm. "We are all Ethiopians. We must find a solution that respects the unity of our nation."

Ezana spoke up. "You talk of unity, but you will only bring more violence to our land. Too many have suffered. Too many have died."

It soon became apparent to Will that the debate was just going in circles, with the parties stuck in repeat mode, while Taneisha kept trying to convince them to at least commit to extending the ceasefire.

Fed up with their ceaseless bickering, Will turned off his earbud and, before he quite knew what he was doing, stood up suddenly and, in a firm voice, said, "Enough."

His phone dutifully translated the word.

With all eyes suddenly upon him, Will wished Deke had stayed behind with him. With his profound talent for negotiation, Deke would have known exactly what to say.

Mulatu, who had been speaking, regarded him with a frown. "You have no place here," he scolded. "While we respect your role in bringing us together, we will not tolerate your interference."

Will ignored the rebuke. "Listen to yourselves. You're so caught up in your desires for control and ownership that you're forgetting what's truly important: the lives of the people who live here."

He looked around the room, letting his gaze rest on each participant. "You're acting like children fighting over a toy while the house burns down around you. The oil shale, the land, all of it means nothing if it leads to more suffering and death."

Seeing that he was having no better luck than Taneisha, he turned his gaze to Abune Tomas, and in a softer tone, said, "Your Eminence, may I have a word with you in private?"

The elderly Patriarch returned a bemused smile, but then nodded and, using his crozier like a walking stick, rose to his feet, his vestments rustling softly. Despite his age, he carried himself with dignity, following Will out onto the balcony. The cool air outside was a relief after the heated atmosphere inside the room.

Will gazed out over the ruins of ancient Axum for a moment before turning to the Patriarch. "Can't you make them understand how important it is to preserve the peace?"

Abune Tomas, his face lined with age and wisdom, his eyes reflecting a lifetime of contemplation and faith, gazed thoughtfully at the phone as it translated Will's words. Then, with what almost seemed like embarrassment, he replied, "I am praying for God to show me the way."

The answer felt like a cop-out. Instead of taking the lead, the Patriarch seemed to be waiting to see who would come out on top of the debate before giving the outcome a stamp of divine approval.

It was time for a game changer.

"I think your prayers are about to be answered," said Will. "I've found something that I think you will be very interested in."

Abune Tomas registered a quizzical expression. "Found something? What is it?"

Will took a deep breath and smiled. "Something you didn't even know you had lost."

EPILOGUE

Tigray National State, Ethiopia — Six weeks later

DR. ELENA RAMIREZ finished restocking her black medical pack and zipped it closed with a smile of satisfaction.

It felt good to be back at the clinic, helping the people who needed her help the most.

She had spent more than a month waiting for the board of directors at Doctors Without Borders to approve her return. A month wasn't really very long for her, but for some of her patients in Tigray, suffering from a host of treatable, but potentially fatal illnesses, it was a literal lifetime.

Still, she had developed a little more appreciation for the board's cautious approach. Her abduction by General Tadesse had brought home to her just how quickly a situation could spiral out of control. As eager as she was to get back to Tigray, she had learned her lesson and was not going to rush headlong into danger. Nevertheless, when she got word that a security expert from Project: RESCUE had completed his risk analysis and judged the condition in the region to be "somewhat stable," she had started packing.

Her new team, comprised of Dr. Amina Ibrahim, a general practitioner from Nairobi; David Kim, an emergency care specialist from Seoul; Maria Santos, a pediatric nurse from Manila; and

Thabo Ndlovu, a community health nurse from Johannesburg, had been in Tigray for ten days now, and in that time, they'd completed the vaccination program, and treated dozens of people infected with the leishmaniasis parasite. The people in the towns and villages they visited knew little of the political situation. They were just happy to be able to go about their lives.

She raised her eyes as Thabo came from the back room, carrying two mugs of tea. "That was a productive morning," he said. "I'm glad we caught that leishmaniasis case early. There's no better feeling than getting out ahead of something like that."

"Makes all the hard work worth it," replied Elena. "Looks like we've got quite a crowd waiting for us already."

As was their custom, they spent the balance of the day seeing walk-up patients, of which there were presently nearly a dozen lined up outside the door. Many of them were suffering only minor afflictions, but none would be turned away without first receiving attention.

Thabo chuckled. "No rest for the weary. But I wouldn't have it any other way."

Elena nodded in agreement, feeling a sense of purpose and fulfillment. "Let's get to it, then. These folks have been waiting long enough."

Just then, she heard the sound of a car's engine roaring up the road outside and was overcome with an immediate sense of foreboding. The arrival of a mysterious vehicle always seemed to precede trouble.

"What's wrong?" asked Thabo, evidently sensing her anxiety.

Elena didn't answer. Bracing herself for the worst, she stepped outside and watched as a too-familiar green Land Cruiser pulled up in front of the clinic.

"No," she growled under her breath.

Squaring her shoulders, she marched past the line of waiting patients, and approached the vehicle, ready for a confrontation. The door swung open and Will Irons, looking rugged as ever, stepped out to meet her.

"No," she said again, this time in a firm voice.

"'No' what?" he replied but was unable to suppress a mischievous grin.

"No, I'm not leaving. Don't even think about trying to make me leave. I don't care what's happened or what the risk assessment says, I'm not going."

Will raised his hands in mock surrender, a playful glint in his eye. "Relax, Elena. I'm not here to make you go back."

"Then why are you here?"

"Well, as you may recall, I promised to take you out to dinner. And as I happened to be in the neighborhood, I thought I'd see if you were free today."

Elena blinked, taken aback. "Dinner. You're kidding."

He shook his head. "Nope. A promise is a promise."

She eyed him warily. "You just *happened* to be in the neighborhood?"

He shrugged. "Truth is, I never left. I sort of got caught up in something that kept me here. In Tigray, I mean."

"Project: RESCUE business?"

"In a manner of speaking. I've been involved in a sort of infrastructure restoration project. We're mostly done, and I'll be heading back to the States soon. I heard you were back here and thought this would be a good time to deliver on that promise."

She crossed her arms, suspicion replacing defiance. "You seriously drove all the way out here to take me to dinner?"

His grin softened into a more sincere smile. "Come with me. There's something I want you to see. Something amazing."

Her skepticism was evident. "Will, I can't just take off." She glanced over her shoulder at the line of women and children waiting at the clinic door. "I have patients to see."

"I can handle them," Thabo called out from the doorway from where he had evidently been eavesdropping.

Elena threw the nurse a withering glance over her shoulder. "I'm not going to leave you to handle this all by yourself," she protested.

"The others will be back soon," insisted Thabo, flashing a broad, Cheshire Cat grin. "Go! Have fun"

"See?" said Will. "Problem solved. Let's go."

She hesitated, her curiosity piqued despite herself. "Where exactly are we going? I don't know if you've noticed, but there aren't any restaurants in Adi Gebru."

"Axum," Will said, his smile widening. "Exactly where is a surprise. You'll just have to trust me."

Elena sighed, glancing back at the clinic, then at Will. The thought of an adventure, even a small one, was tempting. And despite her initial default setting of resistance, she found herself strangely intrigued by Will's offer. There was something about his confidence, his sheer audacity, that was hard to resist.

"All right," she said finally. "But this better be good."

As Will drove up the highway toward Axum, Elena found herself enjoying the easy conversation with Will. They chatted about their respective careers and passions, exchanging stories of their adventures abroad. Will recounted some of his more harrowing missions, while Elena shared her experiences working in some of the world's most challenging and remote regions. Despite the weight of the topics, the conversation flowed naturally, filled with laughter and mutual respect.

Elena couldn't help but notice how comfortable she felt in Will's presence, a marked contrast to the friction of their initial meeting. There was an undeniable chemistry between them, a connection that had sparked during their shared ordeal, and seemed to grow stronger now that the crisis was behind them. Yet, a part of her remained cautious. She knew that dating and having a relationship could potentially interfere with her work and the things she wanted to accomplish in her life. But then again, Will didn't seem the type to demand a stay-at-home relationship. He understood her drive and shared her passion for making a difference in the world.

As they neared Axum, the streets grew increasingly crowded. People dressed in their finest attire filled the sidewalks, their faces alight with excitement and anticipation. The vibrant colors of traditional Ethiopian clothing created a festive atmosphere, and the sound of joyous chatter filled the air.

Elena glanced at Will, burning with curiosity. "What's going on here?" she asked, her eyes scanning the lively crowd.

Will smiled at Elena's question, eyes sparkling with excitement. "What you're seeing is the Timkat festival," he explained as they navigated the busy streets. "It's one of the most important celebrations in the Ethiopian Orthodox Church, commemorating the Epiphany... the baptism of Jesus in the Jordan River. As part of the celebration, the priests carry replicas of the Ark of the Covenant, called Tabots, through the streets to a body of water for a simulated baptism."

Elena listened, intrigued. The enthusiasm in Will's voice made her even more eager to see the festivities up close. "Sounds... interesting."

"It is," Will assured her. "And this year, there's something unprecedented happening. You'll see."

They soon arrived at the Atse Kaleb Hotel, where Will parked the Land Cruiser. "We're walking from here," he said, "but it's not far."

They joined the throngs of people on foot, the air filled with a sense of joyous anticipation. Elena found herself swept up in the excitement.

As they approached the ancient site of the Queen of Sheba's Baths, she spotted a familiar face above the sea of colorfully attired locals.

"Is that Deke?"

Will nodded with a grin. "Yep, that's him."

They pushed through the crowd to join Deke, and Elena was delighted to see more familiar faces. Sanjeet and Maisy were there, along with Taneisha, all of them clearly enjoying the festival. They waved excitedly as they spotted Will and Elena approaching.

"Hey, you two!" Deke called out, his deep voice carrying over the noise of the crowd. "Glad you could make it!"

Elena answered by throwing her arms around the big man and wrapping him up in a fierce embrace.

After an exchange of hugs and handshakes, Taneisha said, "Will, thank you for making all this possible."

Elena gave Will a sidelong glance. "What did you do?"

When Will just shrugged, Taneisha supplied the answer. "During the peace talks, he said something to Abune Tomas, the Patriarch of the Church. After that, Tomas laid down the law. He told both sides that God had answered his prayers, and that it was time for peace in the land where God's glory resides." She looked at Will. "He refuses to tell anyone what it was he said."

"I'm sworn to secrecy," replied Will, solemnly.

"Whatever it was, it worked. Yared and Mulatu agreed to abide by the ceasefire and table the matter of Tigrayan sovereignty indefinitely. Since then, the government has been making progress with infrastructure projects, restoring a lot of the damage done by the war."

"What did he mean about 'the land where God's glory resides'?" asked Elena.

"Ah," said Will. "I'm glad you asked." He gestured toward Sheba's Baths. "This way."

They moved closer to the pond where dozens of people were wading out into the water, sprinkling each other to symbolize the baptism of Christ. Elena's attention was drawn to a large, squarish object concealed under richly embroidered covering cloths, set up in front of the pool.

With a gleam in his eye, Will pointed to the shrouded object. "That's the surprise," he said. "I told you that during Timkat, the Tabots—replicas of the Ark of the Covenant—are usually carried through the streets. But this year, they've brought out *the* actual Ark of the Covenant. It's usually kept in the Chapel of the Tablets at the Church of Saint Mary of Zion, never seen by the public. But this year, Abune Tomas decreed that it would be brought out for the festival, just this once. It's literally a once-in-a-lifetime event."

Elena's eyes widened in amazement. "That's *the* Ark of the Covenant? Like in the Indiana Jones movie?"

Will quirked a smile. "Well, that's hard to say for certain, but it definitely *is* the Ark that's been venerated by the Ethiopian Orthodox Church since the 13th Century. I suppose the rest is a matter of faith."

THE SOUND OF trumpets signaled the next phase of the celebration. A procession of priests, clad in their ornate vestments, approached the covered Ark, raising it on lifting poles and carrying it aloft on their shoulders. The crowd, including Will, Elena, Deke, Taneisha, Maisy, and Sanjeet, followed in hushed reverence.

Ahead of them, the trumpets continued to sound, their clear notes rising above the murmur of the crowd. The procession wound its way through the streets, the faithful lining the route, some reaching out to touch the trailing cloths of the priests' robes, seeking a blessing. The air was filled with a mix of awe and devotion. People pressed close to catch a glimpse of the sacred relic, their faces reflecting a blend of faith and wonder. The priests moved with measured steps, their expressions solemn, as they navigated through the streets of old Axum to its sacred resting place in the Chapel of the Tablets.

As they approached the church, the atmosphere grew even more charged. The crowd slowed, creating a respectful distance as the priests reached the entrance. The heavy wooden doors of the chapel stood open, waiting to receive the sacred relic.

With great care, the priests carried the Ark inside, their movements deliberate and reverent. The trumpets ceased, replaced by the soft chanting of the clergy. The crowd fell silent, watching as the Ark disappeared from view, once again hidden away in its sanctified sanctuary.

Deke leaned in close to Will and whispered, "When did they make the switch?"

"Last night. The replica Ark from the chapel was brought out to consecrate the Tabots that had been brought from some of the other churches in the region. The real Ark was brought in with all the rest, and then, after everyone had left for the night, they switched them."

"Pretty slick. And no one will ever know that the Ark that was in the chapel for the last ninety years was a fake."

"I'm sure not going to tell anyone," said Will. "And I don't think Abune Tomas, or any of the priests will either."

Will recalled his conversation with the Patriarch. When he'd revealed to Tomas the discovery of the Ark in the wreckage of the Esperia in a canyon to the south, the overjoyed Patriarch had not doubted his claim for even a second. Instead, he had admitted the closely guarded truth—that the theft of the Ark by the invading Italian army in 1935 had been covered up, the Ark replaced with an inferior, albeit antique forgery. The secret had nearly been exposed in 1992 when a former professor of Ethiopian Studies at the University of London claimed to have examined the Ethiopian Ark in 1941, declaring it to be nothing more than an empty wooden box of middle- to late-medieval construction—which in fact, it was.

It had taken the better part of a month to recover the Ark from the airship debris. Under Will's direction, Edge Dynamics, an elite international engineering firm renowned for its expertise in classified salvage and recovery operations, had been contracted to stabilize the fragile wreck and erect a tiered scaffold to allow access to Esperia's cabin. Once that part of the job was complete, the engineers withdrew, allowing a select group of Orthodox monks to enter the cabin, and retrieve the holy relic.

From there, under the pretext of a sacred pilgrimage to Axum, the monks carried the covered Ark on their shoulders—a journey of thirty miles over the course of three days, timed to coincide with the Timkat festival, which presented the perfect opportunity to make the exchange without anyone being the wiser.

Will did not know if the restoration of the "true" Ark to the care of the Church would form the foundation for lasting peace in Tigray, but it was a hopeful start.

The doors of the chapel closed slowly, the finality of the moment settling over the crowd. A collective sigh seemed to ripple through the assembly, a release of breath they hadn't realized they were holding.

Will glanced around, seeing the mixture of emotions on the faces of those gathered—joy, reverence, hope. He turned to Elena, who was watching the scene with wide eyes. "It's like something out of a dream," she said.

"It is," Will agreed. "And we're lucky to be here to witness it."

Deke half turned away and stage-whispered to the others, "Let's give these two some alone time."

Elena's cheeks flushed a delicate shade of pink, but she managed a smile as Deke and the others said their goodbyes and began to drift away, leaving her and Will standing together.

The weight of the moment hung between them, a blend of anticipation and unspoken possibilities. Elena faced Will, her eyes reflecting the soft light of the setting sun. "Thank you for this," she said, her voice barely above a whisper. "It was everything you promised." Then she grinned, "But you still owe me dinner."

He chuckled softly, the sound mingling with the fading notes of the trumpets. "I haven't forgotten," he replied. "How about we find a place with a view of the ruins? I hear the sunsets here are spectacular."

Elena smiled. "I'd like that," she said, taking his offered arm.

PHOTO & GRAPHIC ATTRIBUTES

Coming next in the
Project: RESCUE Adventure Series

PHANTOM WIND

Tension ignites as Scott Devlon deploys the FAST Team to the treacherous jungles of Mindanao, Philippines, to rescue hostages seized by deadly Dawlah Islamiya insurgents. But this isn't just a ransom mission – the captives are dragged into a sinister plot hidden deep within insurgent-controlled territory. With danger at every turn and shadowy forces working against them, the team is locked in a race against time to free the hostages and stop a diabolical attack on Manila.

ABOUT THE AUTHOR

CHARLES G. IRION is a man determined to make every moment count. A publisher, award-winning author, successful entrepreneur, adventurer, humanitarian, artist, executive producer, and actor—if Irion can dream it, he can achieve it.

His academic background is as diverse as his passions. Irion holds bachelor's degrees in Biology and Economics from the University of California, Santa Barbara, and an MBA in International Marketing and Finance from Arizona State University's renowned Thunderbird School of Global Management. Now pursuing doctoral studies in the Global Leadership and Management Program at ASU, Irion remains committed to lifelong learning, constantly seeking new challenges and opportunities to grow.

Irion's career began in the pharmaceutical industry, where he earned recognition as the 1977 Rookie of the Region at JNJ McNeil Laboratories. In 1979, he returned to Arizona to launch a regional office for the commercial real estate powerhouse Marcus & Millichap. By 1982, Irion had founded U.S. Park Investments, which grew into a leading owner and manager of manufactured home and RV communities across the country.

Through every chapter of his life, Irion's relentless drive and wide-ranging interests have shaped a remarkable journey of personal and professional achievement.

But business success is only part of Irion's story. His deep commitment to community and service is reflected in over 15 years as an Executive Board Member and International Assessor for Project C.U.R.E., a charity that delivers medical supplies to more than 130 developing countries. He has personally volunteered in many of these nations. After serving as President of the Phoenix Phil-Am Lions Club, Irion received the esteemed Melvin Jones Award from the International Lions Foundation. After graduating from the Citizens Police Academy in 2023, Irion took his commitment to public safety a step further by joining the Board of Directors of the Phoenix Police Department Foundation, where he plays an active role in supporting initiatives that strengthen the community and empower law enforcement. He is also a lifetime member of the Phoenix Committee on Foreign Relations, underscoring his belief that we are truly "One World, One People."®

Not one to rest on his laurels, Irion continues to push the boundaries of his *"DASH"*—that span of time between birth and death. His love for storytelling led him to become a prolific author with 18 books to his name. His works range from the thrilling *Summit Murder Mystery* series to the bold, satirical *Hell* series, the captivating *Murdered By Gods* series, the gripping near-future political thriller, *FOUR*, and his latest venture, the *Project: RESCUE Adventure series*, kicks off with *FREE FIRE* in Winter 2024 and Phantom Wind in 2025.

Irion's creativity extends beyond writing. As an actor and executive producer, he's worked alongside the late Tom Sizemore in *Durant's Never Closes* and on the cult hit *Max Reload and the Nether Blasters*. His next film, *Jackie Fontaine*, is in pre-production, and in 2023, he brought General George Allen to life in the live-action trailer for his novel *FOUR*. Soon, fans will see him in *FREE FIRE*, where he will portray one of the antagonists (and may or may not face a dramatic demise!).

Never one to shy away from adventure, Irion has explored the far corners of the globe. He's summited Mt. Kilimanjaro, tackled the Chinese side of Mt. Everest, and scaled the Bavarian Alps. Whether scuba diving, skydiving, or white-water rafting, Irion lives for the thrill of discovery and the rush of adrenaline. His passion for adventure is mirrored in his novels, where every page is filled with suspense, danger, and excitement.

For more about Charles G. Irion and how he's making the most of his **DASH**, visit:

Amazon Author Page: amazon.com/author/charlesirion
Facebook: www.facebook.com/MBGOneWorld
www.facebook.com/charlesgirion
Twitter: @AuthorIrion
Instagram: @charlesirion
YouTube: Charles G. Irion
Website: www.charlesirion.com
IMDb: Charles G. Irion

Psst, Chuck here. Want a FREE eBook?
Visit www.charlesirion.com/contact-me and sign up for my newsletter. Along with your free eBook, you'll get my latest news, updates and insider exclusives.
Limited-time offer

SUMMIT MURDER MYSTERY SERIES

The Summit Murder Mystery Series explores murders set on the Seven Summits, the highest and deadliest mountains on the world's seven continents.

Murder on Everest
Abandoned on Everest (Prequel to Murder on Everest)
Murder on Elbrus
Murder on Mt. McKinley
Murder on Puncak Jaya
Murder on Aconcagua
Murder on Vinson Massif
Murder on Kilimanjaro

MURDERED BY GODS SERIES

Dragged out of 'retirement', Scott Devlon and other characters from the *Summit Murder Mystery Series* return in the new thriller series, *Murdered By Gods*. Scott is thrown back into the thick of international exploits and intrigue. He must find his way to save the world and those closest to him.

"I could feel the Call of the Wild beginning to ring in my ears once again...."

Machu Picchu
One World
Timbuktu

F四UR
a stand-alone novel

In many Asian cultures, the number four (四) is considered unlucky because the word for the number four and the word for death are the same.

FOUR people have FOUR days to prevent World War FOUR...
and save the world from destruction.
"FOUR . . . MEANS DEATH FOR US ALL."

**The Summit Murder Mystery Series, Murdered By Gods
Series**, and **FⵎUR** are available in paperback,
Audible, eBook for Kindle, and other e-formats.

Amazon Author Page: amazon.com/author/charlesirion
www.charlesirion.com

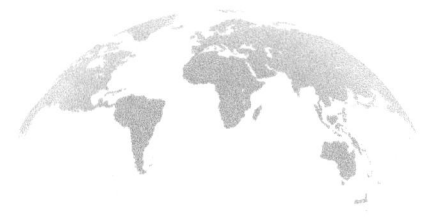

www.ingramcontent.com/pod-product-compliance
Lightning Source LLC
Chambersburg PA
CBHW061541170626
46811CB00001B/42